Race to Riches

Race to Riches

❖

Vicious criminal attacks change
Nurse Sarah's life ambition

Ron McCarthy

Library of Congress Control Number:		2024921484
ISBN:	Hardcover	979-8-3694-9777-7
	Softcover	979-8-3694-9776-0
	eBook	979-8-3694-9775-3

Print information available on the last page.

Rev. date: 10/29/2024

To order additional copies of this book, contact:
Xlibris
AU TFN: 1 800 844 927 (Toll Free inside Australia)
AU Local: (02) 8310 8187 (+61 2 8310 8187 from outside Australia)
www.Xlibris.com.au
Orders@Xlibris.com.au
862738

The Len Gorski Series

Len's a former World Cup footballer looking for his first A-league coaching position. He is continually diverted to protect lives and to help solve crimes.

ACKNOWLEDGEMENT

My thanks go the Editor of WIN News and TV, Alison McCarthy, who helped me with the final draft. Alison acquired this new surname by marrying my younger grandson, Matthew, during the final draft..

ONE

It's 10.00AM and Clem is stirred by banging on the front door of his ground-floor bedsitter in the Gold Coast. He rubs his eyes and is surprised by the rough stubble on his cheeks. He remembers he hasn't shaved for two days; he hasn't been in the mood. He rolls, pushes himself up on an elbow, and slowly rises onto unsteady feet. Pulling on his short satin bathrobe he stumbles over clothes strewn across the floor, and staggers to the front door. *What the fuck now!*

'Oh my God, Sis. What are *you* doing here?'

'I'm here because you're sick. And now you've got Mum worried. I warned you on the phone months ago. Look at yourself. Still in bed at this hour, struggling to stand straight, unshaven, skinny as a rake. Wake up to yourself.

And do your dressing gown up!'

He glances down and turns to cover himself properly, chewing his lip. 'I've come because I know you're in trouble.' She says, getting his full attention by gently taking his arm and peering into his eyes.

'Sarah, you should of let me know you were coming. I worked late so I slept in.'

'Don't take me for a fool, Clem. I'm a nurse. I know the symptoms of drugs and alcohol. I was home when you called mum and asked for a small loan. I heard your voice. The tremors, the slurs, your problem listening to what Mum was saying. I'm worried about you, that's why I'm here.'

Sarah's driven from Millmerran where she works at the local Hospital. It's a small tidy town in the Darling Downs of Queensland, close to where she grew up with her only sibling and doting parents. She's been agonising over recent health turmoil in her family, and she's determined to do something about it.

'Sis. Calm down. I'm doing my best to work my way through this. Don't stress me out. It's not straight forward.'

'I've just driven over 250 kilometres to help. Let's sit down and talk about your problem.' She leads him back to the kitchenette. In her quick look around, she sees a basic cheap rental. A kitchen island bench, stools, the sink against the rear wall, a bed on one wall, scattered clothes near the bed, a TV, and a sofa for viewing. The newspaper on the floor is open at the horse-race reviews, a couple of beer cans sit alongside the sofa, an empty peanut packet is wedged between them. The only frame on the wall is Clem's diploma for automotive engineering. *He's proud of that.*

Clem follows slowly, hanging his head. He switches the coffee machine on then slides onto a stool at the kitchen island bench and rests his face in his hands, his elbows on the benchtop. Sara fusses around searching for biscuits and milk and supervising the machine. She turns to face him.

'I'm on my way back to see Dad.' She says. 'He's in a bad way. His memory's been failing for some time and now he's had a serious accident at the Cobar mine. His manager's got him into a nursing home at Engadine, in New South Wales. Mum's stressed out with his condition and doesn't need any more problems from you. I can treat you Clem, but you'll have to make the commitment. It's really up to you. It's never easy to kick a habit.'

Clem lifts his head to look at Sarah. He's looking through a fog and struggling to find words. 'It's not that easy. As well as repairing cars in my new job here I was asked to deliver tobacco supplies to the shop in Pittsworth when I visited home. Then later, to shops along the way. Well, now I know, they contain hidden drugs. The mate that got me the pay-rise to move here from Millmerran told me this later. He also gave me some to try. How I started. I found I could work longer hours, do more trips, make more money, get high whenever I wanted. But truly, Sarah, now I want out.'

'So why not just tell them you want to quit. Can't you just walk out and not buy more of their stuff? They'd have many users and plenty more knocking on their door?'

'Don't you get it? It's not that simple. I'll be lucky to get out of this alive. I know the whole fucking distribution. The customers, where the shipments are held and distributed from. Some of the bosses. My mate says the cartel will kill me if I try to walk out! I'd be too great a risk.' Clem is shaking, his face livid and hanging over his clenched fists on the bench top. 'I just want to get out of all this and start again.' He pauses, crosses his arms, then grips his chin tightly and moves his head slowly side to side.

'I'm in real trouble with this drug ring Sarah.' He says. 'I know too much.' Sarah slips off her stool, rounds the bench, throws her arms over his shoulders, and snuggles her face in beside his. Her fragrance brings back close feelings they have shared throughout their lives. They've been close, not like friends they've known where boy girl siblings have been rivals and argued over favouritism.

They've grown up in a stable family on a twenty-acre property in a rural garden village just to the west of Millmerran township. Both attended primary school at Millmerran, then high school at Pittsworth, a twenty-minute trip eastward in the school bus. Few locals finished their schooling to graduate and pursue further qualifications like they have. Clem became an apprentice motor mechanic at Pittsworth, Sarah commuted to the large regional centre at Toowoomba to study nursing.

Sarah truly wants to help. What can she do? He's become addicted to drugs, that has to be a priority. Would police help him with security? Would they want to lock him up? Where is it safe from criminals desperate to protect their trade and identities? Could he hide out at Millmerran? It's a big country, but he has to work and have a life. Then her brain sees a glimmer of hope.

'Clem, we've got friends that will help.' She says. 'Len Gorski is a good friend. He's worked with a top-ranking Detective Inspector on two major crimes that I'm aware of. I was involved in the one at the Leyburn resort where illegal migrant girls were held. Len now works in Toowoomba on a new football coaching assignment with Boris helping him. I'm sure Len will help.

Clem rises and turns, taking Sarah firmly into his arms and hugging her tightly. Sarah rests her face on his chest. Neither speaks for some time, each just absorbing mutual support and affection. 'I love you, sis.' Says Clem finally. 'I've been too selfish doing my own thing. I know you saw my problem looming and I should a listened. And who's this Boris guy you're sweet on? I've only just heard about him.'

'We haven't announced it yet, we're engaged. I'm sure you'll like him Clem. He's after an A-league position as a professional player with Len's new team.'

'I'm sorry I haven't kept touch with you Sarah. I'd like to meet him.'

'You'll like him, he's a great guy. Look Clem, we can get you out of this mess. Len's our best hope. Let me talk to him and see what he says.'

After Clem settles down, Sarah prepares a breakfast, and while they eat Sarah tells Clem how she met Boris. 'He travelled from NSW with a football mate for his first go at a pig-shoot. There's plenty of wild pigs in the woods just south of where we grew up, as you know. Well, the ute rolled. Boris was not prepared for the risks involved, was slow to jump free, and the tray of the ute caught his leg. His mate took him to our hospital where I cleaned him up and treated his leg. We hit it off just there and then. I guess it was a case of love at first sight.'

'Good for you Sis. It's about time.'

Then Sarah moves on to talk about their dad. 'The Cobar mine manager contacted me at the hospital and said Dad was searching through a heap of slag at an abandoned worksite and was struck by a large piece dislodged from higher up the rock face. A workmate saw what happened and called paramedics. When Dad stayed unconscious with a bad head injury, they arranged for immediate transport to the Liverpool Hospital, a leading trauma Centre. He was still unconscious on arrival.

'Dad's intercranial pressure was monitored there with a catheter and some fluid drained to relieve the pressure. He's conscious now. It's serious, Clem, I know the first six months will tell how bad. About half of people with this injury decline or die within five years.'

Sarah stops eating and uses a tissue to wipe her eyes and blot the slight tremble in her lip. Now it's Clem's turn to swap sides of the bench and hug Sarah. 'You're under too much stress, Sis. You can't manage all our family problems. I promise to solve my own. You've got to go and help Dad. I don't know much about those tests Dad's had.'

'The mine manager arranged to move him to this nursing home where he knew the head nurse personally. The head wound where he was struck is now okay, it's his memory. I know the first six months is critical. I'm trying to help him remember old times and play simple games. Games like checkers can help. People can go through a confused state and improve over time. Sometimes it takes years. Dad can't even speak yet.'

'You've stayed here long enough, Sarah,' says Clem, 'go back and help Dad. I'll find a way out of my own mess. And I'll call mum and calm her. I haven't been much of a son – I've been too selfish. Your visit's brought this home to me. I do love you sis.'

'Yeh. Me too for you. They've been good parents to us. I still remember them encouraging us to move into the fields we were passionate about. They saw me patching up dolls with imaginary injuries and you fiddling endlessly with motorbikes.'

'They didn't have much money and had to make sacrifices for us.' Says Clem.

'I just learnt Dad's been working on a secret ambition of his own.' Says Sarah. 'I'd love to find out more about that, it could help his recovery.'

Sarah leaves Clem. She sets off for Sydney and joins the Gold Coast Highway heading South. She soon enters the main shopping area of Surfers Paradise. The road's congested, pedestrians are crossing willy-nilly, sidewalks are flooded with young shoppers in happy spirits, and her heart sinks. *I'm too stressed. I need a break before I take on a long drive to Sydney and get there safely.* She spots a parking spot and takes it. She sits for a while watching the activity. She sees extravagance, opulence, sexy clothing, promiscuity. She realises 'Schoolies week' finished only a few weeks ago when adolescent school leavers invaded the place to party. She also knows the beach is walking distance, and this no doubt influences the attire. She senses the effects of drugs and alcohol out there and it's only mid-morning.

Her thoughts spring to her friend Jane's son Phil, who's just finished school and moved to board with three other students to attend uni courses at Newcastle. *Will Phil fall to temptation like Clem has? He's with his friend Liana, Len's niece, and she's a beautiful sensible girl and a good influence. I hope to God Jane's values are respected.*

She spots a café and decides she needs another coffee break to settle down for the long drive.

Two

After Sarah leaves for Sydney, Clem switches the kettle on again. He sits on his stool and leans back, stretching his neck and staring at the ceiling. *What a fucking mess. Why did it take me so long to realise the shops were paying too much for those deliveries? Why did I let myself get suckered in for more money and to try drugs? I'm a fucking idiot! I'll keep working and look for a chance to just piss off overseas without notice. Once I settle, I'll send safe packages back home to help the family.*

The next day he's asked to drive an owner in his newly imported Maserati to his mountain home at North Tumbulgum in the mountains west of the coast. Clem's been told to bring the car back for modifications. He knows these modifications are to build a concealed compartment for transporting drugs. It was one of his first duties to build these compartments prior to him knowing about the drugs.

Clem begins the drive, and travels South along the Gold Coast Highway, through Tweed Heads, Banora Point, and along the Terranora Road into the mountains west of North Tumbulgum. It's the thing Clem likes most with his new job here, to drive these luxury imports. These mountain roads are a challenge, but this Maserati handles the road surfaces and bends with the ease of a knife spreading soft butter on toast. He would love to drive faster but sitting next to the new owner it would be a wrong move. Especially as they climb higher, and he seems to be enjoying the scenery. The huge forest trees and lush tropical growth interspersed with majestic views over the valleys. Enjoying the reverie of the drive the car owner becomes conversational.

He's well dressed in fashionable leisure clothes and says he is a recent migrant to this beautiful country. His previous home was in Italy in a suburb of Florence, the capital of the Tuscany region. He tells

Clem about masterpieces of Renaissance art and architecture. Of the cathedral with a terracotta-tiled dome engineered by Brunelleschi, of Michelangelo's 'David' sculpture, and of Botticelli's 'The Birth of Venus' artwork. He says he would take the hour drive to the coast at Viareggio to relax on the beach. For years he travelled the world and he boasts about his range of experiences and living conditions.

Listening intently Clem urges him to continue. Italy could be an excellent place to escape to. He knows the drug cartel is managed from Columbia so it's unlikely they have contacts there, and the population density should favour his secrecy.

'I find Australia so young and fresh.' Says the owner. 'I enjoy the magnificent beaches on this Gold Coast. I love the hinterland where my new home is located, a beautiful drive away from the surf through these dense hillside forests. I love the variety of trees and the eucalypt scent in the early mornings. The cool breezes and fresh air and the relative isolation are so new and attractive. I want to travel to see more of this country's beauty.'

His ego has been boosted by Clem's interest and he invites him in to meet his partner. She's many years younger, very attractive, and elegantly dressed. He asks her to offer refreshments to Clem before his return trip. *This guy's well-heeled. I guarantee he's been promised good money to explore new opportunities for the drug big shot here. Drugs must be the source of his money. That's why the car's being given a secret compartment.*

On his drive back to the coast Clem becomes aware of a police car catching up, now some two hundred metres behind him. The car then sits behind him. Clem's driving reasonably quickly, thinking now that this Maserati might be the reason for their attention. But he's being careful to drive within limits, and safely for the conditions of this single-lane mountainous road. He keeps close vigilance preparing to pull over to let them pass. Eventually they sound the siren and flash their lights to pull him over just as he is in the process of following a long righthand curve with a precipice on his left. He's not too pleased about this but feels he has no choice. A policeman walks up and asks to see his licence. Then he's asked to step out to be shown a problem with the rear number plate attachment. The moment he steps out he's struck on the back of his head and bundled back in.

* * *

It's dusk as Clem stirs and finds himself dazed and aching all over surrounded by collapsed airbags and partway down the rockface toward the foot of a mountain. With blurry vision, he slowly checks his many bruised parts and looks for fractures. He finds none. There's a large lump on the back of his head. Ouch! He checks his watch. He's been out to it for three or more hours. He squirms his way out from the airbags, finding his seatbelt unattached, and tries to open his door. It's jammed. His only way out is to climb between the front seat backs and out one of the rear doors.

He stumbles out, and discovers himself three parts down a steep incline, and the car is wedged between two boulders. He has difficulty balancing as he works his way down to the valley floor. He has to wend his way through thick brush and huge trees. Some are ironbark gums that must be over a century old.

He finds a small stream and kneels to scoop handfuls of cool mountain water to quench his thirst. He bathes his broken skin patches, a couple on his forehead, and parks himself on a rock. He folds forward with his hands holding his head and tries to think through his predicament. His addled brain has a mixture of depression, confusion, and haunting ghosts spying on him from above.

These bastards mean business. I didn't expect it to be from cops though. But I'm lucky, I've been saved by the quality of this expensive import. I can't go back to Southport. I'll contact Sarah and tell her what's happened and find a way to Sydney – this means a long hike down to the border. He hasn't had a fix for some time, and he doesn't carry any. *I've fucked -up bigtime and doubt this life's worth living with all my problems.* He stays seated until he feels the need to drink more cool water. He then stands and walks slowly on.

Those two cops would have to be cartel recruits. It could take a couple of days for them to find I wasn't killed in the fall. They'll be looking for me. I've got to get lost. This phone could be a giveaway. I'll text Sarah a message to say I'm safe. I'll just tell her I've walked away from the drug scene and will be out of contact for a while. I don't want her to worry. I'll wreck this phone. I'll need identification to travel away, that'll be a problem. I might get a work passage on a ship. First, I'll look for a refuge with drunks. One last hit would help — maybe there's a bit floating around there. I'm going to kick this habit well and good for Sarah's sake.

He checks his wallet. He's got three hundred dollars in notes. At his first opportunity, he'll withdraw as much as he can and find a safe way to hide it. He reasons the flow downstream will take him toward the coast and decides to follow it. He comes to a property fence. By now it's quite dark. He has no desire to be noticed and finds his way quietly through the property to a gravel road. He sets off to walk in search of a main road.

His clothes are not damaged by the fall, and apart from a few minor blood stains, he feels he is reasonably well dressed to continue his trip to Sydney without being recognised as a fugitive. He's worried about the police. How many are involved? He comes to an intersection, the signpost tells him it's Dulguigan Road, and leads to Murwillumbah. *I must be in NSW already.* He knows that town name and thinks there's public transport to Sydney from there. The sign says it's twelve miles away, he should reach it by morning.

THREE

Len was offered a commission to build a new A-league football team for the Darling Downs area of Queensland by Derek Deed, the manager of the Toowoomba State League club. Derek negotiated with other clubs in the area to form a consortium and obtain an owner to support his plan. Len's reputation was well known and his work at Morisset ended when the Local Government Area declined the plan to build the new stadium suitable for A-league in favour of a huge entertainment centre.

Len and his partner Jane moved from Morisset, where Jane grew up, to live in a Toowoomba hotel unit. Len's nomadic lifestyle had kept him unattached until Jane appeared on the scene. Their friendship had budded when Jane was kidnapped, and Len's alpine rescue exposed a devotion that was laying below the surface.

Jane works from home as a freelance accountant and their new relationship can blossom here in Queensland. They plan to marry. Boris, one of Len's star players, agreed to come to help Len select and coach recruits, planning to be a member of the new A-league team they form.

Len carries an aura of pleasant confidence. His body has the olive complexion of his Central Asia heritage. His life as an elite footballer has made him sure footed and agile, a condition he has maintained into his forties where his style of coaching involves him being physically active in training practices. His spoken English was gained as part of his tertiary education in a sports university in Warsaw, and he has worked hard on it since his arrival. He is caring in nature and intolerant of crime due to his experiences growing up in a Soviet military town during their war with Afghanistan.

He has his selected players assembled in the training room for the first time. 'Welcome to our new team. Boris here has helped me select you all from what we saw of you boys in your club games. We liked your ball skills. We were looking for your ability to see problems and opportunities and if you reacted properly. Like if you knew when to use caution, when to be creative looking for penetrating passes, and when to take responsibility to shoot. We're satisfied we have the makings of a very good team here. My plan is to use the first few weeks to instil on you all the basic principles of attack and defence, principles you will need to use to be successful.'

'I'll work hard to get the best results possible with this team. I'll do this to establish you all as competent A-league players. I also want to establish myself as a competent A-league coach. Let's work together guys to achieve this. Get yourselves organised and meet up at the halfway line.'

Boris joins Len on the walk out to the field. 'Len, I'm worried about Sarah. She's not answering my phone calls and text messages. We usually talk together every night no matter where we are or what we're doing. I rang her hospital; they said she called in to take two weeks off to visit her dad in Sydney. That was days ago, and she didn't tell me. I rang her mum. She said Sarah left to visit her brother first and then to drive to Sydney to see her dad. I asked for her brother's number, tried it, and couldn't get any answer. I'm worried they might have had an accident. If it's just that she wanted to spend some time alone with her brother, she would've told me. I got back to her mum. Now she's worried too. She can't contact either of them.

'Where's her brother live?' Says Len.

'On the Gold Coast. He's been crook, so I suppose she called in to see if she could help.'

'Look Boris, I wouldn't worry for a couple more days. In my experience the police won't do anything until she's been missing for longer.' Says Len.

'I can't wait that long. I know something's up. She might've been picked up and taken somewhere. She's attractive and travelling alone, as far as I know, and that makes her a target. We usually talk every night, no matter what. I'm not gunna wait. I'm going in to report she's missing and find out what they're doing. Do you need me here today?'

'No. I'll be right. You go. See me at the pub later to tell me how you got on.'

Len sets up attack versus defence in one half of the field. He serves the ball to one of the attackers to begin play, and watches to see how the defenders move quickly to react to passes. In this session he concentrates on the first two principles of defence.

The first defender must close in quickly preparing to tackle. The nearest defender must back him up calling advice. He has three missions. One is call when to tackle, one to cut off passes, and one to be quick to take the role of first defender if his mate is beaten. Failing that, he must replace anyone that already has.

Len uses the 'freeze-replay' technique, to freeze play then step in to demonstrate how a role should have been played. *A picture is worth a thousand words.* Doing this not only shows what he wants, but his skill and fitness enhances the respect he gains from his players. They have never before experienced this form of coaching, and he takes a while to get players to freeze on the spot when he calls 'freeze'. Games are restarted at the half-way each time the attack fails.

Before long many see the mistake made and volunteer their own interpretation of what should have happened before any comment

from Len. He encourages this. He's pleased with the session. He ends
the session and congratulates the players. Before they break up Len
is asked a question by a player acting as spokesman for the others,
who wait to listen.

'Len, we've been told you played World Cup. Is this why you earned
your reputation?'

'As a player, yeh. As a teenager I was spotted to do a football
scholarship at the academy in Warsaw and then a tertiary course for
sport. I had to learn English. That was the hard part. While playing
I was recruited to migrate to Australia to play as a marquee player
in Australia's A-league competition. It took me a while to master
the way you guys use English. I still can't follow what you call slang
sometimes. I then became head football coach at Australia's Academy
for Sport, and now I'm chasing my own goal to coach a successful
national team. Like I said before, I want you guys to be successful.'

As they walk away Len asks three to stay behind for a chat. Len has
learnt that managing individual personalities is a vital ingredient for
performance.

That evening Boris and Len meet up at the hotel before having their
evening meal together. 'The cops were very helpful and I'm glad I
went.' Says Boris. 'Mrs Fielding had already reported her children
missing. The cops also had a report about a car crash, and their
enquiries indicated Clem may have been the driver. They've alerted
their Southport police to investigate. I rang her dad's nursing home,
and they said Sarah did arrive, but hasn't returned. It doesn't make
sense and I'm desperate.'

'I'm no expert with female ways, Boris. I'm told they often want time
out to do their own thing. My partner Jane has gone to Sydney to do
a short course in accountancy software, and I haven't heard from her
either for days. I *do* know she's missing her son. Phil's lived at home

with her as a single parent for the last twelve years and I'm sure she'll want to visit him at Newcastle on her drive back. He's doing a uni course there and boarding with three friends.'

'I think the girls'll call us when they're ready, Boris.' Len continues. 'The cops are onto it now. If they find there's a problem, they'll call you for sure. We're both hooked up with girls for the first time here. For me, I've found I'm on a new learning curve. Have a break. Let's get a beer before we eat.'

*   *   *

A phone rings in the Pittsworth tobacco shop. 'Is Mr Pickings there please?' A sweet female voice.

"Yeh, speaking.'

'You have a call from Mr Goldman. Can you take his call?'

'Yeh. Put him on. – Mr Goldman, can I help you?'

'Have you seen Clem Fielding?'

'No. As far as I know he's been staying down on the Gold Coast for the last twelve months sir.'

'He lives up there doesn't he.?'

'His family home's at Millmerran if that's what you mean, sir. That's about 30 Km further West down the Gore Highway. This is Pittsworth here. Is there a problem, sir?'

'Of course there's a bloody problem or I wouldn't call. He's been missing and his car's laying idle in the garage here. I'm being pestered about him. Some people here want him urgently. Call me if you get anything.'

The line goes dead. Bill Pickings tobacco shop is empty. He stands at his counter with the handset still held firmly and his free hand drops to scratch his testicles. *What's that Goldman prick on about? He's no garage manager with a sweet private secretary.* He shakes his head. He swaps hands again with the phone and punches in a new call.

'I'd like to speak with Peter, is he on today?'

'Speaking. Who's that?'

'Bill Pickings from Pittsworth. How you keeping?'

'I'm fine. What's your call about Bill? I'm on my own and starting to get a few customers in.'

'Just a quick one. A Mr Goldman is looking for Clem Fielding and I was wondering if he's gone home to Millmerran.'

'He hasn't been to the pub, so I don't think so.'

'If you see him, can you let me know?'

'Will do Bill. My missus knows everything that goes on in this town. I'll ask her for you tonight.'

'Thanks. See you mate.'

FOUR

Clem walks into the outskirts of Murwillumbah at sunrise. The walk's been long and tiring, and his brain's been mulling over his alternatives. Scepticism is prevailing, his stomach is churning, and his legs are feeling like he's run a marathon. The countryside has been picturesque, lush, and green. But his mind has been on other things. He desperately needs to rest his dazed and grazed body somewhere. He's thought of staying a few days to recuperate but rules it out as this being an obvious place for the gang to look.

He sees early morning activity ahead. Vehicles are busy entering and leaving a park some four hundred meters away. When he reaches, it's a large community market being set up in a leafy council garden with lofty trees, concrete paving, and well-kept lawns. There appears to be some thirty or more marquees with all kinds of new and recycled clothing, artefacts, craftwork, tools, and machinery. And food stalls are being set up. It's a hive of activity.

On entering Clem sees a group of young people chatting loudly and laughing as they set up their displays of fancy clothes and colourful shawls. Further along an older group is setting up trestles with tools and farming equipment. This group is less noisy and more intent on arranging their wares tidily and in categories. They're dressed comfortably in well-worn clothes, no doubt their favourites for some years past. Next to them are two recycled clothes stalls. Len pauses here, considering a change of clothes that could better suit his new plan.

The aroma of hot food catches Clem's nostrils and draws him toward a food stall. It appears to be set up for workers, stall managers, and early shoppers. A queue is forming with acquaintances joining for small talk. The barbecue hotplate has a changing variety of sausages, rissoles, bacon, and cooked tomato. The mouth-watering aroma is from the onions in a metal pan on one corner of the hotplate. The smell of the hot food causes his stomach to rumble. It must be close to twenty-four hours since he has eaten.

He's advanced from sixth to third in the queue to the barbecue where the cook is selecting the chosen combination and handing the loaded plate and bun to each customer. Earlier customers have known each other, townies, and their conversations and jokes can be easily overheard. The man in front of Clem is an old geezer dressed in a flannel long-sleeve shirt, faded jeans that could be thirty-year-old but would have been tailored top-range Levi's in their time, and a well-worn Akubra hat. His boots are worn at the heel and loosely tied. All up, it's clear to Clem he's a farmer who's come in for a day off from his chores to enjoy rest and greetings with old mates.

After the last joke, the geezer turns to see the silent customer standing behind him.

'G'day mate, how you going? Christ, you look a bit roughed up. You okay?

'I'm fine thanks.' Clem answers. 'I had a bit of a fall and banged my head. That's all.'

'There's bound to be a first-aid station here somewhere. Get 'em to patch it up for you so the flies don't get to it. I see you're from out of town, well have some fun while you're here.' He turns to make his choice, carefully takes it in both hands to keep it intact, then faces Clem to say Hoo Roo! and wander off.

Clem make his choice, finds a vacant bench seat, and sits to savour his breakfast. His choice is a large bun loaded with sausage, onion, and barbecue sauce. It's still too hot. He licks the barbecue sauce slopping down one side on the bun before attacking the filling with gusto. A sharp pain stabs his jaw as he takes the first bite. He cups his jaw and feels around it. There's a lump on his chinbone where it must have struck something. Maybe the steering wheel.

The park is quickly becoming busy, and seats are hard to find. Another elderly man sits next to him and starts eating. He's friendly and they exchange greetings. Townsfolk are beginning to arrive in increasing numbers and wend their way through the marquees searching for early bargains. Clem assumes this must be a popular monthly event.

'I get here early and look through the recycled clothing tents.' Says his new acquaintance, seeing Clem's eyes following the arrivals. 'Lots are brand new and cost peanuts. I'm not too fussy to wear second-hand clothes either. I always pick up a bargain.'

'That's a good idea.' Says Clem. 'I'm just passing through, so I'll test my luck. Can you tell me some good places to look? Hang on, before you do. Is there a coffee stall somewhere? I'll grab us both a cup to wash down this food and you can give me a run-down of the stalls.' The man looks strangely at Clem then nods. His manner tells Clem no stranger has made this offer before.

Clem returns and while sipping the coffee Clem's companion rattles off his favourites. He mentions a bag stall near the clothes, where last time he bought a cheap haversack to carry his purchases. 'Their bags are usually bargain prices; some are used.' He says.

'I'm off to Sydney but I'm not sure where the coach leaves from. Would you know?'

'Sure. There was a train here years ago. That's long gone. But you're right, there's now a coach, and the booking office is up the road at the old railway station. You'll see the sign. You might have to wait 'till tomorrow though. I don't think coaches run on Sundays.' He wipes his mouth and stands. 'See you later mate. Thanks for the coffee.' He walks away toward the stalls.

Clem leans forward and sinks his head into his hands. He's struggling to think clearly. *I ought to die and come back as a dumb ass. I can't stay here. I can't get out for another day. I need to get money out from a bank, and that can be traced. This is where they're gunna look first. I'll have to find a homeless shelter in Sydney while I look for a passage out, I'll need different clothes. I'll see what's here. I need to look different.*

He wanders over to the recycled clothes. He starts looking for jeans and a jacket. He picks out a well-worn long-sleeved denim jacket with multiple pockets, blotchy light blue in colour, then casual loose-fitting jeans with straight legs and more multi pockets, deeper blue in colour. He chooses items that represent an earlier lifestyle, planning to look more like a small-town worker dressed up to travel. This has taken a while. He moves to the bag stall and buys a cheap haversack and packs it with his new purchases. He hears chatter from the nearby stall selling bright multicolour shawls and casual summer wear. He looks across, and his attention is drawn to old-fashioned hippie wear. The stall is popular with young and old, and he wonders if a commune exists near here.

He drifts in and listens as he inspects some of the shirts. A middle-aged lady is searching on the same rack, and he casually asks if the selections are for her or her daughter. She looks at him, sees a well-dressed and handsome young man, even though he has a couple of facial bruises, and she decides to chat. 'A bit of both,' she says, 'for myself and my daughter.'

'Is it a commune?'

'Yes, the Onetable Falls Community. Years ago, my now-deceased husband helped pull down an old church to get the timber to build us a tidy little cottage there. I still live there, now with my daughter and her daughter after her partner walked out three years ago.'

'I'm sorry to hear that. Are you short of cash? Maybe I could help you out as a favour.'

'I work at the hospital here. I have an income and my daughter has child support. But it was very nice of you to offer.'

'I'm on my way to Sydney, but I've just learnt I can't get a coach 'till tomorrow. I'm looking to make a new life for myself. I'd love to see your commune to fill in some time, would that be possible?'

'It is a different lifestyle, and few are attracted to it. But you're welcome to see for yourself.'

'Do you own a property, or does the community own the homes in some form of trust?'

'I own the house, but the commune owns the land. I've no desire to leave. The surrounding bush and the fast-flowing mountain stream make the area so beautiful and natural. We operate in groups to grow fruit and vegetables. We breed chooks for eggs, and we have a good healthy lifestyle. The nudity, free-love, and drug-taking that the media focuses on are myths in our community.'

'So, you still work and prefer the environment there.'

'Sometimes I question why I live there,' she says, 'and then some really lovely thing will happen, and I realise all over again that I live there for that closeness to people and I guess that spontaneity and creativity that just happens.'

She stops fumbling among the clothes, turns to look him squarely in the face for an interminable minute, then suggests he come with her when they finish their shopping.

I've got no idea why I've just done that. She has a point about relationships though. I don't fancy moving into a high-rise city block of units where no one talks, and everyone walks past without even nodding. I'll respect her and find some way to show my gratitude. Some drugs might still be used in this form of living. I do need a fix to keep me going till I get proper help like Sarah said, but I won't impose or upset her trust. I'm going to kick this shit for good. My mind's set. If she offers me a lift to see this place, I'll insist I need exercise and walk back to town. I'll find somewhere to sleep the night. I've got no real ties to prevent me taking to this commune lifestyle. It's worth thinking about.

They meet when they both have finished their shopping, and they introduce themselves properly. On the drive into the mountain, Brenda says her daughter's name is June, her granddaughter, Seven. 'June gave her that name against my wishes.' She says. 'Some new names for children amuse me, some annoy. Still, I love Seven so much she melts my heart. I *do* wonder what she'll think of it as a name when she's older, though.'

'I've never had that problem,' says Clem, 'I'm sure if I ever marry my wife will be the one to decide.'

'Let me tell you a bit more about what you'll see at Onetable Falls.' Says Brenda. 'I regard it as a well-designed village that creates the right balance of togetherness and privacy. Everyone needs community in their life, and I don't believe it's possible in today's high density residential estates. They have to seek it in clubs of some sort.'

'Onetable is designed for social activities. The central common house has a shared kitchen, dining/lounge area, laundry and other facilities as the community requires. Houses are placed around the common house. The people who live there take responsibility for the community - they are their own landlords. Cars are parked at the back of the living spaces.'

'The community is based on respect, listens to all voices, and has open decision-making. The Native Americans said it well: "If you want to go fast, go alone; if you want to go far, go together".' Brenda stops her description leaving Clem in deep thought.

This could be just what I need. Brenda is intelligent, and qualified, and has grown up in this lifestyle and chosen it with thought. On being introduced to June he feels a hot flush and difficulty finding the right words. She oozes personality behind a clean face free of makeup and dressed in bright clothing covering a slim body with bumps in all the right places. Seven comes running in from the direction of the centre complex to grab her mum's hand, smile broadly, and peer up to Clem's face. Seven's anxious to meet the visitor, full of questions, wanting to know all about life beyond the commune.

Clem's mind flashes back to his own childhood in a remote part of the Darling Downs. He crouches to Seven's level. 'Seven, it's a pleasure to meet such a bright and inquisitive young girl. Your mum's invited me in for a cup of tea and you can ask me all the questions you want to if you join us.' Then June intervenes.

'Seven! Mind your manners, please. Mr Fielding is our visitor. You must be more patient.'

Clem holds his hand up to June. 'Don't worry. It's a pleasure to meet such a bright young person.'

Clem spends an hour enjoying the conversation, answering Seven's questions, and then decides to leave on his walk back to the town after thanking them all for their hospitality. He declines the offer of a lift, saying he needs the exercise. He finds a bus shelter and stretches out on the seat using his purchases as a pillow. His mind is tangled with concerns about escaping the drug net and the opportunity of becoming a recluse at the commune. Could it be an alternative to fleeing the country. He feels his welcome there was exciting. Slumber comes eventually, but it is a troubled sleep.

In the morning Clem is still in two minds as he walks to the station to book his seat. He uses the station facilities to change clothes and clean up and has time to wander back to the local bank to withdraw $2000,00 cash, the most they would do for one day. He knows this will have to do until he escapes the criminals. He doesn't know much about Sydney. He's heard Woolloomooloo is a harbour suburb where commercial and naval shipping operates. He'll look at opportunities for a passage out. He may have to earn his keep.

FIVE

Sarah reaches Sydney after another seven hours on the road. Arriving at the Nursing Home, Geraldine apologises to say there is no suitable bed for her at the Home, but she is aware of cheap accommodation in Hurstville. Sarah makes enquiries and books at the Latitude Hotel on Forest Road, quite close to the railway station. She spends some gruelling few hours coaxing her father to speak and after she shares a pizza with Geraldine, she leaves the Home late to retire. On the way she has the feeling she is being watched and she switches trains at Sutherland to check. By the time she moves into the Hurstville accommodation she flops onto the bed fully clothed, exhausted, stressed by the family troubles, and the suspicion she was being watched. She drops off into a troubled deep sleep and does not stir until three the next morning. It's too late to phone Boris, and she decides to leave it to the next night.

The next day she spends the morning trying to drag information from her father's long-term memory banks. He listens and smiles. He seems to understand her references to life at Millmerran, the animals, the vegetable gardens, the chooks. He nods his head from time to time, but words fail him. Sarah's patience finally gives in for a break.

She and Geraldine share sandwiches and coffee in the kitchen for lunch. 'The hotel suite is right near the Railway station,' says Sarah, 'it's only rated as grade two accommodation, but that's fine, it's only for sleeping. I'm worried because I had a feeling I was being followed after I left here last night. I'm not used to this. Is it a problem Sydney has?'

'Not that I'm aware of.' Says Geraldine. 'It was quite late though for a girl to be travelling alone. You are attractive Sarah, maybe you should take care about travelling so late. Oh, I forgot to tell you earlier, but a man rang for you yesterday after you'd left. He said he is a friend of your brother and asked to speak to you. He said it was urgent and asked where you were staying. I just said you were renting accommodation in Hurstville, and they should call again today. I haven't had a call yet though.'

'That's very interesting.' Says Sarah. 'Did he give a name?'

'No. He sounded strange. As if something serious was troubling him about your brother's health.'

'Clem's trying to kick his drug habit. I've been trying to convince him to get proper rehab. He said he would work on it while I helped Dad. I'm not sure why his mate would ring here!'

'If he calls again while you're not here, do you want me to give him your mobile number?'

'Sure. I'll call Clem now to see what's going on.' Sarah walks to the room her dad's in and phones. She gets a voice message to say the number is not answering. She calls the number she has for the garage where he works. A guarded voice tells her Clem has not reported for work. *Clem's capable of calling me if he needs help. I won't call Mum about this and worry her.*

She returns to tell Geraldine and finishes her lunch, and they continue to chat. 'Would you mind if I asked you to pick up some Chinese herbs for me when you go back to Hurstville?' Says Geraldine. 'The Asian supermarket, Song Li, is close to the station, near your hotel. If you would, this would save me a trip.'

'No trouble. For yourself, or patients?'

'Both, I suppose.' Says Geraldine. 'I believe in some of the Chinese herbal medicines that have been used for thousands of years. I have a book written by Ping-Chung Leung and others and found some that work. I do believe in Western Medicine, of course, but I'm flexible and try to find what works best for me.'

'I find that interesting,' says Sarah, 'could you loan me the book for a read one night?'

'Of course. You might find something to try for your dad. I'll give you my shopping list when you're about to leave. The Song Li Asian market has some Nopal herbs that's prepared for pick-up at closing time tonight, seven PM.

Sarah leaves the train at Hurstville station. It's after six PM and almost dark. She goes to the Asian supermarket and begins to browse the large collection of herbs. Some only have Chinese calligraphy to identify them, others have both this and English. *These latter must be the most popular.* She works her way through the shop taking some time to browse those having English identification, then picks up Geraldine's Nopal herbs. When she leaves the shop and is about to walk past a laneway she is suddenly taken by the arm and pulled into shadows.

She struggles to quickly free herself. 'Sarah, it's me! Take it easy!' It's Clem. She recognises straight away and hugs him, breathing heavily and gasping. Her mind is racing with questions. Blood has rushed to her face and neck and her heart is thumping.

'What's going on,' she cries softly, 'what are you doing?'

'They tried to kill me. I've got to get away. Two cops pushed my car over a cliff expecting to kill me – they'll be searching for me now, knowing I'll shop the whole bloody lot of them and their trade after what they did.'

'You look terrible. Are you trying to go cold turkey?' Why not phone me? Why this?'

'I smashed my phone so they can't trace me. There's cops in this, Sarah. I'm worried they'll be after you as well, thinking I've got nowhere else to get refuge. They could have cops everywhere looking for me.'

'Come with me so we can sort something out.'

In the hotel room, Clem describes the accident and his try to shelter in Woolloomooloo at the Martin Talon Hostel. He found the providers were mostly volunteers. He was shown a dormitory with six other men, all staying for one or two days, unable to afford the cost to stay longer. It's been a nightmare because of his fear of being recognised by cops and he left.

He's wearing his denim clothes and they're filthy. Sarah has no way of washing them and offers to take them to a laundry the next day while Clem recuperates. Sarah offers to go out to buy some food, but Clem says he's already had food at the refuge. Sarah decides to go anyway while he takes a shower. When she returns with take-away food they sit at the kitchen bench. Clem describes the ambush, and they discuss their next moves.

'We're both in trouble now Sarah. I'm so sorry for this mess, Sis. I used a public telephone to call the nursing home as someone else and was told you were staying in Hurstville. I've spent hours watching all train arrivals hoping to catch you. I'm sorry for the secrecy, I'm out of my mind. They'll easily find where Dad is, so neither of us should go there again. This gang will take time to be smashed.'

Sarah sits quietly thinking. Clem goes to the sink and starts preparing coffee. 'I might have an idea,' she says, 'Cheryl works in a nursing home somewhere in Sydney. You remember her? She was at the Pittsworth High School with us. I've got her phone number. I would have asked her to take Dad, but Abel Turner had already booked him in with Geraldine at Engadine. Cheryl might have an idea of somewhere for us to hide.'

'Yeh. I remember her. Your best friend there. She was two years behind me and was in the school netball team.'

'I'll give her a call. We haven't spoken for years. She'll get a surprise.' Sarah walks to her handbag and takes her mobile out.'

'Stop!' cries Clem, 'don't do that!'

'She won't mind me asking. What's wrong?'

'These cops could be monitoring phone calls. I've ditched mine. You should do the same till this blows over!' Sarah turns and stares at him narrowing her gaze. She returns to her stool without a word. 'If you call Cheryl, they'll be able to find you both.' says Clem, 'They'll know where Dad is, it's not safe for you to go there again. That's why I covered my voice and left my message from a public telephone saying I was a friend.'

Sarah switches off her phone and leaves the suite to call Cheryl from the station phone booths. Thirty minutes later she returns. 'Come on, let's go.' She says, picking up her handbag and the herbs.

SIX

Sarah collects her belongings and they set off for the Anna Nursing Home. They travel by train and bus. Hurstville is still very much alive on their walk to the station and Sarah is surprised by the number of shops open in both the main street and the station complex itself. Many people are studying the train schedules. Restaurants and take-aways are busy and hotels are in full swing. Does this suburb ever sleep? And where can all these people be travelling at this hour?

At Sutherland station, things are quieter, and they are fortunate to be just in time to catch the bus. By contrast there is only one other bus passenger. Clem's head has dropped, and his eyes are closed. Cheryl glances at Clem's new clothes wondering what could happen next. The thought of cops working in combination with drug dealers has given her sweaty palms and damp underarms. *What the hell has Clem done to us? She fidgets with her nursing gown picking off split ends of hair. What's Cheryl going to make of all this? Is it fair to involve her with this risk? What will happen next has to be life-threatening.* Perspiration moistens her forehead.

She turns to look through the window. The bus drives past bus stops where no one waits and the scenery flashes by. For the most part, there's little parkland and comprises mostly of dwellings that are either high rise or dense residential housing crammed into blocks of land as small as the local council can prescribe. How different is this city life? She's grown up on a twenty-acre property with fruit trees, vegetable patches, a chook run, and bird baths for attracting and feeding the local birdlife. There she's known many of the locals and town people and everyone you pass in the street acknowledges by nodding or raising the hand. In this city everyone is in a rush to get somewhere and doesn't want to know you. *What will it be like to live in Toowoomba after she and Boris marry?* Her choice would be to stay at Millmerran and commute as needed, but that's just one item of many they haven't discussed yet.

She looks askance to check on Clem. Has the twelve months in the gambling, nightlife, and money packed pleasure-seeking tourism changed him from those roots? *Am I right to believe I can change him back? I know I have the skills for treatment and medication, but my training tells me recovery is best done in social groups. Where individuals gain comfort from seeing others suffering and trying to change like himself. There's some solace in that, but Clem has to be locked away to be safe. I'll do my best. I feel he really does want to go clean.*

Clem stirs and lifts his head and rubs his eyes. He sees her flushed face and puts his arm over her shoulder. 'I'm sorry Sis. I shouldn't have come to you for help. But don't worry about it. The sooner I can organise a passage out I'll disappear overseas 'till these crims are caught. I've been thinking about it, and I've got some ideas. I talked with some homeless guys at Woolloomooloo, and they promised to look around for me. I offered them money.'

'I don't even know if Cheryl can help for long and I'm feeling guilty for jumping into this.' Says Sarah.

'I'll only be here for a day or two. I don't want you in any danger. I'll find a way.'

'You need help with your detox Clem. I want to help.'

They alight at the Menai shopping mall and walk to the nursing home a few streets away. Although it's late evening when they arrive, Nurse Cheryl is expecting them. She has already prepared the two-bedroom suite at the rear of the centre for them to share. The front door is locked for the night and Sarah presses the night button. They don't have long to wait.

Cheryl opens the door and sees Sarah. They jump into each other's arms both crying and trying to talk at the same time. 'Sarah! It's been years since I've seen you. How did we lose touch? How long since we've spoken on the phone? Ages – our calls just drifted away. You haven't changed though. You look so good, and the years don't show. Seeing you brings back so many memories.' These two girls are best friends from school days and when they stop hugging Cheryl welcomes them and escorts them through the Home to the suite.

Sarah introduces Clem to Cheryl. He takes her hand and nods, but his head hangs low, and he shows no desire to join their eager conversation. He says he's struggling to keep his eyes open and excuses himself to clean up, go to bed, and try to relax. He's fatigued and has a headache. He's been suffering insomnia more often since taking drugs, but his body needs to rest and recover from the crash. He's prepared to have to lay awake for some time. He walks away and Sarah turns back to Cheryl.

'You look good too Cheryl and we should have kept in touch. I've worried all the way here because we could mean trouble for you too. This has been sudden. If we're too much trouble, we'll move off. Don't hesitate to say so. I *am* thankful for your offer, but I couldn't say too much on the phone. We've a lot to tell you but it can wait 'till tomorrow. You should leave both of us to unwind for now and get some sleep for yourself.'

Cheryl points to the kitchen island bench indicating she's not ready to leave just yet. They sit opposite holding hands across it for a short chat. 'Thanks so much for accepting us.' Says Sarah again.

'You told me some on the phone,' says Cheryl, 'you should know I'll take any risk for my life-long best friend.' Their eyes are wet as they pause and sit looking at each other. Cheryl speaks first. 'You know, I really missed you when my parents and I moved down here. You were my rock for so many years.'

'Travelling together from our small town to the big school at Pittsworth was the start of our friendship,' says Sarah, 'and It's funny how we both got into nursing, isn't it? I know the school advisor said I should do a medicine degree, but I like the closer relationship nurses have with patients.'

'I feel the same too,' says Cherly, 'but you were much smarter than me.'

'I don't regret my choice,' says Sarah, 'and I'm so glad you've got this job managing the nursing home here and are willing to help us. I've never been this close with anyone since you left, Cheryl.'

As they continue to reminisce Sarah talks about the problem she has before her to treat Clem. Cheryl soon looks at the clock and sees its well past midnight. She says she really needs to get some sleep to be able to do her early morning rounds. They smile at each other, and head for bed.

In the morning the two women continue their chat over breakfast. 'Cheryl, you've made us welcome, but I've probably endangered you too because of this ruthless gang chasing Clem. Clem's destroyed his phone and mine's switched off because Clem warned me about bent cops and their ability to trace phone locations. I called you last night from a public phone to not involve you.'

'Can you tell me more about Clem's big problem? What's going on?' Asks Cheryl.

'There's a gang trying to kill him. They've already had one go and pushed him over a cliff in a car he was driving for work. He's been foolish, Cheryl, and got himself tangled up with a drug gang by doing deliveries for them. He knows too much but wants to leave.'

'I'm sorry,' says Cheryl, 'I'll help in any way I can. I remember Clem differently.'

'I haven't had a proper chance to introduce you yet.' Says Sarah. 'I was too overcome last night. He's not well, but he's determined to fix that now. He'll be okay. I want to help him kick the drug habit he got himself into. I'm qualified to get proper medications for his condition, but I'm scared to go anywhere. I've got both Clem and Dad in need of constant care and it's very worrying.'

'The other night I felt something was fishy, that and I was being followed when I left Dad's nursing home. I jumped off the train at Sutherland and lost him, then went to Hurstville where I was staying. It's very creepy.'

'Then Dad's nurse, Geraldine, tells me about a call from a person looking for Clem. But it was Clem himself, and next, he turns up suddenly at Hurstville and tells me his story. That's when I remembered you had a nursing home. That's what Clem needs, but I'm not leaving him here for you to take care of. I'm staying too because they want me to lead them to Clem. Cops pushed him over the cliff to die, and he says they can get your location through your phone. They can probably monitor calls as well to see who's making calls and where from. It's spooky.'

'Wouldn't it be safer to use home phones then?' Asks Cheryl.

'If they're monitoring calls from family and friends, they recognise voices and get information that way. Clem says a thing called 'calling line identity' works for home calls. Like I said, it's creepy, and even public phone boxes are a risk with calls to numbers they know. If I call home to Mum and they're monitoring her line, they could listen and learn where I am.'

SEVEN

Days later, Jane walks through the Central Station complex on her way to her lodgings after a day of study at the Sydney Technical College. Hordes of business workers are rushing for their trains home, and she has to watch carefully to avoid clashing with others. She'd like to take more time to examine the renovations taking place, the eating facilities, and to read the inscription below the bust marked as the Founder of NSW Government Railways. *I'll do that in the morning when it's not so rushed.* It's getting more congested as she approaches the single down escalator for the Eastern Suburbs and Illawarra line.

She works her way to the top of the escalator from about ten deep and is surprised to see how far down the platform is. She's forced to share her step with two others, but no one is talking. During the long descent, she peers over heads looking for the indicator board to see the timetable for Edgecliff. Her vision narrows. She stretches her neck forward and focuses. *It can't be. That looks so much like Sarah! It can't be. She's been missing for days and hasn't called anyone.*

Jane's heart beats faster. She's oblivious to the screeching brakes and the unintelligible garble from loudspeakers announcing destinations. The blast of cold air pushed from the tunnel by the train emerging doesn't register. The train squeals to a stop and doors open to the surge of passengers for the Illawarra direction. It looks unruly as people force others aside to get a foot on the train. Her neck throbs as she pushes through the congestion and dodges down the opposite side of the platform to those boarding.

The girl's attention is drawn, and their eyes lock. Her facial expression is a mixture of surprise, acceptance, then panic, changing quickly. She moves to step inside her carriage, keeping her eyes on Jane. Jane tries to push closer through the thong, but Sarah shakes her head mouthing 'No! No! No!' She steps aboard. Giving Jane no chance to follow.

She doesn't want to know me!

As the train pulls out Jane staggers along the platform staring through windows at standing passengers. Sarah turns to face her and shakes her head again.

Jane shivers. Her feet are stuck, and her head is spinning. *This can't be. Why hasn't she called someone? Boris is devastated. We all thought she'd been abducted. Police are searching! What is she doing here and without any escort? It must be voluntary.* Jane slumps onto the nearest platform seat, chewing her lip, and staring at the end of the disappearing train.

She didn't want to recognise me. She didn't want to say anything. It couldn't be cold feet for her coming wedding. I've got to let Boris know she's alive. What about her parents? How could she be so cruel?

Jane doesn't know much about Sydney, she's only here to do a short course on accountancy. She's been living with Len in Toowoomba. She expects Len will be spending the day with his new team. She sends a text message saying she will call later tonight – something serious has come up. She'll talk to him from the quiet of her bed-sitter.

Jane's decided a search for Sarah must take priority now. She looks at the railway timetable on her mobile and stares at the possible destinations of interest on the Illawarra line. Nothing takes her attention. Sarah is a nurse, could she be working at a hospital? Jane decides to ask Len to send a photo and tomorrow she'll visit all the hospitals on this line.

She leaves the train at Edgecliff and walks casually down her street. The quality of the housing and high-rise accommodation justifies the elite suburb advertising she read before picking her second-floor unit. She plans to cook for herself and stay in for an early night. She takes off her shoes and stretches out on the bed to rest.

Jane wakes from her short nap with a headache. She rubs her eyes and stares at the ceiling. *How am I going to find one person in a city of over five million people. My only clue is she went somewhere on the Illawarra Line. But she may be visiting. I'll start with hospitals. She is a nurse! She might have a job.*

She glances at her watch and phones Len. 'Did you get my message? I saw Sarah this morning – I know it was her. I've been worrying about it.' She says. 'She's in hiding from all of us for some reason. Why would she run away from me to catch a train? I've got to find her. I've been thinking. She couldn't go to a large hospital and sign on with her registered name because she would know we would look for this. She might be working at a nursing home, or a retirement village, maybe even palliative care. It means I'm on a wild goose chase. I need her photo!'

'Jane. Wow! Calm down a minute.'

'And I've also got that funny feeling that I'm being watched.' She says.

'You've got to think about yourself in this.' Says Len. 'I don't want you getting involved with anything shady. I want you safe. How long are you planning to stay there and search?'

'We know her well enough to know she's straight, and she must be in trouble. I'll call you every night. I'm going to search.'

'I'll tell Boris you've spotted her and she's alive and well. You stay safe. Keep me posted. Promise?'

'Len, you can't say anything to Boris yet. We don't know enough about why. Do you think she could have found him dating someone else or having a past? It's a mystery. I'll call you again tomorrow. Could you look for her photo and send it to my phone please?'

'I'll do that. Jane, if you feel you're being watched, there must be a reason. What's she running from? I'm not happy about this, you've got to be very careful.'

*   *   *

When Jane rises the following morning after troubled sleep, she's not the slightest bit hungry. After one slice of toast and vegemite, she dresses neatly and sets off to the station. The first hospital she visits is Saint George Public at Kogarah. It's a fifteen-minute walk from the station, where most businesses activity is taking place. Her walk takes her along an uninteresting street cluttered with construction works, to a large hospital complex that's being extended and upgraded. A Public and a Private are co-sited on a very large block opposite a multistorey parking station.

The hospital expansion activities are partly commonplace following the Covid virus and the greater demand for services. Sometimes patients are cared for by paramedics at the hospital front door for over an hour before admission to emergency wards. And even then, they are kept on ambulance trolleys until a bed is available.

During Covid the media focussed on hospitals and health services because the pressures were so severe on the emotions of nurses. Nurses have been leaving in droves. Those remaining are holding work stoppages and demonstrations for more staffing and better pay. Jane knows that Sarah would have no difficulty to obtain employment in these circumstances. *But where?*

At the enquiry desk of the Public, she asks if it would be possible to speak with the Chief Nursing Officer (CNA) about a nurse she's searching for. She's put through to an office where a receptionist answers. No new nurse has recently made enquiries about employment.

She moves into the hospital trying to draw the attention of a nurse during her rounds. Twice she is successful but neither recognises the person in the photo. She does the same at the Private with the same lack of success, and she leaves. The next major hospital is the Sutherland Hospital, so she returns to the trains and goes further South.

The line branches at Sutherland, one direction goes further south toward Wollongong and the South-Coast, and the other east to the Cronulla Shire, the location of this Hospital. Jane alights at Caringbah Station and takes the long walk. Her similar approach again proves unsuccessful, and having had little breakfast, she decides to have a snack in the cafeteria. She finds it crowded. She buys her snack at the counter and carries her tray while scanning the tables and sees a group of three nurses sitting together at a table for six. She decides to join them.

She doesn't interrupt their chatter, and while she eats, she places the picture of Boris and Sarah on the table. Sarah is in her nurse uniform. Soon the nearest nurse sees the photo and enquires. Jane describes her hunt for Sarah. The photo is shown around, and one nurse recognises Sarah and asks Jane to come aside to talk privately.

'She was seeking Buprenorphine here, a medication to treat euphoria and craving when being used for detox. She was very distressed, explaining that her brother was in trouble. She showed me her nursing qualification and photo, a Licensed Practical Nurse from Millmerran, saying she was unable to obtain a prescription in her present circumstances. She was pleading. What I did was unlawful, I know, and I don't want anyone else to know. But I believed her and gave her a small supply from our hospital chemist. I could see she was genuine and needed help.'

'Oh God. I'm so grateful to hear this.' Says Jane, dabbing her eyes. She describes how she spotted Sarah at the foot of the escalator. 'Can you give me any directions? I must go to her. She needs my support.'

'I've just finished my shift and I'll be heading home in about half an hour. I can drop you off at Sutherland Railway Station where I dropped your friend. I think she said she was headed to Menai. Will that do?'

'I can't tell you how thankful I am. I'm lost in this city and Sarah will be too. Thank you so much. I'll show this photo around to the staff at Sutherland station and try to pick up her track from there. If they can't help, I'll head to Menai and look around.'

EIGHT

While doing web searches on the bus to Menai, Jane finds the Anna Health Centre. She hopes for success but is not really expecting to be lucky so quickly. Following a few enquiries at the Menai shopping mall, Jane finds her way to the Centre. On entering, the receptionist is very cautious until Jane shows the photo. A nurse comes to reception and escorts Jane to a self-contained unit at the rear of the complex and knocks softly. Sarah opens the door.

Sarah stares speechless at Jane and begins to shiver. Jane stretches her arms out. After pausing for what seems like an eternity, Sarah suddenly relaxes and falls into Jane's arms, squeezing her tightly, and a flood of sobs and tears begin to flow. Sarah sags. Jane and Cheryl grab her and assist her into the unit and sit her on the lounge. Jane crouches at her feet, cups her hands round her calf muscles, and begins a soft massage.

Sarah stares into Jane's eyes. 'Oh Jane. I know you mean well, but you've probably just given my secret hideout away.'

'How? I'm sure I haven't been followed, and I've been very careful. But why should I be?

'It's a long story but you've got to switch off your phone straight away.'

Jane does as asked and moves up to sit alongside Sarah. She wraps an arm around her. 'What's the problem? What's going on?'

'Clem knows there's a gang trying to kill him. They must be able to track calls. They found Dad's nursing home and saw me visit him. Somehow, they thought I was expecting Clem to visit me. It's scary! I was followed the last time I left Dad, but I managed to escape, and found this place for Clem and me to hide until I can fix his habit. I've had my phone switched off ever since, and I make sure I lose anyone trying to follow me.

'Where's Clem now? Is he okay?'

'Clem's in the bedroom here. I dosed him to sleep off another craving and anxiety attack. He's on the run and worried, but he seems to be okay and keen to kick the drugs and alcohol. Drugs were offered to him by one of his mates as a favour. Before long he became a cocaine user.'

Sarah continues to explain to Jane the circumstances of Clem's addiction, the action of the bent cops, and the dangers they are facing. 'This is terrible,' says Jane.

'The big problem is cops are involved. Contact to or from family and friends could trace us. They might even be able to monitor calls.'

'This is not fair on Boris. He's out of his mind. He's got to know you're safe.'

'I'm desperate to let him know too,' says Sarah, 'but my priority must be to protect Clem. Dad should be okay for a while. He's in bad shape and doesn't remember who I am, just smiles when I go in. My problem now is that Clem needs my full-time care to get him clean and let him find a safe place to live. Maybe overseas somewhere. If you tell Boris he'll want to come here, and that'll give our secret away. I'm not even game to call anyone from a public phone.'

'Now I know where you are I'm sure I could bring Boris here safely.' Says Jane. 'We could leave our phones somewhere and find our way here making sure we're not being followed. Where is your dad? What happened to him?

'Another long story.' Says Sarah. 'He had a bad accident at Cobar where he worked advising on the chemicals to extract minerals from tailings. His head accident at Cobar was serious and he was taken to a nursing centre in Engadine. The accident caused total loss of memory and he needs full-time care. I went to Engadine to check on his treatment before Clem's problem came up. Dad was dedicated to his work and even when home he carried out private experiments at a historic plant at Sundown Creek, not far from Millmerran.'

'The nurse here has no experience with addiction, detox, and stabilization.' Sarah continues. 'She's helping me treat Clem. Cheryl's a quick learner. I think Clem's already taken a liking to her. Depending on his mood and his craving he can be a nice guy.'

'I'm going to talk to Len again tonight.' Says Jane. 'He's worked with Detective Inspector Beryl Stone to help solve crimes in the past. It would be far better to clean this gang up properly.'

'I know Beryl Stone,' says Sarah, 'I was involved. That could take ages though. I've got to concentrate on Clem for now and can't afford to take risks, or he's dead!'

Clem wanders out from his bedroom wondering who the visitor chatting with his sister can be. He's dressed respectfully in short leg pyjamas that Cheryl purchased for him at the Menai shopping mall, but his hair is unkempt, and face unshaven. Jane is introduced to Clem, and they chat together until Jane senses that Sarah wants to attend further to Clem's detox program. She departs, saying she will now be extra careful about her movements and contacts. She will tell Boris that Sarah is safe. She won't disclose the location and she'll find a way to get Boris here secretly, making sure nothing leaks.

*   *   *

'Mr Goldman's office, can I help you?'

'It's Bill Pickings here with information for Mr Goldman. Can you ask him if he wants it now or will he call me back?'

'Hold the line please.'

'Bill, what do you know?'

'Mr Goldman, I've had a call back from my friend at the Millmerran pub. His missus knows everything going on out there. Clem's mum's in a bad way and she's getting home care because she's had no word from Clem or his sister. Her husband had a bad accident in a rock fall and lost his memory. The daughter went to Sydney to support him, she's a nurse. The daughter did go to the coast to visit Clem and that's the last thing she knows.'

'Thanks. It confirms other reports I've had.'

The line goes dead and again Bill stands there staring at his handset. *He's an ignorant prick. No thanks no favours. Thinks he's a fucking bigshot. Why do I do any fucking chores for him.*

*   *   *

Goldman phones Abel Turner, the manager of the Cobar Mine. 'Abel, Caleb Goldman here. Two things. First, I heard there was an accident and George Fielding was badly injured. He was telling me about his experiments and about the impact they could make. I'd like to get an expert opinion about them to see if he could use his ideas as an investment. I could help him there. I'd like to know his condition to discuss the prospects'.

'Second, I'm looking for his son Clem who seems to have disappeared from the face of this earth. Has he been there looking for his father or collecting his belongings?'

'Clem hasn't been here. George has a complete loss of memory and he's in a care centre for him in Sydney.'

'Would you know where George keeps the records for his experiments?' Says Goldman.

'He's got a locker here. There's only one key for it. I suppose his daughter's holding it for him. I've met her. She's a lovely girl. She's a nurse and anxious about getting proper care for him.'

'Would you know where she is or how I could contact her?

'Sorry Mr Goldman. I only can only give you the address and phone for the Millmerran home if that would help.'

'I already know those. If you hear from the daughter, would you ask her to call me? Let me know if you get anything.'

Abel slowly restores the handset to its cradle and sits back in his seat gazing blankly at the opposite wall. *I've had chats with George for years. He's never mentioned Caleb Goldman to me, nor said anything about getting help with his work. That guy wasn't all that interested in George's accident or his condition. I wonder what it was really all about. I wasn't going to give anything away till I know more.*

NINE

Jane arrives at her Edgecliff unit. She sits on her bed, takes a deep breath, holds it, then breathes out slowly and bends to remove her shoes and massage her legs. She has a tight feeling in her chest and throbbing above her eyes. Something new is worrying her. That sinking feeling that she's being followed. Is this just imagination after listening to Sarah's distress? Sarah didn't mention her mother either. Was that because bent cops might be monitoring her line?

I've been calling Len. Does this implicate us already? Would they know I've been searching for Sarah? How can I contact Len to tell him what I've just learned? Would it be safe for me to contact him by a call to his hotel from a public phone? I'd have to make sure I wasn't followed to that phone. I'll sneak out the back of these units and go to Bondi Beach by bus to make this call. That way I'll know if I'm followed.'

She leaves the rear access to the units and follows the lane to the back street. It runs parallel to the front street, so she turns and walks toward the station, keeping watch. *If I'm being watched, where would they wait. Or could they have someone at the station keeping watch, expecting all my movements to be by train? When would they know to expect me? How long would they be prepared to watch? How many people would be involved? It could be a parked car, but surely no one could be that patient. Or could they have another lodger keeping watch and keeping them posted? They must already know I've found Sarah and are waiting for me to lead them to Clem. If that's the case, they don't want me to be suspicious, and they're not likely to harm me in the meantime. I hope I'm right with that. To be sure it's not someone at the station I'll walk to the next bus stop.* She wends her way through side streets to get back to the main drag and looks for a stop.

'Toowoomba Gates Hotel, can I help you?

'Yes, it's Jane here from unit 303. I want to make a private call to Len. Would you be able to contact him in person and ask him to talk to me on one of your house phones in the reception area please? I know this is a strange request, but it's really important for me.'

'No problem, Jane. It's Simon here. I saw Len come in. I'll duck up to tell him and set it up for you.'

'I'll hang on here. I really appreciate this Simon, it's urgent.'

'Jane love,' says Len, 'What's going on? Are you in trouble?'

Jane has a tremble in her speech. 'Oh Len. Sarah's hiding Clem and they're in big trouble as we expected. She's safe for now. She's in hiding with Clem because he's being chased by a gang that have corrupt police involved. That's why absolute secrecy is needed.'

'Good God,' says Len, 'Jane, whatever you do make sure you're not involved in this. You have to leave this to me from now on. Do you understand?'

'It may be too late. I've spent hours today with her and Clem and now I feel I may be followed. Not right now, I've taken precautions to make this call from a beachside public phone. I'm sure it's safe, but I'll have to limit the details in case our hotel line is being monitored. This is so scary!'

The situation is explained, and they prepare a plan. Len will confer with Boris who will be over the moon to know Sarah is alive and well. Boris will be keen to go to Sydney once he knows how to reach her. Jane is to wait until Boris arrives at Edgecliff and be told secretly how to reach Sarah. Jane will return to Toowoomba. Len will try to get advice from Detective Inspector Beryl Stone, who he knows well on a personal basis. He has previously helped her with a sabotage plot and the attempted assassination of a government minister. He's sure Beryl is straight and will help.

Len calls Boris who is still back at the football ground kicking the ball around with some of the team members. He asks him to come back straight away to the hotel where they both stay to discuss an urgent football matter. This is an unusual request from Len, so Boris knows something serious has come up. He quickly tells the others he's been called away, he grabs his gear, and heads for his car.

Len leads him to the side table, presses him onto a chair, keeping his hands on his shoulders. 'Boris. Sarah's alive and well. She's doing this to protect us all from a gang. She hasn't deserted you. It hasn't been safe for her to call anyone.'

Boris jumps up grabbing Len's arms. His face is ghostlike, and he glares at Len. 'Why?' Boris raises his voice.

'Steady old boy. It's true all right,' Len says, 'She hasn't called us because the gang has bent cops who can access our calls and trace her. She's in hiding with Clem. Settle down and listen to my plan.'

'Just tell me where she is so I can go there.' Says Boris.

'You'll have to go there in secret. Only Jane knows where. You can't use your phone or mention this to anyone if you want her safe.'

'What's your plan?'

'Phone Jane and tell her you would like to call in to see her on your way to talk to Liverpool Rangers, that new Sydney football club.'

'I'll kill any shit-kicker that touches Sarah!' Boris says. 'Has that fucking brother got her into this?

'Calm down mate,' says Len. 'Sit back down again and I'll tell you everything I know.

Boris calls Jane to say he's about to drive down to Sydney, and why, as planned. It will be about a seven-hour drive plus finding his way through city suburbs. He says he will leave straight away for her unit no matter what time of day it is when he arrives. He'll call again as he gets close.

Toward the time Jane expects him, she walks out to her balcony and scans the street from her second-floor unit, hoping to see his car arrive. There's a familiar car parked opposite. It's one she saw when she returned yesterday. It's not directly opposite but sitting where there is a clear view to the front of her unit. There's a hollow feeling in her stomach and there's a new tension above her eyes.

She leaves the door to the balcony open so she can hear street noises and she sits in a chair nearby. Boris rang from the end of the motorway and could arrive any minute. She waits patiently. A car door slams, she swallows hard and nearly overturns her chair as she rushes to look. It's not Boris. Two policemen join the stranger, and they walk to the front of the units. *This looks bad. Is it for me? What can they know?*

She checks the deadlock and puts her ear to the door. Her heart sinks as she hears footsteps coming along the corridor. There's knocking on the door. She freezes. They knock again, harder this time. She covers her face with her hands and backs away. There's a raised voice.

'This is the police. We know you're there. We have an urgent message for you from a nursing home. Our plain clothes detective has been waiting to make sure you would be in when we got here. It's serious, and we must speak to you in person.'

'What nursing home?' Jane shouts back.

'In Engadine. This is urgent, please open the door.'

Could this be true? I'll plead ignorance. I'll act normally. There's no reason for them to suspect me of anything. She steadies herself and unlocks the door. The three men enter and close the door.

'Is this news about Mr Fielding?' She says.

'We're looking to contact this person's daughter to advise her of her father's death. The nursing home says his daughter has been there to visit him, and we've been unable to find her. Our investigation has indicated that you know the daughter well and she may have contacted you while you're visiting Sydney.'

'What you're talking about is all a mystery to me. I'm only here to attend a week-long accountancy course at the Sydney Technical College.'

'We don't believe you're telling the truth. Please be cooperative or we will have to take you to the station.'

One of the uniformed men takes her by the shoulders and forces her onto a settee.

'Lady, we're serious about this.' He says. 'We know you spent most of yesterday in the Illawarra area. We know you've asked questions at hospitals along that line. You've just lied to us. We won't leave this room until you tell us what you know, even if we have to use force.'

'You're fake cops to suggest such a thing.' Says Jane, twisting away from his hands, struggling to stand and make a dash for the door. The other policeman grabs her arm and slaps her savagely across the face. She spins, stumbling back. Jane kicks his knee and makes another dash for the door. The plain-clothed man blocks and takes her into a bear hug. Jane back-heels him in the shin and screams.

There's a loud bang and the door swings open on one hinge with splintered wood flying everywhere. All eyes turn to see Boris burst in and he crosses quickly to the one holding Jane. He gives him a kangaroo punch to the back of his neck, and he crashes forward smothering Jane beneath him. Boris delivers his best drive into his kidneys. He rolls in pain and will piss blood for weeks. The two in uniform move on Boris. Jane struggles to her feet and makes a dash for the balcony to raise the alarm. One cop turns to chase. Boris follows. The struggle continues close to the railing. Boris tries to drag Jane away from her captor, she stumbles, the top of her body overbalances and she begins to slip over the railing. Boris dives to grab her. His momentum forces them both to overbalance and they tumble over. They land heavily on the concrete pavement below, Boris partly across Jane's body, partly softening his impact, but adding to her injury. Neither moves.

The two in uniform adjust their clothing and run down the stairs. People are gathering to try to provide help and one is speaking to 'emergency'. Jane and Boris are both unconscious. Jane has blood trickling from one ear. By the time the two police reach the scene they explain their presence because they received a report of a domestic tiff in the unit. As soon as the paramedics arrive, the police talk to them and leave the scene.

The paramedics check breathing and circulation. They check their eyes, looking for dilated pupils. They check for fractures. They're more concerned about Jane's head injury, she needs urgent hospital attention. They stretcher Jane first to an ambulance. A second ambulance arrives, and the new paramedics attend to Boris. He's begun to stir, but he has fractures. He could have spinal trouble indicated by the agony he experiences as they try to move him.

Jane is admitted immediately to the emergency ward at Saint Vincent's Hospital. She's still in a coma. The doctors are concerned, and they arrange an MRI to check for bleeding of the brain.

The registrar asks Admin to try to contact the nearest of kin. Jane carries no identification, and police are requested to go to the Edgecliff unit to look for her purse to get contact details. Admin is annoyed to find police have not recorded the accident and they have to learn the location from the paramedics. Boris can talk by the time his ambulance reaches the North Shore Mater Hospital. He's been taken to a different one to Jane because of bed shortages and his injury didn't look as serious as Jane's.

*   *   *

Goldman receives a phone call. 'There's been a stuff-up boss. The bird at Edgecliff fell off her balcony trying to escape. But it's not all bad news. Her phone travel was traced to some place in Menai in South-Western Sydney. We have a rough location and will have it investigated ASAP.'

'I got a call earlier telling me the nurse was thought to catch a Menai bus before contact was lost. That looks promising. Don't muck around, you know what to do.'

TEN

Len starts his morning coaching session on defence again. He's worried that Jane hasn't called again. Her phone is probably switched off because of what she said the previous night. He begins as before and soon stops play when a failure occurs. He steps in to replay the move. The team physio is minding Len's phone, and he rushes onto the field to give Len a message.

'Hotel reception called. Police are there looking for you. They want to speak with you urgently as soon as you can get there.'

'Oh my God. It's got to be Jane! You'd better take over here Mark. The boys know what to do, just keep them at it. Make them discuss it when defence breaks down. Tell them I've been called away.'

His heart is racing as he drives back. *This must be serious. God help me. I shouldn't have let her stay in Sydney. Fuck - could these be more bent cops?*

He invites the police up to his unit. His agitation is obvious, and they ask him to sit while they describe the situation for both Jane and Boris. Len presses both hands to his temples. The police pause to allow Len to settle down. Then they begin to question him regarding Boris's relationship with Jane. Could there be a basis for a quarrel? Len is guarded, *Keep it cool. Just ask for details of the hospitals.*

'They are both close friends of mine. Jane is in Sydney to attend an accountancy course. Boris was to call in to see her on his way to see the Liverpool Rangers football club. We are all the best of friends.'

'We have a report there was a tiff before they fell.'

'I can't believe that. Look, please give me the details of their hospitals. I want to get there as quickly as I can. Jane and I are about to get married.' He says.

The police show empathy. Len is convinced that these cops are genuine and thanks them for their help. The police are satisfied with Len's response and depart on a friendly basis.

Leaving for Sydney, Len almost side-swipes cars he's overtaking, and he speeds through yellow traffic lights trying to beat the red. He grits his teeth each time, but his thoughts rush back to Jane. *How could I let her get mixed up with bent cops? She told me about being followed. Fuck! I should've done something straight away!*

He chooses the New England Highway, expecting this to be the fastest route. It's a scenic highway that follows the Great Dividing Range with mixtures of dense forests and grassy plains, but they are no more than a blur to Len who has eyes only for the road ahead. He's caught in periods of slow traffic behind heavy transports and punches the steering wheel several times. One, a timber jinker, carries huge logs some twenty metres long up a steep incline with double lines and blind bends. Other times his passage through the many towns is slow and he takes risks whenever he can with the speed limits. Some have 50 Kph speed signs and while Len is confident he can travel much more quickly and safely, it becomes a balance between speed and being caught. Then some towns have traffic lights, and he sits drumming his fingers and gritting his teeth. He's not looking forward to the final stretch through the suburbs of Sydney to the central business district and then looking for the hospital. He's been told it's a nightmare with congestion, one-way streets, multiple speed signs, round-abouts, traffic lights, and give way signs.

Len doesn't have an eTag and gives toll roads a wide berth. His car is not equipped with GPS, and he can't manage his phone and drive at the same time. So, he relies on road signs and gets horribly confused and finishes up completely lost in a crowded suburb just north of the harbour. He looks for a service station to get fuel and ask directions. He's given a map to study and told his best way is to cross the Harbor Bridge, look for William Street, turn off into Victoria Street, which is one-way only, and then turn into the entrance to the main hospital foyer where he can access the parking station.

It's taken him several hours to reach Saint Vincent's Hospital and find somewhere to park. He goes to reception and looks for advice. His nerves are on edge, he's thirsty, his head aches, he's shuffling from one foot to the other, and he's told to wait. He won't take a seat and continues his pacing around until he is finally met by the Registrar. He stares, holding his heart, only to be told that Jane is still in coma. An MRI test has been taken and surgeons are currently discussing her condition. He's taken to the ward where she is under constant surveillance, hooked up to several monitors, and a drip. He's allowed to sit with her. He holds the hand of the arm which has the catheter attached and reaches over to whisper in her ear. He continues this while stroking the arm but gets no reaction. His eyes are wet, his stomach churning, his heart racing.

He's taken aside and asked to wait outside a surgeon's office for a briefing. After a short wait the surgeon invites him in, offers him a seat, and turns to face him. He asks to describe his relationship with Jane. Following a few pleasantries, he begins to describe Jane's condition. 'I'm sorry to say the news is not so good. Your partner has had an MRI taken to study the condition of her brain. Her fall has caused serious head injury, which of course you know. The test has shown she has suffered an acute subdural hematoma, burst blood vessels pressing on the outer layers of the brain, which will require draining. There is also intracerebral hematoma, blood pooling in the tissues of the brain. I've discussed the treatment required with other surgeons and they agree that I should tell you that there is real danger that she won't survive this injury.'

'I'm sorry I have to pass this possibility on to you. Keep your chin up though, we're doing our best and we have the very best surgeons on hand for her treatment. There's a coffee shop next to reception, I suggest you take a break as we expect it will be some time before Jane could regain consciousness.'

Len is thankful that he's sitting. His legs feel weak. He closes his eyes and presses his palms to them. He leans forward to rest his elbows on his knees. He's at a loss in this situation. In the past he's been able to resolve most stressful situations with brute strength and street-smart skills. Skills he acquired in his youth growing up in a town housing one hundred thousand Soviet troops during their war with Afghanistan. Several times he came to the aid of young women in distress. Until now he's had no lasting female relationships due to his nomadic life trying to fulfil his football ambition. Len and Jane discovered their true love for each other only recently during an escape from criminals in the Himalayan snowfields. The traumas experienced at the time caused them to realise the depth of devotion each held for the other.

Len returns to her bedside and continues to speak gently to her and stroke her arm. His eyes begin to droop, he lays his head on the bed, and he drifts off. He stirs when he feels her arm move. *Is this true or am I dreaming?* He rises from his seat, reaches over, and stares into Jane's closed eyes looking for movement. She's breathing slowly through her mouth and trying to speak. He places his ear close to her mouth. He speaks softly to her. Her eyes remain closed but she's trying to say something.

'Save - - -Sarah - - at - - - Anna' - - - is what he makes of it. Her face goes still again, and she continues to breathe slowly through her mouth. *Is her brain working? Is this a good sign?* Len rises intending to look for the doctor who spoke to him earlier.

The surgeon intercepts him, a lab assistant moves to the bed, unlocks the feet with his foot, and begins to move the bed. The surgeon tells Len they are about to operate.

'But I've just heard her speak. Her brain is working. Isn't that a good sign?' He says.

'I'm afraid not. The brain damage is increasing and must be attended to. Be assured we know what is needed. Take a break, the operation may take hours. You look exhausted, find somewhere to sleep and we'll phone you when the operation is over.'

Len is unsteady as he walks to the reception area again and takes a seat. He wants to be with her. He has the address of the Edgecliff unit, so he decides to walk there and rest for a while. Then he thinks of Boris. *Where is he??* He walks over to the hospital counter and joins the queue. When the receptionist eventually checks the records for him, she finds that the paramedics attending the accident advised that they were admitted to different hospitals because of the indication there was domestic violence.

He's told Boris was admitted to the Mater Hospital in North Sydney. Len is given the address. He searches for where he parked his car and drives off to North Sydney. He finds Boris and is pleased to see him awake, but nevertheless, in pain. Breaks to an arm and a leg have been set, but now there is suspected fracture to his vertebrae. He grimaces if he attempts to move his body and he's been strapped down.

Boris describes the scene he found when he arrived at Edgecliff, what he did, and how the fall resulted. 'Jane didn't have time to tell me where Sarah is hiding,' he says, 'she was going to drive me there secretly as soon as I arrived. I don't know where she is.'

'I'm going nowhere till I know how Jane is.' Says Len. 'I have a feeling she was trying to tell me something. They were the only noises she made. I'm very worried about her. Look Boris, I'm glad you seem to be well looked after. I want to get back to check Jane's unit and grab a couple of hours sleep before going back to Saint Vincent's. I'll see you again as soon as I can.'

Len checks in with the manager of the units before he climbs the stairs. The door is standing but leaning off the jamb, broken by Boris. He enters cautiously. *If they're smart, now they would want to see if I could lead them to Sarah. The cops don't know that I know they're bent, and they'll be watching me closely.*

He wakes from a troubled slumber. He's missed a call - could he please come to the hospital. He goes directly to the observation ward where he had been with Jane. The same surgeon leads him to where they had the previous discussion and sits him down. He takes a seat himself and faces Len with a blank expression. 'I have more bad news for you I'm afraid. Your partner is still in a coma and may be for days. We've operated, but I'm afraid that in many cases like this we have to rely on the healing powers of her own body. I'm terribly sorry, but I have to repeat, there is slender hope that she will pull through.'

Tears run down Len's cheeks. He hasn't cried since his early childhood. His recent association with Jane changed all that. He quenches his sobs and looks tearfully at the doctor.

'I want to sit with her.' He says.

'Sure. You'll have to wait until she's moved to a ward. The hospital has a lot to do yet. Can you help with the next of kin?'

'Both parents are dead. She has a son, Phil, a young footballer I coached. Now he's going to uni at Newcastle. I can give you his mobile, but I would like to break this news personally.'

Len eventually sits with Jane, stroking her arm again. His mind is still spinning. He lays his head on the bed and has an occasional sob. *I'll get these bastards if it's the last thing I do. Boris will be out of action for a long time. I'm going to take on the task of finding and protecting Sarah and bring these shit-kickers down.*

ELEVEN

Sarah, Clem, and Cheryl are sitting at the dining table of the unit at the Anna Health Centre having breakfast together. They're unaware of events happening elsewhere since Jane left for Edgecliff.

Clem's feeling better than he has for some time and is grateful for all the attention he's getting from both Sarah and Cheryl to speed his recovery. Glancing sideways at Cheryl his memory goes back to school years. He does remember her from then, even though he didn't pay much attention to her. She was two years behind him at Pittsworth High School. She and Sarah were like two peas from the same pod. Both were intent on their schoolwork and obtained good marks each year. Both were private without many other close friends, seemingly intent on obtaining results to boost future employment. He thought his sister was a bit of a swat. He knew she wanted to be a nurse. But surely you don't need top qualifications for that. Maybe they both just enjoyed studying and each other's company. He knew Sarah loved reading classic novels.

Study was not his forte. He was captivated by mechanical things, and he only referred to books when they were manuals for whatever he was working on. It was practical, hands-on learning, for him. By his final year at school, he was working part-time in a car recycling workshop in Pittsworth. Instead of payment, he could take replacement parts for whatever project was current. With his dad's money, he managed to get a crashed car for peanuts, and he was doing a full reconstruction using the tools at the workshop. He eventually had it registered and would drive to school in Pittsworth. Sarah was now chauffeured there instead of having to catch the bus.

'I've been thinking back to school times, Cheryl'. He says. 'You and Sarah helped each other with schoolwork and projects, and you played netball in the school team too even though you were two years younger than the others. I know some of the boys had the hots for you. You were very athletic and attractive, and they thought you were a bit of a snob because no one could pick you up.'

'I remember you too,' she says, 'I thought you were a bit of a tearaway with that bike of yours. And then the car. Sarah would tell me how you souped it up and made modifications to improve performance and the ride on rough trails. When you got that car some girls in my year wanted your attention, but you didn't seem interested in girls.'

'You probably remember more than I do. I was more intent on getting an apprenticeship to be a motor mechanic.'

Sarah leaves the table and starts cleaning up. It's her turn. Clem faces Cheryl across the table, and they continue to chat about their school years and other interesting students and teachers.

Sarah leaves for the bedroom and returns in her street clothes. She interrupts their conversation.

'I'd like to visit Dad.' She says. 'Cheryl, would you mind looking after Clem's medication while I'm away? It could be late by the time I get back.'

'Sure,' says Cheryl, 'you go. I'll look after him.' She winks at Clem.

Sarah blows them each a kiss and leaves. Neither of the remaining two speak as Sarah walks out through the Home and closes the front door. The silence is like the gap that follows a lightning strike waiting for the thunderclap. Both are consumed by what has just happened and are deep in thought. Clem is surprised that Cheryl gave him that wink during Sarah's parting comments. Could it have been a slip?

Clem's feeling better due to her presence. He's more comfortable, and calmer, and their conversations have grown longer. He feels some sort of magnetism. He's been dreaming about her and waking with an erection. He considers this to be part of her nursing skill, not an emotional attraction. But it's time to make a move. *That wink might have been subconscious, but it could carry more and tell a story. She might have the hots for me, and this could be how girls work. My mates have always taken whatever chance they can get.* He's new at this but there's something about her. She's been very attentive and for days has tended to take over from Sarah.

He pushes his chair back, steps around to take both her hands, and pull her into an embrace. She looks up. Clem cups her face in his hands and kisses her. This is a first. 'You've been good for me Cheryl. Your help with Sarah to try to mend my selfishness last year has given me new hope. I didn't chase girls at school, but I *was* attracted to you. I thought you were too popular for me to have a chance. You were admired by too many others. I'm surprised to find you unattached.'

'I'm very choosy waiting for Mister Right to turn up.' Clem's surprised that Cheryl is content to let him continue his embrace. His body is experiencing a hot flush sensation, and his heart is pounding. Cheryl moves her arms higher on his back drawing him closer. Clem hugs her and kisses again, this time harder and longer.

He picks her up and carries her to his bedroom and sits her on his bed. He sits next to her, wraps one arm around her drawing her into another firm embrace, kissing her again. He slips his other hand under her uniform to gently feel her breast.

'Stop.' She cries. 'It's too soon for this! I like you Clem, but we've only just met. I need more time.' He stands and sways on his feet with a bulging erection while Cheryl stands alongside and adjusts her uniform, feigning to not notice.

'I'm sorry, I'm sorry.' He says stepping back with blood rushing to his face and neck. 'I made a mistake. I understand. You need to know I can kick the drugs. I understand that.'

'I *do* like you Clem,' says Cheryl, 'but I've seen too many cases where it takes much longer, and I need to know it won't bounce back for you.'

'I'm sorry I've upset you,' he pleads, 'but I do understand. I *will* convince you, Cheryl. I've never felt this way before.' He pulls her to him again and they hold a long embrace in silence. Cheryl then leads him back to the kitchen for more coffee. She leaves to check her patients.

Clem decides he needs some exercise, and he changes clothes to take a street run. It's time to try harder.

TWELVE

Sarah reaches the nursing centre to find George has been given a seat on the front porch, sheltered from the sun, but in a position where he can watch the traffic and the parking lot. She knows Dad is reliable but worries about the opportunity this gives him to wander off. She enters the home and looks for Sister Geraldine to express her concern.

'Good morning,' she says, 'Dad looks comfortable out front, but is there a danger he might wander off?'

'Oh, hello Sarah,' says Geraldine, 'what a surprise to see you. I've been worried because you haven't been back since I asked you to pick up those herbs. Don't worry about your dad, he loves the chance to look at the people and the traffic. It seems to be his only interest. He's very settled and quite happy just to sit quietly by himself and think. Goodness knows what about. I feel sorry for him, but he shows no interest in having company.'

'I've got your herbs here for you now. Sorry about the delay. Can we have a chat about another family problem I've got now? I might not be able to visit Dad much for a while and I need to explain why.'

Later, when she walks up and sits facing her dad, he smiles. It's clear to Sarah she isn't recognised. He looks at her charmingly without inviting conversation. She pulls her chair over and sits closer to him. 'Dad, I'm Sarah, your daughter, how are you feeling today?'

His brow falls slightly, and he mumbles, 'Nice – here - isn't - it.'

It's clear that messages are confusing him. At least he's spoken. She moves closer, takes both his hands, and begins to describe joyful memories together from her childhood. The story about the pet dog he brought home for her third birthday. Some of the bedtime stories he would tell her before she went to sleep. Stories like the one about a young girl living on a remote country estate, having to ride her horse to school through woodlands and across a creek ford. He's listening intently and silently. He peers deeply into her face. She is surprised when he starts to mumble again, and she moves closer to try to understand what he's saying. It's something about a secret bed. She has no recollection of any story about a bed and assumes his mind is wandering. His smile disappears and he stares at her and nods his head up and down slowly until he gets her returning smile.

This is a new twist in his reaction to Sarah's visits. He looks healthy enough and he's clearly being well cared for, but the improvement is negligible. Her heart is at rock bottom. He closes his eyes and slips into sleep as she continues her story. Sarah slumps, idly picking a stray hair from her skirt. Tears form and she rubs her forehead waving it slowly from side to side.

Geraldine looks through the front window and sees Sarah's distress. She goes out to comfort her, then walks her inside to sit at the kitchen table. 'He's not improving Geraldine.' Sarah says. 'If anything, I think he could be getting worse. I'm so worried.'

'Don't give up,' says Geraldine, 'he eats well and sleeps well. Our visiting doctor checked him only yesterday and gave him a good report and said you can't hurry these things.'

'I suppose you're right. I know you're doing your best and I appreciate it. Abel Turner was a close friend of Dad and knew what he was doing when he organised you for his care. Have you known Abel long?'

'I cared for his mother two years ago. He made a special trip down from Cobar every month to see how she was going and told me he was impressed. He brought me a special gift every time he came. He's a gentleman, Sarah, and I know he was very distressed about your dad. He holds himself responsible, I think.'

'What happened with his mother?'

'She recovered well and Able found a retirement village for her. When he rang me about your dad, he said his mum was flourishing, had made several new friends, and they went shopping every week in the village bus. I'm sure he was hoping for an outcome like that for your dad.'

'Working at the hospital in Millmerran I've met lots of busy mine managers. The majority are too focused on their business to spend much time in these matters of the heart. It's sad, isn't it. Do you find that?

'I certainly do. That's why Abel is such an exception. He's a good man.'

After visiting for an hour, Sarah decides to return to the Anna Health Centre, taking all the necessary precautions. When she arrives, she finds Cheryl attending to other patients and gives her a wave as she continues through to their unit. She finds Clem soundly asleep, a good sign. The room looks like it needs a clean-up. Clem hasn't left clothes on the floor like this since she visited him at the Gold Coast. Something has unsettled him.

She moves to the kitchen section, switches the kettle on, and looks for the biscuits. She's still being very cautious about being followed, even though she takes the best precautions she can. She had a suspicion of being followed again from Engadine Station back by train to Sutherland Station. When she alighted, she searched around and saw no follower, then caught the Menai bus.

*　　*　　*

The person trailing Sarah makes a phone call. 'Mr Goldman. I've called to give you feedback on why it's taking so long to find Clem. I lost their friend days ago at Caringbah when she got a lift from another nurse instead of returning to the train. I looked up the nursing home for Clem's old man and kept watch for a few days. I saw Clem's sister there today when she visited, and I trailed her. I thought I was on a winner this time. She got off at Sutherland station and walked to the bus shelter and waited there. She looked frightened and kept glancing around. I wasn't game to show myself because she might've remembered me from the train, become suspicious, and caught a taxi. But she caught a bus.'

'For God's sake, get on with it and tell me what bus it was.'

'A bus to Menai. But she could get off anywhere along the way. It could take some time before she visits her dad again, so I'll study the Menai bus route.'

'I don't want long-winded stories, just get to the point next time. What you've just told me agrees with other information I've got, so good work. Get to it and start at the Menai end. She'll lead you to Clem, keep trying. Call me then.'

THIRTEEN

Returning from the hospital Len wends his way to the Edgecliff unit. He slumps into a chair. He doesn't have the energy to drive to Newcastle to talk to Phil, but he feels it's his responsibility to tell him his mother is seriously hurt and not responding to treatment. He's in two minds about suggesting Phil should travel down to see her. It wouldn't help Jane, and it's bound to devastate Phil to see how bad she is. It's bad enough for himself, how much worse it would be for Phil. And what's to gain?

Jane raised Phil, her only child, as a single parent after his father was killed in an explosion in the mine where he worked. There was controversy over the cause of the explosion, which Phil only heard about recently, and it partly explains why Jane has not found another partner for all those years. Not until Len turned up for a coaching assignment at her lakeside village.

Len saw Phil, a member of his new Morisset team, as a young player with great potential. He was a gifted striker and Len believed he was capable of advancing to A-league, even into the Australian team, if this became his desire and he was prepared to work at it. Gifted strikers are hard to find, are keenly sought, and Len was prepared to provide special coaching to advance his skills. If interested, he would be a shoo-in to Len's new team. In the past Len saw he had a problem with Jane's motherly protection. He needed to escape her apron strings, be his own man, and toughen up. This might happen now. At Morisset Len took a special interest in him and invited them both to visit his sister at Khancoban in the Kosciusko Mountains so he could take him bushwalking to toughen him up and improve his endurance.

Len's sister Samira and her daughter Liana migrated to Australia four years ago to live in the new family home at Khancoban. Liana and Phil became good friends during the Mount Kosciusko holiday, and that's where Len's close friendship began with Jane. Liana has matured quickly in the last two years during which time the two children have been snow skiing, water skiing, sailing, and mountain biking together. They both have just enrolled for different courses at Newcastle University and are sharing a nearby flat with two other friends.

Len wants to help Phil. He wants to free him of the responsibility of completing all the rigmarole tied to his mother's business as an accountant, and the management and maintenance of her house at Morisset. Both Jane's own parents died years ago, and Len knows of no other family members. He needs to check this out, collect all the information he can, and free Phil to live his own life. But this can wait for now, Jane's condition is the immediate problem, and he needs to talk to him.

For now, he will just pass the news of her fall in a phone call. Liana is very capable, and she will be a big help. He phones her first. 'Liana? It's uncle Len here. I've got some really bad news for Phil. Please tell me if he's there with you before you pass the phone.'

'Yeh. He's here Uncle. What's happened?'

'You both know his mum had that bad fall. I visited her last night and she's in a very bad way. I told the hospital I wanted to be the one to break the news to her son and prepare him for whatever might happen next. I know Phil will be worried and I'm pleading with you to do your best to comfort him and prepare him for the worst. I'm not able to drive to Newcastle yet, but I'll pay you both a visit as soon as I can. Can you do that?'

'Oh God. Of course. I'll do my best. I'll get help if I need to. Don't worry, you've got a lot on your plate and I'm sure I can handle it here for now.'

'You're a gem, Liana. A credit to your mum.'

He kicks the stool away and falls back onto the bed, pressing his palms to his eyes to stop bursting into tears again. His head aches, an unfamiliar condition because of the hardened life he's lived. He witnessed the worst of human behaviour growing up in Termez. Hardened soldiers returned for breaks after plundering and raping captured territories, not knowing if they will survive when they leave camp to return to the front. This left some undisciplined with their treatment of women and youths in the town. Len acquired his street-smart skills to survive, and he would always help those being harmed, usually the women. He can handle the rough stuff but feels useless to cope with these new emotions.

He can't sleep. He feels blood punching his eardrums. He needs to do something. *Save Anna, was it, or save with Anna, or save at Anna?* He mulls it over. He's heard of Anna Bay, looks it up, discovers it's north of Newcastle, and rules it out. Could she have a friend called Anna? He has Jane's bag. He takes her phone from it and scrolls through the contacts. Not one called Anna. He looks at the web. There are two young Anna students looking for accommodation to either study or sight-see. Forget them. There are three Annas offering psychology treatment at different inner suburbs. With their father's memory problem could there be a possibility that Sarah's being helped by one. Sarah must be very stressed herself. These are worth exploring. It has to be a personal visit to be trusted.

Len takes off straight away. Without appointments he has to wait at each one to talk to someone with authority, but it proves to be a disappointing waste of three hours. On returning to the city, he visits the Anna International Hotel to check if Sarah rooms here to visit her father daily. Another lost cause. *Where is her father? I'm not thinking straight, this is where I should have started.*

Len phones Mrs Fielding. A carer answers the phone to say Mavis isn't taking calls unless it's about either Sarah or Clem. 'It's Len Gorski here. Mrs Fielding knows me well; would you please tell her this is Len, and I'm after the address and phone number for the nursing home George's at.' There's a long pause.

'Len. Do you know something? I'm worried sick about my children. I've heard nothing back from them or from the police who are looking for them.'

'I'm trying to find them myself Mavis. If Jane found them before her accident she's still in coma and hasn't been able to tell me. She's in a bad way, and I've been warned she may not make it. Could you tell me where George is staying? I should have thought of this first but I'm not thinking too clearly myself at the moment?'

'Oh Len. I'm so grateful you're trying to help. George is at a nursing home in Engadine and the home is run by Nurse Geraldine. I've spoken to her, and she's worried too. Sarah was expected to return one morning but didn't turn up. I can give you her phone number.'

Len takes the number and phones Genevieve to find the address so he can visit. Geraldine seems reluctant to talk too much over the phone about details for some reason. Then he remembers the bent cops. He decides to take the train to the Home and is invited in to chat with Geraldine over coffee. They talk about a hideout, but she doesn't know the whereabouts herself for all the secrecy. She says Sarah first stayed at Hurstville at the Latitude Hotel but moved out on the second night leaving no message. She does mention that Sarah was worried about being followed when she left here and switched trains for safety.

On the train ride back to Edgecliff Len puts the pieces together and remembers Jane's phone call to him. Sarah's a nurse, and she needs income, she may work as a nurse. He searches for likely places on the Web and finds the Anna Health Centre. *This is it! I'm going there as soon as I get back to my car. I'll call Beryl Stone too. She's bound to be interested in the drug ring and might help with Clem's problem. These bastards are serious, but they don't know what they've started.*

He looks up the shortest route to take. He leaves both phones on the bed. After leaving the central business district he notices that the same car has been following him. Sometimes a few cars away, sometimes distant, but consistently behind as he sticks to the main arteries. He decides to divert to a side street. The car is distant but turns to follow. Len pulls in to stop in front of an old federation brick building. The car passes and stops a further five houses up. The car is occupied by two large men wearing checked winter shirts. Len's first reaction is they look like bushmen. He waits and watches. They remain seated. *They might think Clem's hiding here. If I drive off, they'll follow me again. I've got no doubt I'm expected to deliver them to Clem.*

Len gets out and walks toward their car. When he looks in, they too get out and come to face him. They don't speak, just stare. 'You guys are following me. What's going on?' Says Len.

'I think you know.' Says the dominant one. He looks sternly at Len. 'There's nothing in this for you? We want you to stay right out of this for your own good. It's not your concern.'

'You guys are small fry and doing what you're told. I've got no quarter with you blokes, it's your leaders I want. Just tell me who your boss is, then piss off and say I got away from you in traffic.' Says Len.

The leader lurches forward aiming a two-handed grab of Len's shirtfront. The other pulls a knife. Instead of trying to back away, Len surges forward and head-buts the leader, cracking his nose, and causing blood to squirt everywhere. When he covers his face to stem the blood, Len drives his knee into his groin, sending him reaching and rolling away in agony. The second attacker quickly swings the knife at Len's stomach. Len sweeps it away to his own left and in one twisting motion lunges closer and delivers a savage karate chop to his left neck. He collapses alongside his mate. Len learnt this skill in his youth from his best friend's father, a black belt Karate instructor. He knows that this delivery to the carotid sinus will immediately disable an opponent and affect his vital nervous system and heart. If delivered with too much force it can kill. This is not his intent. He wants to show them his anger. But he wants the 'mister big'.

Len steps over the unconscious one, pulls his wallet from his hip pocket, and takes out his driver's License. After a quick look to compare the licence photo to the attacker, he pockets it and drops the wallet. The leader is just conscious. Len drags him to a sitting position against the front fence of the house. 'I want to know more about who's behind all this. Who's your boss?'

'Get fucked.' He says. 'You're wasting your time mate. You're just small fry yourself in this, you don't know what you're up against. Stay right out of it or you're dead like your girlfriend.'

'Yeh! We'll see about that. You can tell your leader I'll find him. Tell him I'm going to thrash him senseless before I hand him to real cops for raiding my girl.'

Len picks up the knife, plunges it into the sidewall of a rear tyre, pulls it out, moves to the other rear wheel and plunges the knife in again and leaves it there. He walks to the driver's door, takes the ignition keys, and tosses them deep into the unkempt long grass at the front of the house. He walks back to his car and drives off.

Before turning into the street of the nursing home he does a trip around another block to make sure he is not followed. He parks around the corner and walks to reception and pushes the buzzer.

He's met by Cheryl. 'Can I help you?' she says.

'My name is Len Gorski, I'm a close friend of Sarah Fielding. My partner Jane is very sick in Saint Vincent's and I'm trying to find if this is where she said I would find Sarah.'

Before speaking Cheryl crosses her arms over her chest and stares looking for another sign that could identify him. She glances at Len's unkept clothing. She's looking at a distraught man. The tone of his voice tending on incoherent. His face is gaunt with signs of fatigue, on edge and shuffling his feet from side to side. It's a plea, not a question.

'I can see you're worried.' She says. 'Is she in trouble?'

'I understand your question. I don't carry a phone to make sure I'm not traced, I'm trying to protect both Sarah and her brother Clem from a drug gang. Their home is in Millmerran. I promise you; I am legit.'

Cheryl's heard so much about Len. This man's age, profile, and attitude are convincing. After eyeballing him all this time she is prepared to take the risk and asks him to sit while she gets Sarah to come to reception. He takes a seat and sits patiently with his hands in his lap. Sarah peeps down the hallway, screams and runs forward. Len springs to his feet, catches her and takes her into an embrace as she sobs uncontrollably. 'I knew you'd find us Len!'

Len holds her tightly with Cheryl looking on until the sobbing subsides, then he puts an arm around both nurses and walks them through to the dining area of the unit. He sits them down and is about to close the door when Clem comes running through the hall in a lather of sweat wearing football shorts. Introductions are quickly made, and they sit around the table with each starting to tell their story.

This is the first time Len has met both Clem and Cheryl. He expected he wouldn't like Clem because of his weakness and his sink to the use of drugs, as well as for all the strife he's caused. His detest is amplified because in some way he was responsible for Jane's accident. On first impression, he likes Cheryl, the way she speaks, the way she pampers Clem, and the respect she shows for both Sarah and himself. She sized him up quickly at reception and was quick to respond.

Clem cools down from his run and excuses himself to change out of his running gear. Len looks at Sarah. 'How's his detox going? Is he making the effort? I'm pretty sure I could get Inspector Stone to find a safe house for him, but I hesitate to ask her for his rehab as well.'

'He's committed to it, Len.' Says Sarah. 'I've now got a source in the city for the proper medication. That's where I'd been when Jane spotted me. Cheryl's coping with him now, but it's my qualification that's needed to purchase some of the medications.'

'If there's a problem about finding a safer place for his care,' says Cheryl, 'I'd be prepared to go with him. I think he's doing so well those special drugs won't be needed for long.'

'I'm impressed with how you two are so willing to help him.' Says Len.

'Don't forget he *is* my brother!' Says Sarah, glaring at him.

'I'm sorry,' says Len, 'I just don't know him well enough, I suppose. I'm not myself, I can't move on from thinking about Jane. I'm sorry for jumping to conclusions.'

The conversation continues in a more sober tone. Clem returns and Len begins questioning him for information about the drug ring. He explains his relationship with Beryl Stone and the warning she gave him about interfering, but says he's not satisfied to wait for ever to get the people responsible for injuring Jane and Boris.

'Len, you mentioned Boris. I haven't seen him for ages and would dearly like to visit him at his hospital. Could you take me there for a short visit?' Says Sarah.

'It's too risky,' says Len, 'I'm not sure it would be safe. The crooks might have Boris under surveillance.'

'Surely not.' She says. 'He's not wanted. It's Clem they're after not me, and they wouldn't expect me to visit Boris openly in a public hospital. Couldn't we make a flying visit? I want to see him. I want to know he's recovering from his injuries. Please?'

'These are members of an international drug cartel we're up against. They've got lots of money, lots of connections, and lots of users to ask favours from. They might have someone working at the hospital who they're paying to call them if Boris gets visitors.'

'You go.' Says Clem. 'Make it short and make sure you're not followed when you leave. I'm just sorry I got you guys involved in my troubles.'

FOURTEEN

Goldman speaks to the garage manager where Clem worked. 'Duchy. I've got an urgent job for you. It could take one of the drivers a few days, but it's the only safe way to do it.'

'You're the boss. What do you need that's so important?'

'A light aircraft has arrived at a small airstrip in Central Queensland with two important shipments. One is more product. The other is two of the crew from Colombia because of trouble they caused with a rival cartel. Their names are Grigor and Gustav. I need them picked up. They don't have passports.'

'How urgent is this?'

'The small shipment helps, but the urgent need is the two men. I learned that the partner of that girl on death's doorstep is a football coach. He's cosy with some high-ranking detective broad in Sydney. The syndicate told me they want him kept out of the equation and told me to get rid of him ASAP. I sent two boys down to Sydney with deliveries and told them what to do. But he's a tough nut. He cleaned them up big time. He even took one's driving licence. Because we attacked him, he must know we're after him now. He's a risk because he knows that broad and he'll be all riled up and dangerous. The boys said he was capable of killing them but let them off boasting about what he will do to their leaders. We can't have that. I'm sure our boy whose licence was taken will clam up if questioned. Those boys value their lives. These new Columbians are good and will handle it.'

'So how are these two going to get rid of him? What's so special about them?'

'They have a reputation. Grigor's nearly two metres tall and over 150 Kg', he says, 'he's all muscle and delights in pulverising athletes and gifted players because of their fame and all the attention they're getting while he's just a nobody. He satisfies his hatred by showing his own strength.'

'Gustav's a different kettle of fish. He's a lightweight. He's a spastic and getting worse because of his decrepit skin condition. He's got a very rare skin disease. He was born with it and has thick, hard plates covering his skin.'

'He takes pleasure disfiguring people.' He continues. 'He carries a fancy knuckle-duster capable of ripping strips of flesh off torsos, legs, and arms to satisfy his craze. He's able to do this in a way like beasts capable of devouring human flesh. Animals such as lions, tigers, crocodiles, and even feral pigs. He leaves no gunshot or knife wound, so if bodies are found there's no hint the injuries were caused by man. He contracts to slaughter unwanted enemies.'

He hangs up, leaving the garage manager with a damp chill down his spine.

*   *   *

The following morning a limousine parks in front of a small cottage in the rural suburb of Cypress Gardens, just to the west of Millmerran. A well-dressed man knocks on the front door and waits for a response. He knocks again, harder this time. With the security chain still attached a puzzled face peers out. Mrs Fielding is still dressed in a nightgown.

'Mrs Fielding. I'm sorry to disturb you without first calling, but my firm is trying to help your husband. My name is Doctor Dane. As you know George is in a nursing home in Engadine and he wants his notebook computer so he can to do some work on his research project. May I come in?'

She pauses, casting her eyes over at his expensive suit. Then she sees the polished black limousine. 'How is he now? My daughter hasn't given me any reports for some time, and I've been relying on her. The nurse there says he hasn't made any progress yet. She says he's not likely to improve. I'm really worried about him and why Sarah hasn't called.'

'I don't know the answer to that. My firm specialises in helping people with brain injury. I believe we can improve his condition considerably if we can take him his laptop.'

'I don't have any computer. He never brought any of his work home. It must be at the Cobar plant where he worked.'

'I run a clinic at Inglewood. As you would know, it's just 30 kilometres away, and I would like you to come to see how my patients are responding to my methods. I'll show you first-hand how effective my methods are. I operate as a charity, so it wouldn't cost you anything. Could you come? I could take you there now.'

'I'm not very well. I'm worried about my children too.' She pauses. 'I suppose I should look at what you could do to help George.' She stares ahead then covers her eyes. 'Okay. Wait outside and I'll change.'

She returns dressed in her street clothes, unlatches the chain, and opens the door to let him in. She directs him to a seat at the dining room table.

'My clinic at Inglewood is only one of a small network I have dealing with head trauma.' He says. 'I've found treatment similar to that for dementia patients is very successful, but it needs something of keen interest for the patient to stimulate the brain neurons. For every new stimulus, neurons go searching for connections, and a subject of vital interest speeds up recovery. Do you understand what I'm trying to say?'

'I think so. Medical knowledge has increased so much I have difficulty even keeping up with what my daughter talks about. She's a nurse you know, and a very good one I'm told.'

'Quite so.' He says. 'Well, your husband's research is no doubt very complicated, and his need for concentration during this process I offer will help speed his recovery. If you come to Inglewood with me, you will see firsthand how successful this process works. But it's important we take something of vital interest for your husband, that's why his computer is so important.'

'Well, I don't have that. My daughter would be the best person for that. She's in Sydney with George now as far as I know.'

'I'd like you to come with me to Inglewood. I've selected this location for George's treatment because it would be far more convenient for you all to visit him there. I think you will be impressed.

'I'll come with you if you wish. I suppose that's best for George.'

The main road to Inglewood is via Millmerran township and the doctor suggests they stop at the local coffee shop for refreshments and the chance for him to describe more of the care he would provide to help the recovery of George's memory. He dazzles Mavis with stories about the use of head caps that can trace the brain neurons that light up to sensory inputs. How the first stimulus sends signals through the thousands of neural pathways looking for connections relevant to the input. The more these pathways are energised, the greater benefit it has to recover connections lost due to the head trauma.

'The brain has two different hemispheres, you know, and even if one part of the brain is damaged beyond repair this process can cause the undamaged hemisphere to take over functions. It's amazing how these networks can be refigured. The brain is still capable of growing.'

Mavis listens intently, trying to absorb this description. She nods her understanding, although she really finds it's a complete mystery. After talking for a while, the doctor summons the waitress to their table. The waitress takes their order, and the doctor excuses himself to visit the washroom. He walks away down the corridor, through the back door, back to his parked limousine, and drives away.

He connects his mobile phone to the limousine and punches in a frequently called number. 'Okay boys. She says she doesn't have it. Maybe she didn't trust me. Maybe she told the truth. Take a look to be sure.'

Millmerran is a small 'tidy town', recognised for the way the streets, shopfronts, and houses are well maintained and cleaned. There's only one hotel, and most functions and meetings are held there. There's also a small post office and police station, the main lock-up facilities being located at either Dalby or Pittsworth. The café is in the small shopping centre on the main road, the Gore Highway, that runs from Toowoomba, the large regional centre, to Goondiwindi on the NSW border. Years before it was a tourist attraction, having a railway station terminating a line from Toowoomba. That has been unused for years. Mavis Fielding waits patiently. The coffees are delivered. She has a few sips and looks down the corridor and waits. She begins to fidget. The coffees are getting cold, and the sweets have not been touched. She twists the ring on her finger and rolls it back and forth.

She looks slowly around the tables and glances down the corridor again. Eventually, she summons the waitress and asks her to check that the doctor is okay. She's soon told there's no sign of the doctor and his car has gone. Her immediate distress concerns the waitress who calls the police station straight away. Mavis is well known in Millmerran and the local police turn up quickly to investigate.

They advise her there is no **Dr Dane** in Inglewood and she has been duped. They offer to accompany her home and to check if possessions have been stolen. They suspect a well organised crime gang. Similar cases have been reported in other shires. Upon arrival, they find the house ransacked. Every cupboard has been searched, all drawers emptied, and all beds stripped with mattresses tossed onto the floor.

Mr Goldman receives a call. 'Nothing there boss. The daughter must have it hidden.'

FIFTEEN

Len and Sarah enter the hospital and are directed to the gymnasium. On reaching the entrance they see a nurse supervising Boris with his exercises. He has one leg in a cast, a crutch under the armpit on that side, the other in a sling, and he's halfway along an exercise mat trying to correct his balance by leaning against the railing as he moves slowly along. He's making hard work of it. Sarah clasps her hand over her mouth and sways back on her heels. Len grabs her elbow to steady her. They stand and stare, unwilling to interfere and interrupt his intense concentration.

Soon Sarah can't restrain herself and she rushes toward him. Boris sees her and drops the crutch to reach out to her. She ducks the railing while trying to clear her wet eyes and hugs him tightly. He sways. She steadies his balance and stretches up on tiptoe to kiss him, and kiss him, and kiss him. Boris has his good arm wrapped around her, and with no crutch he is unsteady. They are saved from toppling by Len.

Len manages them to a padded bench. Sarah is sobbing and Boris is covering her face with more kisses. Both are struggling to get a word in. The nurse asks Len if there is anything she can do. He explains their relationship but says that their stay will be very short because of other problems. The nurse says she will take a quick visit to the hospital café and come back with coffee for Boris. Len says he will pay a quick visit to the washroom to give the lovers time to talk.

'I've missed you so much Boris. I had to twist Len's arm to bring me here. He's been a great help in spite of his worry about Jane. She's not getting any better and is still in a coma. He's worried about being followed back to the nursing home by someone, or else my being recognised here could lead to trouble. They must have contacts everywhere, this gang, they already tried to follow Len's car. He hasn't told me how, but he said he gave them treatment for their trouble. I don't know what that means.'

'That treatment would give them something to think about.' Says Boris. 'You look so good Sarah. I've been missing you so much. I'm glad you came. If only I could help somehow. I'm busted up pretty bad, but I want to get out of this place and support you. I've never met Clem, but he'll be part of my family soon and I want to help. I've got no idea what Len's done about the football blokes at Toowoomba.'

'Len says he'll get Inspector Beryl Stone to help. I'm sure she will.'

In a few minutes the nurse returns with coffees for both herself and Boris. After another long embrace and leaving Boris with the nurse, they walk to the exit. Len asks Sarah to wait for him there at the pick-up area while he sets off for the parking station.

On returning he sees two vehicles already stopped in front of him at the pick-up. He joins the queue. The front vehicle is a car which soon drives off. The second is a large black double-cab utility which moves up. Len moves up, he now has cars behind him. Sarah is called to the rear window of the wagon. A man runs from the other side and grapples with her trying to push her into the back seat. Sarah is twisting and kicking. She forces an arm free and scrapes her nails across his face. He drags her arm away and slaps her hard across the face.

Len slams his handbrake on and runs to pull Sarah free. He grabs the attacker from behind, but another arrives at his back, pulls Lens arms free, and wraps him in a bear hug. Len twists sharply, one arm comes loose, and he drives his elbow back into his attacker's ribs. His head drops forward. Len spins and strikes him with a vicious right cross that sends him stumbling away. Len turns back to the other who's still struggling with Sarah, and he delivers a karate chop to disable the arm holding her. Len is struck a heavy blow on the head from behind and folds to the pavement with blood trickling down the back of his neck. The ute screeches off with Sarah.

Len stirs and rolls over, seeing it speed off toward the exit. He feels the back of his head and his hand comes back covered in blood. A nurse saw the incident through the front door of the hospital and is quickly at Len's side with a pad to slow the bleeding. Bystanders phone emergency, sit Len up, and pass a phone to him so he can describe the vehicle and explain Sarah's danger. They help Len to his feet and the nurse takes Len's arm to escort him back into the hospital for treatment.

He's reluctant to go, and quickly phones police emergency again on his own mobile giving a more complete description of the vehicle and the assailants. He stresses the urgency of catching the fleeing utility because a dangerous drug gang is behind the kidnap, and Sarah's life is in immediate danger. He sags and his rescuers rush to seize a wheelchair near the entrance, and they soon have him to a doctor in the emergency ward. The blood flow is soon stemmed, his head wrapped in a tight bandage, and he is given a tetanus injection because the condition of the weapon is unknown. The doctor hands him a strip of painkillers and says the wound may worry him for a couple of days, he should rest up for a while. There's no way Len will follow this advice.

Following his treatment Len phones Beryl Stone at the State Crime Command. 'Beryl, I need your urgent help. Sarah, a nurse you've met, has just been kidnapped from the front of the North Shore Mater Hospital in a four-wheel drive. We know bent police could be involved with the gang behind this. I've given your emergency call number the description of the four-door ute, fitted with a Spotlight overhead and a large antenna on the front bumper. They've got Sarah in the rear seat.'

'Len, are you okay yourself? You sound flustered and groggy. Are you getting treatment?

'I am, it's just a blow on the head from behind with something heavy. I'll be okay. But finding this wagon is urgent because I know the gang has murder in mind.'

'I'm so sorry to hear this. Stay there. I'll have you picked up and brought to me so you can tell me everything you know. I'll have a message sent right away to all our vehicles to intercept utilities with your description.'

'I'll come to talk, Beryl. It's Sarah's brother they're after and they want him dead. But I want to go looking for this ute' myself for Sarah's sake. There's one other thing, the guy that just snatched Sarah has a Nazi insignia low on his neck. Could you give me what you know about them when I get there?

'Okay Len. Take care. Don't take it all on yourself like you usually do. The white supremacists are more active in other States. Their flags, posters and signs are banned in NSW, but groups do exist here, and we do our best to keep a close watch on them. The main problem is the influence they have on young people who are not familiar with history that can lead to violence.'

'There's a drug gang behind all this,' says Len, 'I'll fill you in when I get there. This is really urgent. I want to find this bloody ute' soon. It's like a bushie ute' and set up for hunting. The only other clue I've got is that tattoo.'

'That may not be a useful clue, Len. Some youths attracted by the rituals and the symbolism find out later about the genocide during World War II and leave the cult. I will do some research for you though.'

'Tell me more when I get there. I've got another request too. I want to borrow a GPS tracking device. I want to find my way into the drug ring that's causing all this strife. Could you loan me one?'

'That's something you should not be doing. It's a police matter. We are very active in searching for drugs. We're anxious to know where they're coming from and working with overseas intelligence. Disruption of a local ring could jeopardise this.'

'Beryl, the lives of two of my best friends are at stake. You know I'll do my best not to interfere with police work, but I want to save my friends lives. I need a clue to Sarah's whereabouts. You'll remember Sarah, she gave us entry to that sex trade last year. With her and her brother's lives at stake, I can't just wait for police action. A tracking device could be very useful.'

'I'll see what I can do. I know the federal police will object violently, but I'll check what's possible and tell you more when you get here.'

Len's relationship with Beryl is a tricky one. It began with criminals from Uzbekistan, Len's home territory growing up. The gang stole Australian research material belonging to a UNSW post graduate player for Len's then Sydney team. Len's knowledge was a critical factor for solving that crime. Their relationship developed when he moved for another assignment to coach the Morisset Premiership football team and climate activists created havoc and murdered a local teenage girl. And that was followed by an assassination attempt on a government minister residing on the Lake Macquarie foreshore. Each time Beryl sought Len's help to provide local knowledge and intelligence. One night Beryl, divorced, and with a child she had someone mind for her back in Sydney, stayed overnight at Morisset while making enquiries. Last minute accommodation problems led to Len inviting her to share his unit overnight.

At the time Beryl saw Len as handsome, fit as a fiddle, the perfect gentleman, and not prepared to form a permanent relationship because of his frequent travels and tireless football ambitions. Their sleep in separate beds was innocent enough. But by morning the relationship spiralled, and Beryl tempted Len back to bed. Both later regretted their action, and it went no further. They both knew a long-term close relationship was doomed to fail. Beryl has a full-time intensive job requiring urgency at all odd hours of the day, as well as a young child needing stability. Len will work for periods of two or three years at different locations that could be a thousand kilometres distant. They both felt guilty and agreed it was to be their one only one-night stand.

What Beryl does understand, is how devastated Len must be feeling right now. She knows how thoughtful he is to others with problems, how responsive he is to help, and how passionate he can be if called upon. She was surprised by his transformation when Jane came onto the scene. She concedes that Jane is lucky because she works as a private accountant and with the new technology now available can work from home, no matter where that home may be. She did not have that luxury herself.

SIXTEEN

Sarah is subdued and held between two heavies in the back seat of the wagon. The one on her left is holding a pad to his bleeding cheek. He has a nasty scowl and is twisted sideways to keep a close eye on Sarah. She's casting glances at prominent landmarks for future reference. She's not familiar with Sydney and surrounds. She's heard crime reports for Sydney many times on the news. Most of these crimes have taken place in the western suburbs. She's not surprised when the wagon heads west, but when they cross the Hawksbury River and start a long climb into the mountains she begins to shiver. *Why would they want me? why not just follow us back to our hideout? They must surely want Clem more than me. Do they believe Clem's described the gang members to me? And details of their drug distribution too? Will they try to force me to tell them his location? Could they want something different. Think. What on earth could it be!*

The road twists and turns following a railway line. Sarah takes note of as many station names as possible. The car passes Katoomba, a name she knows, and she realises they've been following the Great Western Highway which goes across the Great Dividing Range to Orange, another town name she knows. At Blackheath, a town at the top of the range, they turn-of and negotiate their way onto a minor road and drive to the last few houses where the road ends, close to a cliff-top. It stops in front of an unkempt front yard and a twisting path to a solid stone building set well back from the road. She's taken inside and offers no resistance. The one with the swastika forces her into a chair.

'We want some information about your old man.'

'What do you want to know?'

'We want your father's records. It's stuff we don't want to get into other hands.'

'This doesn't make sense. Dad wouldn't know anything about you or your mob. Why would he want to give anything to a bunch of crims anyway! He's sick and struggling to survive and he's in no condition to do any deals if that's what you want.'

'Just tell me where your dad keeps his records and you're free to go as soon as we get our hands on 'em.'

'I've got no idea what you're talking about. All I know is he's devoted a lot of time to mining – why would you be interested in that?' Sarah knows there's no way they would let her go free.

'He's been in your care since the accident. We know you've spent time with him. You must know where this info is.' Sarah shakes her head.

'I've got no idea,' she says, 'You're asking something I know nothing about. I can't help, even if I wanted to.'

Following more questions and no answers the white supremacist tells his offsider to take Sarah for treatment. Sarah springs to her feet as the offsider reaches out with his right hand to grab her left arm above the wrist. Sarah swings her right hand across to clamp his hand to her arm. She drops her arms quickly down to her left for balance, then quickly swings them both back over the top and down to her right, changing her weight, forcing the attacker's wrist into a position where she can then push him down to his knees to save his right wrist from being broken. He winches and lets go. Sarah makes a dash for the door.

The supremacist chases and tackles her face down to the floor and lays on her prone body. His helper takes her panties down over her kicking legs and throws them onto a table. The men grab one arm each and they force her down the corridor and into a back room.

They work together to strip off the rest of her clothes leaving her stark naked and hurry out the door, locking it behind them. Sarah folds her arms across herself, stumbles to the corner farthest from the door, and squats. She surveys the room. It has no furniture, just a thin mattress laying in the centre of the room. She shudders. *That's not there for comfort. They'll probably torture me and then have their way with me before killing me.*

Sarah was able to defend herself the way she just did because of her training in Karate and self-defence in Toowoomba. Her nursing course was there. She boarded mid-week and twice a week after classes she took self-defence lessons. At weekends she would take the long bus trip home to Millmerran. Now, squatting naked in the corner she begins to shiver and feel humiliated. She knows to be left like this is a form of torture. This does not auger well. As a nurse she's seen many nude bodies but shudders at the thought of herself being seen like this. *I'm not going to show my feelings to this scum, and I won't give in. I'll get my chance.*

The swastika man talks to his mate. 'We'll leave her in there and let her freeze. It'll get bloody cold up here tonight and she'll suffer enough to talk by morning. Someone's after the brother as well and I've been told they might bring him here too. Then we can torture one in front of the other if we have to get them to spill the beans. We'll get what we want one way for sure. I suppose they'll want us to get rid of the bodies as well. I'm not too keen about that though. We'll have to make it look like they've met their end in some sort of an accident. Could be a cliff fall. But they'd have to be bumped off right before the drop. Before we kill the girl, we might be able to have some fun of our own. She's a good-looking sheila and would be a good root.'

'I'm not real comfortable about all this Bro'. Says the helper. 'I've never been part of anything this bad. I don't mean the sex. I mean the rest. I don't know your own background, but I didn't even think about things like this. I was happy to be part of riots and disputes and causing damage to property. If there's a good cause, I'll be in it. But what the fuck is this all about? Where's this sheila come into it?'

'Does it matter?' says insignia man, 'if we want our money and more of the stuff, it's a living. Grow up mate, we're living in a shit country where bureaucrats and corporation bosses live in luxury and all the rest of us are peasants.'

'I thought we were trying to build a better life for all of us.' Says the helper.

'For sure.' Says insignia. 'That won't happen while jews control our money, while Muslims, Catholics, people from Central Asia, and other races run the country. Big changes are needed. We've got to convince all of us smart white paupers to get together and clean the place up. We need a new leader like Hitler to bring power and a better race.'

'You might be right, but I don't see much hope. I'll just look after myself thanks.'

Seventeen

Sarah is shivering. Outside the mountain air has fallen to sub-zero, and although the walls are solid sandstone, they are not offering much insulation. She suspects the cold air is entering from open windows in other rooms, whereas her room has only one sealed window high in the wall. She's curled up in the corner, lying on her side protecting her vital organs, with her knees held tightly up to her chin. She's been lying in this position for hours and is beginning to cramp. Her thoughts are jumbled. She's been unable to understand the reason for their questions, unable to understand if her dad has done something or knows something that's important for them, but about which she knows nothing.

She's been close to her dad all her life and doesn't believe he would keep secrets from her. Especially her. She's treated all his ailments, provided advice for medications, vitamins, and exercises, ever since she became a nurse. She knows she has a special place in his heart. Then she becomes aware of her own freezing condition. Could she benefit by dragging the mattress over and using it for cover.

She's been unable to get any sleep with her mind so active and the cramp. She thinks it must be about midnight by now. They haven't left a bucket, and she knows she might soon have to use another corner to have a wee. She rises and does some stretches and exercises to increase circulation and warm up. She wants to be ready and try to overcome whoever comes in. She doesn't expect any food. Starving would have to be part of this torture. Will they harm her if she still denies any knowledge? *Is that footsteps outside?* She rushes back to her curled-up position.

The door opens and the helper enters with a small tray holding two mugs of steaming coffee and carrying a dressing gown slung over one arm. He places one cup at each end of the mat. He throws the gown to Sarah, and signals for her to come to her end of the mat for her coffee. He sits down in front of his own coffee.

'If I get up, I'll wet myself.' She says. 'I need to go to the loo.'

'You can't leave the room. I'm not supposed to be here, but I don't like to see you suffer this kind of treatment. I respect the nursing you do for others, and I've brought you something to help warm you up.'

'Well bring me a bucket too.' She says.

He takes a time staring at her. 'I don't want to be caught out, so don't make any noise. Stay put and I'll get you one.'

As soon as the door is closed and locked again Sarah rushes to the mat and swaps the mugs over and returns to her coiled position. He returns with the bucket and places it in front of her. She signals for him to turn away. She puts on the dressing gown and uses the bucket, still in her corner, with the noise breaking the silence of the room. He smiles and walks over to retrieve the bucket and he places it at the door. He returns to his end of the mat.

'I don't like to see a pretty nurse treated like this. You do such caring work for all kinds of people. I respect that. I'll do my best to help you, but I can't let you out. Please enjoy this coffee then I must leave you again. If I'm able to help you in any way, I will, but I'll have to take the gown.'

Sarah takes her time to sip her coffee. *Should I try to take him down now while the door's not locked? Let's just talk a while to see what I can find out. If my coffee's been laced, he has other intentions.'*

To keep him there she asks about his reason for being with this group. He talks about his troublesome home life with a brutal father who persuaded him to join his group of supremacists. He did what he was told to avoid being forced to leave home, where he believed he was needed to protect his mother. Then his dad was jailed for his involvement in an attack on a Synagogue and his mother left home to return to her parents. This is all he has until he can find something better. Sarah listens intently to keep him talking, unsure if she is being strung along with claptrap.

The more he talks the more his eyelids start to droop. He rubs both eyes with his palms, sways, then topples forward onto the mat on top of his empty mug. *Just as I thought. He was going to have his way with my body, the bastard.*

She wraps the gown tightly, prises the door open, and peeps out. Complete silence. She returns to the front room, sees her clothes, grabs them up, and sneaks out the front door. She hurries to the nearby bus shelter close to a precipice where a bus must terminate. She scrambles into her clothes and puts the gown back on. There's a path along the edge of the canyon. There's just enough moonlight to follow it. She comes to a signboard with the inscription "Govetts Leap", below it "1.2 Km Grade 4 descent. 9 Km 45-minute loop track. Leads to Blue gum Forrest tracks in the Grose Valley," An arrow points to the edge. *This is the last place they would expect me to go. I'll chance it before he wakes up and sounds the alarm. There must be another way out of the valley where it's safe to find help.*

The air is still and cold, with a slight eucalyptus tang. Mist makes vision difficult. Looking down, all she can see is darkness. She begins the steep descent on a zig-zag rock path weaving through overhangs covered with moss and cold dripping water. It's slippery and her shoes are not right for conditions like this. She grits her teeth and feels the excitement coursing through her body. She finds it's much more difficult descending than climbing on an incline as steep as this. Her legs are straining and she's tiring. In her hast she stumbles, twists her body to fall backwards onto the last rock step, and wrenches her ankle. The pain sears up her calf and brings tears to her eyes. She leans forward to massage her ankle, trying to increase circulation and stem the pain. Then she rises gingerly. She struggles for balance and tries to continue down. Each step is painful, but she has no option but to keep going.

She still can't see the foot of the descending track, but she grits her teeth and hobbles on downward. At the bottom she finds a well-defined track that follows a fast-flowing brook. She stumbles to the sandy bank and gulps handfuls of fresh water. She takes deep breaths and finds a grassy patch against a tree. She settles into the coat and closes her eyes. Her head soon sags forward, and she slips into a troubled slumber.

She's dreaming of her childhood, sitting in icy cold water in a small plastic pool. Her eyes search for a parent to come and lift her out. There's no one in sight, everyone has gone to shelter from the rain. It's raining heavier and the water in the pool is rising. There's no one she can call.

She wakes, trembling, and soon realises heavy rain has caused the brook's banks to burst and water has spread to where she slept. Fortunately, her bare feet had sensed the water rise and her clothes and coat are only damp from the rain. Her sprained ankle is still painful, her weight is being taken by one leg. She must find another place to rest. From her training she knows she must avoid activities that cause pain, swelling or discomfort. Elevation and compression are needed to stop or reduce any swelling.

She puts her shoes back on and notices the ankle is beginning to swell. She hobbles back to the cliff face looking for an overhang shelter from the rain. She knows she has to treat the ankle. It may take days of rest, but the trickle of water from above should be enough for survival until she is able to move on. *Surely, they won't think to search down here.*

EIGHTEEN

Len wakes after a few hours' sleep. Instead of jumping out of bed as he normally would do, he lays there staring at the ceiling. He feels the lump on his head through the hospital dressing. It's sore to touch. He rubs his eyes then cups his hands behind his neck and lays back. Jane is constantly on his mind. He decided to stay in the Edgecliff flat so he can visit her first thing before he begins a search for the kidnap vehicle. He visits the hospital. Jane's condition has shown no improvement and after a shortened stay he decides to leave. He needs to keep busy, even though he's reluctant to leave her side. He wants to start visiting four-wheel-drive equipment shops, but he can't take his mind off the only person he has ever felt so close to. She doesn't deserve to be like this. She's such a caring person. She's changed his life and introduced him to real emotion. He loves her dearly.

I knew I shouldn't have taken Sarah to see Boris. I wasn't thinking about kidnap. If we were watched I thought their best plan would be to follow us to where Clem's in hiding. I could have fixed that. It doesn't make sense. Do they plan to torture her? God – what have I done. I've got to find these bastards quickly.

He scans locations with his phone. There's three in the western suburbs of Sydney, the most likely area to look. He visits the first one in Bankstown. He parks next to three vehicles in the service area in front of a large display shopfront, they're all four-wheel drives, but none equipped like the one he's searching for. He enters and sees every conceivable accessory for four-wheel drive vehicles on display around the walls, including the two he is interested in. He walks to the line of three men waiting for service. He waits patiently and begins a casual conversation with the man on the end of the queue.

'I've been travelling around overseas and just got back,' he says, 'I've been away a while and at the airport a guy said he knew where I would be able to find cheap long-term lodgings. He was there to pick someone up and I lost him in the turmoil in the departure lounge. All I saw was the ute he drove away in. I can describe it well. It was black, a four-door utility with a spotlight mounted on a cabin bar and a telescopic antenna fitted to his front bumper. I've got no idea of his name, so I suppose I'm on a wild goose chase looking in a city like this. But I'm giving it a go. I'd like to find him 'cause I can also tell him exactly where to find the stuff he said he was looking for. You can't buy it in shops.'

A second guy in the queue overhears the conversation but neither can help. Len pushes on with the tale at the front counter. There he's told there would be hundreds who could fit this description and not to waste his time.

Len spends the rest of the day on this mission at the two other service centres and finished with same result. He drives back to Edgecliff and sits in his car. His headache has worsened. All he's eaten so far has been snacks. He doesn't feel like a proper meal. He eases his head back into the headrest, closes his eyes, and takes deep breathes slowly through an open mouth. He leaves the car and walks back to Saint Vincent's Hospital.

He spends the next two hours slowly massaging Jane's arm and whispering into her ear. There's the occasional eye flutter, but that's all. His eyes are blurry, and he rests his head on the bed. Before long he falls into another troubled slumber. He is eventually woken by a nurse shaking his shoulder. She says he should take a break, return to his flat, and take it easy.

These sentiments don't rest easy with Len whose mind is searching for ideas. *These bastards will be made to pay for all this.*

On his walk back he gets a call from Beryl. 'Len,' she says, 'any improvement with Jane?'

'None at all.' He says. 'Still deep in coma but there are signs to keep me hopeful.'

'I'm glad.' She says, 'We have no reports for that vehicle yet, and we're still searching. I've had a look at our supremacists' records, and we do have a case of violence for one that resides at Blackheath, a railway suburb in the Blue Mountains.'

'Can you tell me where he lives?'

'We don't know exactly, he's with a group of men who move around and keep squatting in vacant residences. There's a risk that they're no longer in Blackheath, but they seem to like that area.'

'Thanks for doing this Beryl. I'm going to head up there now.'

'Well take care. If these are the ones, they'll be ruthless, remember. If you recognise the person you're looking for, get police involved.'

Len collects a few warm clothes and a blanket and sets off to do surveillance at Blackheath. He knows his chances are slight, but he's got to do something. He won't forget the face he's looking for and he knows the vehicle. Now he's wide awake. His stomach rumbles and he looks for a burger outlet on the drive West. His heartbeat has returned to normal, and his headache has gone. When he reaches Blackheath, he drives around the streets looking for the wagon. No luck. He returns to the shopping centre, finds a parking spot in the main street where he can see the hotel front and several of the main shops.

He can't relax. As darkness closes in, he enters the hotel and orders a beer. He takes a good look around at the patrons, then he gives his same spiel to the barman. He claims to know no person or vehicle to fit Len's description. Len uses the washroom and returns to his car. He has no accommodation booked. He intends to spend the night where he is, hoping that his target will eventually turn up.

After remaining alert for some time, he begins to rub his upper arms briskly. He wraps his lower body in his blanket and lowers himself into the driver's seat far enough to allow him to still watch vehicle arrivals. He soon drifts off.

Early the following morning, the town stirs, and Len is woken by cars with early shoppers beginning to park near him. Len's heart skips a beat. He spots a wagon with the right description pull up in front of the butcher shop. He can't get a good look at the man who gets out to enter the shop. He dons his cap, pulls up his collar, leaves his car, and walks slowly past. *It's him.* He sees him clearly at the counter being served. Len returns to his car. He watches the man place his purchase on the back seat of the utility, then turn to enter a small-goods store. When the wagon finally leaves, Len follows at a safe distance. The wagon drives up the side of an old stone building until it is out of sight from the road.

Len parks several houses back and ambles toward the placard at the precipice. Passing the house in question he takes a good look. It's large. The front window has heavy curtains. The driveway the wagon took is along a windowless wall. The house is old and in need of maintenance. The front lawn is unkempt, and the garbage bin on the nature strip has a strong dank odour. Len turns at the railing along the cliff face and ambles back toward his car. He makes a quick entry up the driveway, stops at the far corner to make sure it is safe to proceed, then sneaks to the closest rear window. It too has heavy drapes and there is no view in. He moves to the back door, listens, and tests to see if the door is locked.

He senses someone behind him. 'Step back.' He's ordered as something is pushed hard into his back that he senses is a gun. 'Don't make a move if you want to live!'

Len is quick to act. He takes the odds that the gun is being held in the right hand. He spins around to his left brushing the gun arm

away with his own left arm and moves in on his attacker. He delivers
a right cross to his jaw. As the attacker sways back, Len unleashes
a right foot kick toe first into his groin, a kick with years of football
strength. As his attacker bends forward grabbing for his privates, Len
locks his fists together and delivers a two-fisted uppercut sending him
sprawling. He doesn't move. He will be out for a while. Len takes a
closer look at his neck and is confirmed to see the Nazi insignia.

Had the attacker used his left hand to hold the gun Len knew how
to handle that too, but it's riskier. He assumes his attacker must have
sensed him following his wagon and waited. Len scolds himself for
not being careful to first check the wagon.

It's time to venture inside. The door is not locked. The first room on
his right is a vacant bedroom. The one on the left is unlocked too,
but something further on catches his attention. He creeps along the
corridor and hears talking. From the noises it sounds like they're
eating. It's breakfast time. He listens intently and hears only two
voices. Time to act. He barges in. It's a kitchen dining area with one
sitting at the table and the other standing at the bench pouring hot
water to make tea.

'It's that fucking coach' shouts the one at the sink.

The other springs from his chair quickly drawing his gun from his
belt. He holds it up to point at Len's head, and advances slowly. Len
raises his hands above his head in surrender.

'Hold fire!' He says, 'I'm only looking for a friend not a fight.'

The man moves closer still pointing the gun at Len's head. 'The girl's
not here mate but you've made a bad decision to look for us.'

Len lurches forward dodging his head to avoid the gun. He grabs the
gun with both hands forcing the attacker's arms above his head and

knees him in the groin. He rolls to the floor. The gun goes sliding along the linoleum.

The man from the sink runs at Len swinging a chair at Len's head. Len steps aside, grabs the chair, and uses the momentum of his rush to pull him down onto his face. Len kicks him hard in the kidneys. He passes out. Len's kick is hard enough to rupture, maybe even cause failure. There's no sympathy given.

The first man rolls back onto his knees and crawls for his gun. Len kicks the gun away and treads on his hand, cracking bones. As he grabs it in agony with his other hand Len kicks him in the side of his head and he blacks out.

Len quickly checks the kitchen drawers, finds some plastic ties, and binds the two men hand and foot. He pulls them back to seating positions against a wall, with their hands behind them. He does a quick check of the other rooms. All are empty. He goes outside to bring in the Nazi insignia guy and ties him up the same way.

He calls Beryl's home number. After several rings there's a bleary voice. 'What is it that's this urgent?'

'Beryl. Wake up. It's Len. I've found the Nazi and his hideout. I'm in Blackheath. I'm sure Sarah was held captive here, there's a bucket with urine just inside the door of one room with nothing else but a mattress. I've got three crims tied up and I need police. Can you organise help? I'm in the stone house three up from the bus stop near the track down to Govetts Leap.

'I'll do that straight away. You're taking too many risks again Len. I asked you to involve police once you found them. I'll contact the Katoomba police and make arrangements.'

'I had to take my chance before I lost it Beryl. I know these are the mongrels that snatched Sarah, and they have to be drilled for information about her. They might have given her to someone else before they left here, but I don't think so because of the bucket. I think she's got away. This is urgent because there are others that fear she knows too much and will kill her.

'If Sarah has escaped from these mongrels,' he continues, 'she's sure to contact emergency. Please make sure the police here are alerted and are reliable. They should be asked to search the area as well in case she's injured. If we get her, we need a safe house for both her and Clem that's close to the family home for their mother's sake. I've been thinking about the resort.'

'I've done my best to leave the drug kingpins out of this Beryl. Please trust me and get me that tracking device. I'll use it to look for connections back in the Gold Coast. That's where all this trouble began and I'm confident I can do this safely.'

'I may be able to arrange it through my Queensland counterpart. I'm sure I can ask her to provide a safe house at the resort too. That's a good idea, Len, it would be easy to make that place secure with minimal police presence.'

'I'll get on to these things straight away, and I'll make sure we get all we can from these three crims. You've done well and I appreciate your help, but you must look after yourself and Jane. Take my advice. Don't take unnecessary risks again.'

'I won't. But I'm determined to smash the scum responsible for the damage they've done.

Len stays until police arrive. They've brought paramedics with them to treat the captives before they are incarcerated. They contact Beryl to learn where she wants them.

Before Len leaves Blackheath he receives a call from Saint Vincent's Hospital. He's asked to come as quickly as he can.

NINETEEN

Len climbs into his car to leave Blackheath and heads for the hospital. As he leans forward to slip into his seatbelt, he has a burning sensation in his chest and throat, and a sour taste in his mouth. He sits back to settle the feeling and takes deep breaths. Once on the road again he periodically steers with one hand using the palm of the other to pump his forehead. *It's got to be Jane.* His mind is not thinking about the road. He's running through the bush chasing thieves and shadows.

Twice he pulls to the side of the road to vomit. Arriving at the hospital he grabs a reserved spot in emergency between two ambulances, leaves the keys, and hurries for the ward where Jane was being monitored. He finds it empty. He enquires and is directed to the surgeon's office.

'Take a seat Len,' says the surgeon, 'I've got bad news, we did our best but I'm afraid Jane didn't make it.'

Len sinks forward, closes his eyes, and clasps both hands to his face. *I knew it would come to this. I just couldn't accept it.* The surgeon is silent. Eventually, Len looks up with red eyes to face him. 'Can you take me to her?'

'Of course. I'm sorry we couldn't save her Len, but I thought it best to warn you earlier so you'd know what could happen. We did our best, but her injury was too severe. I'm sorry.'

Len rises and sways. The surgeon takes his arm and leads him to her new cubicle where she's laying covered on a low hospital trolley. Len leans over Jane's body intending to kiss her. He sinks to his knees, pulls back the cover over her face and upper body, holds one hand, and buries his head beside her. The hand is cold. But she looks peaceful. The surgeon apologises once more but says he must leave. 'Come back to my office when you feel able, Len. We need to discuss a few things.'

Hours later, the surgeon describes to a distraught Len the procedures that will be necessary.

In a daze Len rescues his car, which has been impounded, and returns to the Edgecliff unit. He falls onto the bed, and gazes at the ceiling. He's never felt more miserable. Jane changed him from years of selfishly chasing his football dream, never settling down with a partner, feeling unable to commit. He played a role of protecting women in his family and placing others on a pedestal, but had never felt committed to anyone. This relates back to his youth in Termez, and the Soviet soldiers' behaviour. Jane created feelings he'd never felt before. Hours later he rises on weary legs and moves to the kitchen to boil the kettle. He needs coffee but has no desire to eat.

Len has no energy to face a two-hour drive to Newcastle. He phones Phil to give him the sad news about his mother. Phil answers. Len asks him to sit down, he has some bad news. Liana has walked over to hear the conversation because of Phil's reaction. Afterward, Len asks for the phone to be passed and he asks her to comfort Phil. They chat shortly. He will visit at his first opportunity. He explains that he's unsure about a will, Jane's assets, and her wishes. All possessions should be left to Phil, her only survivor so far as he knows.

'There's sure to be a lot of red tape to sort out.' He says. 'All this can wait, but Phil will need help. I'm willing to take charge when Phil feels well enough to talk about it. I can make all the necessary arrangements. Explain all this to him after he settles down. He'll need your help, Liana.' He says. 'I'll visit soon.'

Len returns to his bed, collapses onto his back, and closes his eyes. He loses sense of time until he is stirred by his phone ringing. *Where did I leave it. Will I answer or leave it for a voice message. I don't feel like talking to anyone.* He hears a voice message being recorded and believes the noise is coming from the kitchen bench. That must be where he left the phone. The message is unintelligible and sounds like an unfamiliar voice. Silence again, and Len slips exhausted into another doze.

*   *   *

Clem and Cheryl have not been able to eat a proper meal worrying why Sarah has not returned, nor any message from Len. A letter finally arrives, delivered by a policeman. It's from Inspector Stone to tell Cheryl about Sarah's kidnap. Clem, who's just returned from a street run, saw the policeman leaving and when he enters the nursing home sees Cheryl opening the letter. She shows it to him. He sags at the knees and stumbles to the bench staring at the letter.

Cheryl moves to his side, sits, and hugs him.

'This is a disaster!' he says, 'all my bloody doing. Poor Sarah. Why would the bastards want her? She's done nothing!'

'Len was worried about going to see Boris. He was right.'

'Len's tough Cheryl, I know that much. I know he can handle himself and would do his best. Inspector Stone didn't mention Len, so he must be okay. He's bound to be working on it. I know the two of them are very resourceful. I pray to God Sarah doesn't get hurt before she's found safe.'

'It gives them a new lead for them trying to find you, Clem. You're in more danger yourself now. I think you need a new safe house. I wonder why Inspector Stone hasn't found one for you already now she knows about our problem.'

'There's no way Sarah would tell the crooks about this place. I want to be with you Cheryl. I'll clean up and change first, then we need to sit down and make a plan. I want to talk to this Inspector Stone myself to see what I can do to help find Sarah. Did she give a phone number in the letter?'

'She did. But it's you they're after Clem. You don't want to go running around. You need to stay put. Inspector Stone knows where you are now, she's bound to be working on a safe haven.'

After he returns to the rear unit, a stranger walks into the nursing home and rings the reception bell. Cheryl returns from a patient's room, hesitates, then says, 'is there something I can do for you?'

'Yes. That young man I saw just back from the street run. Is that your partner or a patient? I think I know him. He ran past me when he was turning the corner. Can I talk to him?'

'Do you know his name?'

'Yeh. Clem Fielding. We went to school together.'

'Where was that?'

'Pittsworth in the Darling Downs. He's an auto mechanic working in the Gold Coast now, I believe. We were good mates.'

'What's your name so I can let him know?'

'Just tell him 'Spud'. He'll know straight away.'

He sounds convincing. I'll warn Clem and if he's a fake Clem can escape the back way while Spud waits here. 'He's gone to freshen up and shower. Sit over here and I'll get him to see you when he finishes.'

Cheryl turns to walk away. The stranger pulls a revolver from the belt under his coat, rushes up behind her and strikes the gun on the back of her head, knocking her out. She collapses. He steps over her, walks to the back unit, and knocks. Clem has already dressed and is ready to return to Cheryl when he hears the knock.

'I'm on my way.' He shouts as he tightens his trouser belt and opens the door. The gunman fires a shot into Clem's heart. A spray of blood blotches his shirt front as he falls onto his back. The killer returns down the hall, steps over Cheryl, and walks casually away toward the shopping complex.

Cheryl is shaken roughly by a patient who's screaming. 'Nurse. Come quick. Your friend's been shot.' She stoops to lift Cheryl slowly to her feet and help her to the unit. Cheryl sees Clem and runs to kneel at his side. She rips the buttons off his shirt and pulls it open to see the wound. Her gaze narrows. A bruise is forming above the heart area, but the blood is flowing from a score across the left side of his chest. She checks his pulse There is none. She starts CPR periodically checking for breathing.

'Call emergency.' Cheryl shouts as other patients come to see what's happening. She's excited when he begins breathing and she feels his heart come to life. *Oh my God. He wasn't meant to live through this.* He hasn't regained consciousness, but Cheryl's heart rate is starting to recover, and she leans forward to listen closely to his breathing. She's satisfied that the crisis is over, takes a pad from the pocket of her uniform, and compresses the wound. There's a furrow from the bruise across his chest to another graze on his left arm. She asks a spectator to get a pillow to place under his head and waits for the paramedics.

His vitals are checked by the paramedics and the police arrive just minutes later. Police find the bullet in a corner of the room, and study the blunt nose, a compression from striking something solid. They ask the paramedics to check the pocket of his shirt. There they find a pocket size sheet of plate metal. It's a thin two-layer thick lightweight plate with a compression dent in the centre. Studying it, they find it engraved with a 'best wishes from Dad' inscription.

Clem opens his eyes and blinks rapidly. He opens his mouth, but words fail him. The paramedics lift him carefully and lay him on his bed while he tries to clear his head and take in what has happened. They dress the wound and the graze and tell him how lucky he was. Had the bullet not been deflected he would've been dead within minutes. They show Clem the metal plate and tell him it saved his life.

'Dad sent me that when I left home to come to the Gold Coast.' Says Clem, as he begins to slowly recover from the shock. 'It's one of the things he was experimenting with. I put that in my pocket as a lucky charm after Sarah told me he was taken to the nursing home. I was hoping it might bring good luck. He's very creative, but he keeps secrets to himself. He has a life ambition to invent something that will benefit our whole family. I really miss my chance to keep in regular touch with him.'

'Well, it has brought *you* luck.' Says the Senior Sergeant. 'Do you mind if we take it with us for examination?'.

'No. But I want it back.' Clem says.

Cheryl asks the police to contact Inspector Stone and she tells the police about the problem the family is having with a drug gang. She says she wants police protection wherever they take Clem. She can't go with him; she must stay here with the other patients. She tells them she too would like to speak with Inspector Stone herself.

The paramedics are directed to take Clem to a secure ward attached to the main hospital at Liverpool. Cheryl says she would like to arrange a replacement for her at Menai so she can continue treating Clem. Maybe Inspector Stone can influence the travelling nurse organisation as an emergency. Police say they will deliver the bullet and the metal plate to the forensics laboratory. When Stone speaks to Cheryl, she says she and Len have already spoken about the resort.

TWENTY

Sarah is still sheltering from the rain beneath the overhang. She's fashioned a vessel from hardwood bark off a fallen ancient gum tree to collect the water dripping from above. It tastes cool and fresh. She knows if she is able to stay hydrated, she can survive for days without food. She decides to stay there and make herself as comfortable as possible, elevate her swollen ankle, and rest. She rips a section from the foot of her nurse uniform and uses it to make a compression bandage for the ankle. She is resigned to rest, thinking it may be difficult to find another suitable spot if she moves on. From her position she looks out at a dense forest of tall stately blue-gum trees, green vegetation, and the brook.

She leans back against the rockface and closes her eyes. Her brain won't rest. *Why did they want me? Have they already found Clem? How can I help them – as a hostage? Mum must be worried, and I haven't called for safety's sake. I wonder if she's called the home about Dad's progress and all this tumult in her family. Does she know about the gang? Has Dad's condition changed? How can I escape from here? If I could phone Len somehow, I could tell him about this house in Blackheath. I wonder if other bushwalkers will pass this way and I could borrow a phone. Would there be any reception down here?*

In spite of her stressful day and late night, sleep is denied. Her rambling mind goes back to her conversation with her dad and his mumbles. *Something about a bed. Surely his mind was savouring those bedtime stories with me. Is this part of healing?*

The rain ceases and the sun peeps into sections of the valley. There's been no traffic down the leap and Sarah wonders if authorities have closed the descent for safety reasons. If they have, this could be a God send. She decides to test the ankle and scavenge for food. The soil close to the brook has been deposited by heavy rains over millions of years and is fertile. She hasn't spotted any animals and assumes that any here must be nocturnal. That source of food is out. She knows First Nation people were mostly nomads and used berries, flowers, and yams for sustenance. Lighting a fire is out of the question due to the dampness and no matches.

She starts sampling berries and flowers. She has no idea what they are and relies mostly on smell and how they taste. One bush has berries ranging in colour from green, yellow, and purple. The purple taste good, the others bitter. She eats a small number of purple berries and waits to see if there is any aftereffect. When satisfied, she fills her pockets with these and begins trying flowers and seed pods. She finds a yellow flower that is quite tasty. She tries weeds. She's heard onion weed has white flowers and edible bulbs. She searches. Both the bulb and the flower are tried and liked. Even the white base of some grass is okay.

Her ankle is beginning to pain again. She folds her nurse skirt up, picks as much as she can manage to carry, and limps back to the overhang to enjoy more food. The patch of sun reaches her, and she hangs the coat out to dry. She looks for a comfortable spot to settle down to enjoy the warmth of the sun. Although her body is benefiting, her mind is still in a whirl.

Rousing, and feeling refreshed, she decides to press on down the track looking for a way to reach safety. After a short distance she comes to a junction showing a climb back to the top, but the sign says it returns to Blackheath. This is too risky. She takes the left-hand option and continues down the William's Track along the brook.

Sarah's ankle swells and becomes more painful as she goes. It's difficult to walk. She knows it will only get worse to continue along the brook. She settles down against a gum tree, closes her eyes, and leans back, stretching her neck from side to side. *Could I try to continue with a walking stick made from a branch or should I try to make a shelter and rest for another couple of days. I'm not going back to the cave, that's giving in. I've got to stay positive. I've got the brook and still have berries and flowers, and there's bound to be more here.*

She struggles to her feet and uses a broken branch as a walking stick to begin to gather fallen branches and lean them against the tree she selected earlier. It's rough cover, but it might help, so long as it doesn't rain again. She's tiring because of her injury and lack of food. She settles down, folds the coat around herself, and slowly dozes off. Her thoughts drift to Boris. Her dream state has visions of them trying to reach each other through a thick fog with bikies fighting.

She is stirred by someone touching her shoulder. Her eyelids lift to see blurred images and her heart pounds. She tries to rise. She's surprised to see two school children and settles back.

'Oh my God – what are you two doing here?'

'We saw you here and wondered if we could help. Are you lost? Are you in trouble? You don't look comfortable, and your shelter is bad.' Says the older of two young aboriginal girls dressed in school uniforms.

'You can't know how glad I am to see you. Thank you so much for stopping. Yes, I injured my ankle coming down Govetts Leap and I'm trying to walk out further down the track. I needed to rest to ease the pain. I might have to spend another couple of days here. My bushcraft is hopeless, I know. Why are you two here?'

'We are from the Medlow Bath school and walking here for a meeting with Uncle Jimmy and Aunty Nellie. They're tribal elders who visit our school, and they asked us to come to their humpy to listen to stories and enjoy some bush tucker.'

'Is it far to Medlow Bath from here?'

'Oh no, only a couple of kilometres. But you have to climb back up to the top. You've already come most of the way, but going up would be impossible with that ankle.'

'That's what has me worried.' Says Sarah. 'That's why I built this cover to rest.

'What food do you have?' One asks.

'Only berries and flowers. I've never done this thing before.'

'I don't think we could get you up the climb. Uncle Jimmy's humpy it near here, could we help you get there. Your cover is no good and you need food. You must be starving!'

'Are you sure? He won't be upset, will he?'

'He will want to help. He will look after you and help you to Medlow Bath when your ankle is ready.'

With the walking stick and help from the two girls, she is led a short way from the brook through a dense grove of gum trees and thick scrub into a wide clearing with a humpy sitting on the far side. During the walk, the girls explain Jimmy and Nellie return to this spot every year to visit the ancestors and return for a few days living on bush tucker. They say how in dreaming when spirits created the world they transformed into trees, rocks, watering holes, and rivers that became sacred places linking people of the past and the present. How when the girls usually visit, they spend hours learning about dreaming, guidance, insight, and connections to the spiritual world. They've learnt this spot and the stream have sacred memories for them.

The slow hobble has taken them about thirty minutes. The two elders are sitting cross legged on a cushion of gum leaves at the opening to the humpy accompanied by a skinny brown dog. Sarah has never seen a humpy before and is surprised to see how large it is, and how well it is protected from weather, with a heavily thatched roof folding over walls of branches and bark. It backs onto a standing tree for support, the whole front is open with a forked branch supporting the centre opening. It's more like a dome than a room. Inside Sarah can see some skin throw rugs, a few artefacts, pottery, and bark dishes.

The girls introduce her and explain her problem. Uncle Jimmy directs her to enter the humpy. There's room, only just, for all to sit. Uncle Jimmy listens to Sarah's detailed story and reaches up to pick an eagle feather from thatching overhead. While she sits, he puts on a mask taken from the side wall and begins to wave the feather slowly over her head and chant aboriginal language in a mournful voice. At first, his voice is harsh, summoning his ancestors. After time, his voice slowly descends in volume and becomes monotonous. Aunty Nellie and the girls lower their heads in silence. Sarah's muscles relax, her eyes close, and she's looking at white puffy clouds slowly drifting overhead. Her breathing is slow and deep. She's floating.

Several minutes later the chanting ceases and the girls softly explain the rich culture of her elders. One of belonging, obligation, and responsibility to care for their land, their people, and their environment. Uncle Jimmy has just introduced her to his ancestors in dreamtime and asked for help. The girls explain the chant is from the Dharug language from the South-Western areas of Sydney.

Uncle Jimmy asks the girls to lay Sarah down, make her comfortable in her coat, and elevate her sore ankle onto a piece of broken stump covered with a cushion of leaves. He explains to Sarah that she must lay still while he and Aunty Nellie prepare some food for nourishment and healing. He leaves the humpy and walks to a fire pit. He fills it with combustible bracken and bark, and lights it with matches. Nellie is asked to stoke it while he and the girls gather food.

The girls search the nearby bush collecting native seeds and nuts, then they use pointed sticks to dig up roots and tubers. They return to the humpy to show their collection to Sarah through the open front.

'These are tubers,' one explains, 'they're mostly starch. They're the resting stage so they can outlast winter. We're going to keep some for baking and grind some more mixed with our nuts on these smoothe stones to make a damper. Aunt Nellie is stoking the fire pit for hot coals where all the cooking is done. You'll be able to watch from the humpy and get all the lovely smells.'

'I'm getting a good lesson here. Thanks girls.'

Uncle Jimmy takes a sharp metal hatchet and searches for witchetty grubs in saplings. He looks for the tell-tale holes, slices strips of wood from the trunk, then uses a slender stick with a hook at one end to drag the grub from its hollow in the heartwood. He returns to the fire pit which has burnt down to red coals and cooks the witchetty grubs, held by sticks over the hot coals. The solid tubers are roasted close to the hot coals, then a thin layer of earth is laid to cover the coals. The damper mix is wrapped in paperbark and laid on top. Jimmy fills in the pit with soil to bake the damper.

Cooked lightly, the grubs are high in protein. A mixture of fresh nuts and raw roots is given to Sarah to taste, which she savours, then the grubs. Sarah scrunches her nose to examine the finger size grubs. She takes a small bight and tastes somewhere between scrambled eggs and banana. Quite tasty. She licks her lips and eats more.

'What do you think?' One girl asks.

'I'm still not sure. I know I'm hungry and I enjoyed them, but I don't know about making them a long-term delight.'

'They're high protein and best eaten as a snack before a main meal.' Says one.

The roasted tubers and roots are offered next, waiting for the damper to cook. Sarah relishes these. Delicious, more like her staple diet. The others have joined for the meal and Uncle Jimmy explains the healing powers of the grubs.

Sarah lays back down, satisfied, and slips into a contented dream state. Something she hasn't felt since capture. A feeling of well-being, refreshed for the challenges ahead. When she rouses, she tells Jimmy she's anxious to push on, but he insists she must eat the damper and continue to rest for a couple more days. From her nursing she understands his advice, but she knows that movement should not be delayed too long. It's a delicate balance. The girls depart after the damper is shared, wishing Sarah good luck with her ankle and her return to friends.

*   *   *

On the morning of the third day Sarah wants to test it. The swelling has gone, and it feels strong. She leaves the humpy and walks to the opposite side of the clearing with her walking stick. She looks down the valley. She's distracted by a low buzzing noise. It's coming from way down the valley and getting louder. She walks back to the centre of the clearing to see more clearly. It's a light aircraft flying low above treetops and coming toward her. *Has Len organised a search? Has he figured out what happened? She stands in the clearing in plain view as the plane passes overhead.*

She waits, wondering if it will return. The noise abates and her head droops. She wipes moisture away from her eyes and cups an ear, hoping to hear it again. Her heart beats faster as she senses the noise now increasing. She waves her stick wildly it as it passes overhead again. *If it's me their looking for, where did they come from? And who are they?*

Her decision is made quickly. She wants to set off downstream. *The girls said I was close to the climb to Medlow Bath. I'll go on.* She hugs the elders to thank them for their help, her eyes become moist, but her decision has been made. She wraps her coat around herself and returns to the track alongside the brook.

Using the stick for support, she gains confidence. After a while she feels the need to rest her ankle, and sits back against a forest gum, closing her eyes. Her meandering thoughts are disturbed by her heart beating stronger and a chill rising in her spine. She listens intently. *Am I hearing voices?* Her eyes open and are drawn downstream.

Two hikers emerge carrying backpacks and sleeping bags. Seeing hikers causes mixed feelings. Hope's gone for a search party, but there's the possibility of help. She rises to speak to them. They look surprised to see her in shabby clothes and no luggage. They ask if she needs help. She says she is desperate and asks if they have a phone she could use. One hands her his mobile, takes her elbow while they walk to a clearing, searching for reception. She splutters on about her situation. He shows his concern and offers to help her back to Medlow Bath. Sarah finds weak reception and phones Boris. Quality is poor, she briefly says she's safe and in good hands.

Following Sarah's short call to Boris the hiker and his friend help Sarah back to the track and they set off for Medlow Bath. When they reach the foot of the climb the leader asks Sarah if she's ready to start up, or should she rest first.

'It's a tough climb.' He says. 'When you're ready you should lead, and I'll follow close behind in case you slip again. Your shoes are a worry.'

'I'll find it much easier to climb up than it was to come down. It's good of you to help, but I'm confident.' She holds her head high and owns the middle of the track. She reaches the top in under fifteen minutes, breathing heavily. Her attention is drawn to a light aircraft sitting on a disused airstrip, quite close to the top.

'Is that *your* plane?" She asks.

'It is. To hike to the Blue Gum Forrest, we used the plane to check conditions first. Govetts Leap is closed, and this was the best way to hike there. But look, listening to what you've been through we're keen to help you out of this mess. We'll fly you directly to the military base at Kurrajong and your friends can pick you up safely there where you'll be protected. Here, call your mate again to tell him. My pilot's gone to warm the engine and arrange the flight.'

He walks back to the plane. 'It worked mate! She hasn't got a fucking clue. Get the plane started and arrange a pick-up at the Camden airstrip. I'll go back and bring her to the plane. We'll have to get going, her earlier call could get someone here soon.

TWENTY-ONE

Len phones Boris to let him know about the attempt to murder Clem. He gives him the details of Clem's survival and the new arrangements for his security with police supervision. He describes how he traced Sarah and found she had already escaped. She has not shown up, and police are now interrogating the culprits and searching for Sarah's whereabout.

'Don't dismay old boy,' says Len, 'things are looking up. Sarah's smart and will outfox these bastards, I'm certain of that.'

'I'm sorry about Jane,' says Boris, 'I feel responsible. I know how much she means to you. I know how she's changed your life. It was my fault we fell off that balcony. I'm so sorry'.

'Enough of that, Boris. I'm very grateful you were trying to save her and I'm sorry you were injured trying.'

'Len. It's just struck me. The cops at Edgecliff had the same uniforms as Queensland cops. You know, dark navy short sleeve tops. Down here street cops wear a dark vest over light blue short-leeve tops.'

'That's telling info Boris.' Says Len. 'At last, we might have another lead back to Queensland and a clue for their ability to track phones.'

Neither want to chat about their miseries. Len says he will visit the hospital later to see how his rehab is going.

*   *   *

Len spends the next two days working on funeral arrangements, advising friends, and taking time out to recover. He drives to

Newcastle to pay a visit to Phil and Liana to try to ease Phil's suffering and to tell him what arrangements he's made. Jane's funeral service will be at Ryhope, a suburb in Lake Macquarie where Jane spent most of her life until meeting Len.

On his return to Sydney, he decides it's time to visit Boris again, to chat, and to check on his progress. He has concern for the torment Boris must have over Sarah's disappearance again, knowing these people are murderous. When he arrives, he finds Boris in the gymnasium, sitting on a bench watching another young man going through the same exercises he had.

'That young guy,' Boris says, 'was victim of a hit-run car driver. What bastard would run off after hitting someone.'

'You know like I do, they don't want to be picked up and taken for testing.' Says Len.

'I guess you're right. I reckon there should be a big penalty if they're caught for that though. The penalty after staying should be less than the penalty for being caught later. That would fix it.'

'Depends on what they want to escape from.' Says Len. 'Look at the drug dealers we're chasing. What evidence could cops find in one of their vehicles.' They walk together to the canteen. Boris gets a phone call. He answers but reception is bad.

'Boris – I'm safe!' she screams.

'Sarah. Sarah, I hear you,' he responds, 'where the heck are you? How are you? Are you injured?'

'I'm having trouble hearing you. I've met hikers and I'm using their phone in the Gross Valley. I sprained my ankle and for days I've been cared for by aboriginal elders. They must be rewarded after all this is over. Can you hear me?'

'Just. Where in the valley are you?

'They've offered to help me up the climb to Medlow Bath.'

'Take care and call again as soon as you get better reception. I'll get Len to arrange to pick you up. Tell me the details later.'

'You hear that, Len? Sarah's safe and is being helped to climb to Medlow Bath. You know where that is?'

'Yeh,' says Len, 'that's a suburb just this side of Blackheath.,

*   *   *

Len phones Inspector Stone's office and has to wait several minutes before she can take his call. Boris is punching the air. He's skipping around imitating an Irish Jig and tapping with his sore leg. Len grabs him to stop him falling.

Beryl answers. 'Len, I suppose you've called to learn what we've got from the Blackheath criminals.'

'Not so Beryl. Listen carefully and you'll hear Boris letting off steam. He's just heard from Sarah. She's safe and being helped to climb up from the Gross Valley to Medlow Bath. Would you be able to have her picked up safely? I believe they don't have far to go.'

'What great news.' Says Beryl.

'No details yet. Reception was bad and she was in a hurry to get proper protection.'

'I'll fix that straight away. I know the police in that region, and they're reliable.'

'Don't hang up yet Beryl.' Says Len. 'there's more news. Boris has just remembered that the police they fought at Edgecliff were wearing Queensland uniforms. That thought struck him when he saw NSW street police wearing a dark vest over light blue short sleeve tops.'

'Good find. That licence you sent me is also for a Queenslander. I've been in touch with my Queensland counterpart and we're on good terms. She wants to help in any way she can. She says she will loan you a tracking device when you return. I've had difficulties to get one down here. Now I can ask her to check records to try to identify Queensland police visiting Sydney at the time of the break in at Edgecliff.'

'We're getting somewhere Beryl. Now Sarah's safe I'll go home and pick up that device to learn more.' Says Len. 'Could you also ask her if she could make enquiries with the local telco about calls being traced and some conversations monitored?'

'I will.' She says.

'Have you learnt anything from the Blackheath crims yet?'

'Nothing. The people doing the questioning are convinced they would sooner do the punishment and come out alive than give anything away. They thought they were just being used to do a favour and be able to continue their supply.'

After the call the two friends talk about how so many of the gang's players are such different types and so widespread. The focus must be the Queensland Gold Coast but there's a hunger for drugs elsewhere that gives them willing workers.

Len's deep in thought. He expects Sarah to be picked up safely. Clem's in safe custody under police protection, and he's done all he can for now for Phil. He suddenly finds himself at a loose end. He's short on money and needs to get back to work. With Boris unable to assist with the A-league team, it's up to him alone for now. Len contacts the Toowoomba manager. He tells of Jane's death and how it's affecting him, but he needs to get back to work and this might help him take his mind off Jane. He would like to return and continue to coach the team. The manager shows sympathy, offering to advance some cash to see him over.

Len has plans to use the GPS car tracer Beryl secured for him if he gets a chance. He's still determined to revenge all the damage these mongrels have caused. He knows Clem collected his tobacco from the distributer in Southport. He'll do some surveillance there looking for a vehicle to tag. He takes the long drive back to his Toowoomba Hotel.

TWENTY-TWO

Len's coaching return is a challenge. The morning after his return he tries to conduct the first training session on attack. But his mind is not on the job, and he sets up a small-sided game just to observe the way various players attack. He returns exhausted to the hotel. The following day he begins the morning session without a proper plan. He's working mostly from memory. A method so often employed by other coaches, but foreign to his approach. He addresses the group.

'This morning I'm going to coach the principles of attack. Your ball skills are good, or you wouldn't be here. So, the emphasis is going to be on understanding the role every player has when your side has possession.'

'In general, passing in the back third has to be ultra-safe. Any intercept could be fatal. The number one rule there, is if you're in doubt, kick it out. If you're able to pass safely, do so, if not punt it forward or kick it out. The midfield is where you build play up and where your peripheral vision looks for good passing opportunities. The front third is where you take risks, use your creativity, and take responsibility to shoot at every opportunity. After this first game set-up, I'll take the twin strikers for a functional practice in the goal area.'

'Like with defence,' he continues, 'the moment your team takes possession of the ball, you will all be attackers. The moment of interchange can offer the best opportunity for a quick break-away, but I don't want possession wasted. If there's no clear chance, play safe and build it up.'

'Now for the principles. The man with the ball must be supported. He must be able to make a safe back pass. He should take-on his first defender if he's confident, especially if he's in the front third. He should look for a penetrating pass to a mate in a better position to advance the attack. Other players must strive to offer passing opportunities by moving into clear spaces looking for the opportunity to receive a penetrating pass.'

'We'll start with attack versus defence from the half-way as before, this time I'll use freeze replay for the attackers. If the defenders win possession their target is to get back to the half-way line with a foot on the ball. I'll coach only the side that has possession.'

Len then realises he's given too much talk and not enough action with the ball. He can't expect all this talk to get home. He bites his lip. *Lift your game. Players will learn more when you freeze the game and demonstrate a replay.* But he knows he can't interrupt too often and take away the enjoyment of the contest. It will take weeks, by which time the players will anticipate what his replay will be. They will already know what went wrong. *I'm not travelling well with this. I've got to get with it.*

They start their game and Len watches on. When an attack breaks down, it's restarted again at the half-way. After the third restart Len freezes play and demonstrates how the attacker on the ball had no rear support and lost possession. Players have maintained their freeze positions. Len takes the role of the player who should have provided support and play restarts from just prior to the break-down. He sprints past a defender into correct position, takes the back pass, and slips the ball through to another player who has made a penetrating run into the space he just created.

Play stops. The players begin clapping Len's demonstration. He raises his hand for recognition but sinks to his knees and lurches forward for support from his outstretched arms. He's helped to his feet, but he has trouble maintaining balance. Players support him and they all return to the change room. He sits on a bench and rests his face in his hands, his elbows on his knees. Len is heartbroken. The manager is called down from his office upstairs.

'Len, do you feel okay or do you want me to get medical help. Have you got pains in your chest or anything?

'No Derick. I'm okay. I'll be right in a few minutes. I'm disappointed with my own performance this morning. I'm still struggling with Jane's death. I'll be right soon.'

'To be honest, I wasn't sure about you starting back so soon.' Says Derick. 'I'd already arranged for our physio to take the boys for a few days of team bonding down at Miami Beach and giving them fitness training on the sand. How would you feel about being part of that?'

'That's a bloody good idea Derick. The exercise will be good for me too. I'll get the chance to learn more about each player. I haven't had a chance to talk to all of them individually yet to understand what makes them tick. I'll travel down on the bus with 'em.'

The next morning Len and the physio, Mark Ranger, accompany the players by bus to Miami Beach, a Gold Coast suburb between Southport and the NSW border. On the trip, Mark describes the venue. Accommodation has been arranged for all to stay in a scout hall hired for the purpose. It has dormitory sleeping, a common room for meals and talks, and a small kitchenette. It sits on a one-acre block with a grass area behind the building large enough for Len to conduct specific short passing drills for groups that play in the various areas of the field.

On arrival, beds are assigned as carefully planned by Len and Mark to provide improved communication and interaction. 'Breakfast and lunches are for yourselves to manage,' says Mark, 'the bread, cereals, eggs, and a range of fillings for sandwiches will be available in the kitchenette. I've arranged for all our evening dinners to be provided in the surf club on the beachfront. Len will hold some instruction sessions on some nights after dinner, on other nights you're all free to go your own way.'

'Good facilities are available at the Burley Heads Bowling Club where you can play billiards, darts, or bare-foot bowls.' He says. 'I've arranged this with the Club and made a donation. Please use it and don't abuse it. Curfew is eleven o'clock. The bus is available for travel to and from Burley Heads. Otherwise, you can walk back from the surf-club to the Scout Hall. You will all be trusted to limit your alcohol.'

'Every morning at six o'clock we all go on a road run. After breakfast it's to the beach for fitness training followed by a swim.'

After settling in, Len has a few more words to say. 'Guys, as you know this trip is for team bonding. At A-league level excellent team spirit is vital. I want to get the best out of you as individuals, I want you to support each other, and I want you to understand the team strategy and support it without fail every time you play. I'll do my best to develop our team's own style of football, based on the players we've got, and I'll do my best to make the right minor changes to our game every time we play based on my assessment of each opposition. I want you all to enjoy this break from routine and take the opportunity to benefit from Mark's efforts to improve your fitness.'

Mark takes the players on a jog to the beach for their first beach run and fitness session. Len joins in. The first run is South along Miami Beach, across the headland to Burley Beach, along that beach to the next headland, and then return. Most of that run has been relatively easy going on the edge of the sand made wet from the waves. On return, Mark uses a structured 20-minute Fartlek approach which has an added difficulty in the loose sand. He sets several sprints along the dry sand, with a walk back before repeating the next sprint.

This is repeated a number of times, designed to improve endurance, speed, and mental resilience, by gradually building up the milage and intensity. Len does a few runs with the players, then takes a break to talk privately with individuals. His aim is to work out the type of approach needed to motivate each individual.

Then it's back to the hall for lunch and recovery. The afternoon is spent at the hall, some exercising with gymnasium equipment set up in the common room and supervised by Mark. Len takes small groups in sequence for short passing drills on the grass.

It's been a successful first day. They all walk back to the surf club for dinner. A range of options is provided after that. Alcohol is available and the majority remain to chat over a couple of beers. Some play the slot machines. Others walk back early to the hall and watch TV, to read, or to call their partners and friends. All meet the curfew.

TWENTY-THREE

Len works hard with the group for the first three days, then declares a one-day break to allow them to pursue their own agenda. Some choose to travel down to the border by bus, some visit the bowling club, others go with mates to the casino at Broadbeach.

Len decides to hire a car and drive to Southport and use the tracking device. He knows where Clem would collect the tobacco for transport to various shops as far away as Pittsworth. This Southport manager must be a distributor, but likely to stock small boxes with the drugs carefully camouflaged in packets of tobacco. There would have to be a storage shed somewhere. It would be good to locate it, something must eventually lead to the Mr Big running this operation.

Len visits the tobacco shop. He kneels on the footpath verge to adjust his shoelaces and secretly attaches the tracking device to the shop manager's car, an imported MG ZS 180 that's standing in front of the shop. Len thinks it's an expensive vehicle for a shop owner. He programmed the tracker, a sophisticated police device. It's linked to his mobile and GPS, the route information shows on his phone. The car was obviously purchased from the import garage where Clem worked. He sits in his own car close by to watch the customers.

He doesn't see anything suspicious. There's a café not far from where his car is parked and he walks there to buy himself a snack. It's lunchtime, and the tracker begins to vibrate his phone. Len watches the screen. The car's heading north toward the business centre. Len's anxious to see what happens if and when it stops. He goes to his own car to follow at a safe distance. Driving past the tobacco shop he sees it's closed with a notice hanging on the inside of the door. Len keeps his eye on the tracker's progress.

The MG stops and Len drives by to see what's there. It's parked in front of a Thai café. Len parks and wanders inside. He spots the manager sitting alone at a table eating his Thai lunch. Len takes a table where he can watch discretely, and orders coffee for himself. The manager finishes his meal and returns to his shop.

At five o'clock the manager closes shop and drives to a home in Falconer Street, Southport. Len drives past later. It looks similar to other residences in the area, nothing special. Len returns to the hut at Miami to sleep. He's accepted that his search will take longer. He's learned little so far.

During the night the tracker begins vibrating in his tracksuit top. He checks his watch. 1.00 AM. He sneaks out and sets off to follow. He tracks the car to a headland. His GPS names the headland as Shutterstock Beach. He drives there straight away. It's very dark with no moon, the location is on a cliff top overlooking the ocean. Len thinks it unlikely that this location would have access down to the shoreline and wonders what's going on. *Is it a meeting place?* He parks well back and walks to the headland car park through the scrub. Approaching the parking area along the cliff-face he can see there's a long twisting walkway all the way down to a small beach.

His attention is drawn to flashing lights way offshore. There's a long pause, then more. He makes out the shape of a large vessel. Then he sees white foam streaming from the freighter and heading to shore. *A small powerboat. Jackpot. A delivery.* He retreats to his car and drives some distance away from the carpark, stopping where he can just see the activity. A large van arrives. He sits patiently watching the van being loaded with heavy cartons.

The car leaves first. As it passes, the inside light is on, and Len sees the two occupants. The driver is the shopkeeper, the other he doesn't recognise, he's reading something. Len chooses to wait, carefully follow the van at a safe distance, and keep track of the car on his mobile.

The truck takes him to a warehouse.

He parks some distance away and walks toward it. It's in a large industrial area and there's no other activity at this late hour. The van is inside, and the double doors are still open. Len watches them unload the cartons. He hides and waits for the van to leave and for the front doors to close. People must be still inside. He sneaks up and listens. Nothing. What should he do? He's been directed not to jeopardise the hunt for Mr Big.

He sneaks up the side to look at the rear of the warehouse and sees a set of footsteps to an upper section. He sneaks across to see what's down the other side. Nothing of interest. While returning to the steps a light turns on upstairs. He silently climbs the stairs and listens.

There's low level talk and the sound of crockery. He doesn't expect Mr Big to stay in a warehouse, so he leaves.

Len arrives at the hut just as the players are rising for breakfast. Some heads turn to watch him enter, but no question is asked. There's another group of players whose heads droop, their eyes focussed on their toast and jam. Mark rises to walk over and sit next to Len.

'What's the problem?' Len asks.

'Five boys went to the casino yesterday and got into some strife. Police took their names, and the boys were told to report to the police station this morning.'

'Were they drunk?'

'No. They were stone cold sober when they returned to the hut. Two had injuries to their face. There could have been bruises below the belt as well. They're so fit they could ride most punches.'

'So, what did they say happened?' Asks Len.

'They said they want to talk to you about it and clammed up.' Says Mark.

Len signals for those involved to follow him to the dormitory and asks them to sit around him. 'Soapy' Cellarman, the stand-in team captain, acts as their spokesman and tells the story. Prior to joining the team Soapy worked in a hotel as the odd-job man which included the heavy work of handling the kegs and supervising club behaviour. He's been around, can handle himself in any fight, and is well respected in that tough environment of a country pub.

The boys had been gambling on the slot machines, Soapy and another moved to the blackjack table. Soapy is good at counting cards and playing the odds. Before long a club supervisor tapped him on the shoulder to invite him to a back room where an illegal two-up game was being run. Soapy assumed the club wanted to get him away from the black-jack table where he was cleaning the croupier up and making a decent profit.

Soapy is also an accomplished two-up player and would act as 'Boxer' when the game was played in the pub each Anzac Day. The Boxer's job is to supervise play, to stand in the 'ring' and ensure the 'toss' of the two pennies is three meters high and that the two coins land safely in the ring. The two pennies are placed on a wooden paddle called the 'kip' and the 'Spinner' tosses the coins after bets have been made against the spinner.

Winners are determined by whether the pennies land with two 'heads', two 'tails' or 'odds'. Two 'bagmen' stand in the ring to collect and pay the winners after each toss. The Spinner continues to throw until he lands an odd, one head, one tail. Then a new Spinner is called in. Soapy asked if the other boys were invited too, and they all went to the back room.

'Before long,' says Soapy, 'I could see the game was rigged. They had this two-meter-tall guy in the circle of 'Jack Spinners' that had the ability to throw a double at will by introducing a double headed penny.'

'I could see what he was doing.' He says. 'The crook spinner holds one of the good pennies with his thumb and he's already slipped the double header under the kip. That's the penny that goes in the air. He always throws the crook penny high above his head and the real one out a bit to the side. If anyone in the crowd calls out bad toss, being so tall he grabs the crook penny and in the same movement releases the good penny to the mat. He was as good as I've seen.'

'I can't believe it.' Says Len. 'The Club could lose its licence if this was caught out!'

'I know,' says Soapy, 'I didn't know what to do. They would most likely know friendly cops on duty that night, one's taking a bit on the side. But somehow, I had to stop the game.'

'Noble of you. I suppose I would have done the same.' Muses Len. 'What did you do?'

'I went alongside this tall guy when someone else had the kip. I told him I knew his game and said I didn't want to see him take on Spinner again. He was a quick thinker. Otherwise, it had been planned, I don't know. But quick as a flash he's into me with right and left crosses, the bastard. I'm not usually slow to see one coming. He was good at this too. But I returned the fight and I've had plenty of practice in pub brawls, so it wasn't all one sided. A couple of the boys here tried to drag him off and copped a few for themselves. Others joined in and we had a good barney going. Security guys came running and before long we were locked up being interviewed by cops.'

'Did you get a chance to see the double-headed penny?' Asks Len.

'Better than that, I've got it.' He hands it to Len. Len turns it over; he's never seen a double header before.

'I'll come to the cops with you. We should get you out of trouble, but it may need a promise to take this matter no further.' Says Len. 'I'll go back to the Club and threaten them to not let that guy operate there again.'

'The cops might claim that double-header is my own if I show it to them.' Says Soapy.

'Did you get a go as Spinner?'

'No way.' says Soapy.'

Mark takes over for the morning training while Len and the boys report in at the police station. The matter is dismissed in short order, and the boys are ordered not to return to the casino again. It's apparent the cops have decided the matter is over so long as the boys want no further action. On the way back to the hut Len calls to see the casino manager and tells reception it's regarding last night's barney.

'I'm Bob Cooper, what can I do for you Mr Gorski?' Says the manager, alone in his spacious office.

'I coach those five boys that were attacked here last night. I have reason to believe the fight was started because of you employing a corrupt spinner at what I also believe is an illegal game of two-up.'

'They're serious allegations,' says the manager, 'what evidence do you have?'

'The word of my five boys is enough for me.'

'Well, let me advise you that this casino has acquired permission to conduct games of two-up. Furthermore, my security staff can verify that your boys began the violence.'

'So, it's the word of your security staff, none of whom were present, to that of my five boys?'

'That's correct. I know which group the police would believe if it came to that.'

'I won't go into that. I believe the two-up game could only be allowed with the proviso that the game would be strictly supervised. Why were no security people present?'

'There may have been a serious breach of security somewhere else.'

'Do you intend to employ this spinner again?'

'That's really none of your business. I'm responsible for the run of this casino.'

'If that's your intention, let me warn you I have a scout hall full of players who can attend your games, as well as their friends and relatives. We have a photo of this individual. I'm sure his practice will be recorded in police files for the many places he's been reported. If he's spotted in here again the gambling authorities will be advised. The risk for you is the prospect of losing your employment at any casino.'

Len sees blood draining from the manager's face and his hands begin to tremble. Len doesn't feel the need to involve Inspector Beryl Stone, he's sure the message has been received and understood. He rises and walks out, mission accomplished.

TWENTY-FOUR

Sarah is hurried into the plane. The passenger enters first and takes the rear seat. He takes Sarah's hand to help her up to sit alongside the pilot, next to the door. 'That seat'll give you a better view.' He says. This is a plan so those waiting at the landing site can grab Sarah and drag her straight into a waiting vehicle. 'Have you flown in a light aircraft before?'

'No, only in commercial jets.' She replies.

'You'll enjoy this then,' he says, 'you'll get more excitement this time because we fly much lower. See that waterfall over there? That's the Minnehaha Falls – funny name isn't it. You won't see the Wentworth Falls, they're on the other side of the main ridge. So are the Empress Falls. It's a magnificent country for hiking. We enjoy nature away from the rush and bustle of town life. Soon we'll fly out of this lush valley into developed townships. Do you know this area well?'

'No. I'm from much further north.' *I feel rushed. Why is he trying to keep me talking? Why were they so anxious to fly me to Kurrajong instead of waiting for me to be picked up at Medlow Bath? Then they could have continued their hike? They're pleasant enough, but the more I think of it, it doesn't make much sense.*

The pilot starts listening to chatter on his VHF communication set. He switches to different channels listening for information in this flight path. As he leans forward and twists, Sarah sees a low Swastika on the side of his neck, just below the collar of his jacket. Blood rushes to her neck and face. Her throat shuts tight. To avoid gagging she swings away to face the window, shading her face. *Oh God! What have I done? They took days to search the valley – they must have tried all other outlets first. They're smart bastards to work this plot! Now I'm back to square one! What a fool I've been not to realise this earlier. Where will they take me? Concentrate girl! I've got to make a getaway.* Her heart is racing.

She struggles to hide her anger and frustration and continues to stare at the scenery from close to the window. *Now it's my turn to sound friendly and talkative to lower their guard.*

'Where do you two usually do your hikes? You seem to know this area pretty well.' She asks.

The back seat one answers quickly. 'We've only been here for two weeks and making the best of it.'

'Where are you from, then?'

'We're Queenslanders. We're out of our territory. We were told this is a good part of the country for a break and we can take in Sydney as well. We won't be staying long. You were just lucky we planned our hike this way after learning that Govetts Leap was closed.'

'It's very kind of you then to be going to all this trouble just for me.'

'No trouble at all for the damsel in distress.'

'I've heard that before and there's often an ulterior motive.'

'Our motive now will be to take a ferry trip around Sydney Harbour. Just a reshuffle of priorities.'

'You're kind to do this to help me, and I'm very grateful.' Sarah turns and sees that his cheeks have turned rosy, and he drops his eyes. A young friend of hers does this when he's guilty or embarrassed. Sarah returns to gaze at the panorama as it changes to scattered properties and small settlements. She tightens her resolve to take new risks.

She sees the airport in the distance and knows straight away this is no military base. Their small plane passes close to the airport and then loops to approach a smaller field nearby. There she sees a hanger with a powered glider out front, a car, and two men standing next to it. Two other gliders sit off the runway. There is no other activity. Sarah believes the car must be there to pick her up.

The plane lands and taxis to the far end to turn around. As the plane turns, she throws her gown over the head of the pilot, swings her door open, and jumps. They're not moving quickly. She hits the ground and rolls. The pilot swings wildly in his seat trying to escape the gown blocking his view. In his darkness his elbow strikes the black throttle knob bursting engine revs, and he stamps his foot aiming for the upper section of the brake pedal but hits the lower section instead. This frees the brakes from taxiing. The plane spins wildly out of control and Sarah sprints into the dense scrub.

By the time the men get out Sarah has disappeared. She runs as fast as her ankle allows directly away dodging trees and comes to a small creek, too wide to jump. She looks along it and sees a small crossing further upstream and lopes toward it. It's two long hardwood planks jammed between two iron poles on each side. Safe enough for young children's adventures, but hazardous for adults. She takes the risk, spreads her arms for balance, and runs across. Glancing back, she sees that the men have spotted her and are running along the bank.

Sarah enters a settlement of small cottages arranged in narrow streets running away from the creek. She chooses the first street where property fronts have low picket fences. She is breathing heavily, and her knees feel weak. She looks back – no sign of them. She can't go on. She spots a house halfway along where there is a long pivot hedge inside the fence. She hobbles to it and climbs over, and taking deep breaths she snuggles in at the base. Her heart is pummelling her ribcage. Her mouth is dry. She closes her eyes and begins to pray.

The two men reach the settlement, but a quick look up the streets shows no sign of her. 'That bitch is quick,' one says, 'what do we do now?'

'Take a street each and search. She's got to tire soon, she's not fit.'

'If she manages to get help, we're fucked.' Says the other.

They separate and jog along the first two streets. Sarah hears the one casing her street and holds her breath. He passes. A wave like relaxing in a warm sauna rises from her thighs to her chest and flows to her neck and cheeks. She starts breathing again. Her eyes open but she's not game to lift her head.

She hears a sound like something hissing. Her attention is drawn to the house. She sees movement behind the front window. The curtains have been slid open, accounting for the noise, and an elderly lady is staring at her. Sarah gazes back at the woman, her brain scrambling with possibilities. The woman moves from the window and opens the front door. Sarah is still too scared to move. The woman is looking at a dishevelled girl in a torn nurse's uniform.

'Are you okay?' She calls softly.

Sarah buries her face in her hands, still too scared to move and unwilling to raise her own voice. The woman stands and stares.

'Why don't you come inside and calm down, my dear.' She says. 'You look very stressed. I'm sure you'll feel better if you settled down safely in here for a while. I think some of my own clothes would fit you, you're about my size, and you could change out of those torn clothes of your own.'

Sarah creeps to her knees and peers in both directions above the palings. She rises and rushes to the woman indicating she wants to get out of sight. The woman lets her pass and looks both ways before closing the door and following her inside. Pulling out a chair she directs Sarah to sit at the kitchen table.

Sarah sits and takes a deep breath. 'I hope I haven't brought you trouble.' She says. 'I'm being chased by ruthless criminals. They'll stop at nothing.'

The woman goes back to the window and looks up and down the street. 'They've gone, my dear. If they come here, I'll talk to them while you go to the bathroom and lock the door. Now, tell me what it's all about.'

'I'm Sarah, and I'm a nurse from Queensland. They're chasing my brother because he stopped delivering their drugs and he wanted out. They want to kill him so he can't squeal. I've had him in hiding and now they're chasing me too. I know nothing about their organisation, I'm no danger to them, and I don't know why they want me too.'

'My name is Martha.' Says the lady. 'Let's clean you up first, you can tell me more after that. Come and look at some of my clothes. Then you can have a hot shower and freshen up. I can see you've had a hard time.'

Martha has another look and there's still no sign of the chasers. She prepares food for when Sarah's ready. Sarah comes back to the kitchen a new woman. She's dressed in a blue calf-length spotted skirt and open neck blouse to match. She's carrying her own underwear and asks if she can wash them and hang them out. The two soon form a friendship and Sarah unwinds. This is the first time she has felt safe for days and is recovering her verve. Martha sits open-mouthed to listen to Sarah's story, periodically cupping her mouth and shaking her head. It's like hearing a twisted tale from Robinson Crusoe.

Hours pass before Sarah has completed her story and eaten some sustenance. 'Martha, I don't know what to do now.' She says. 'Calls to my friends could give my location away. I'm worried about both my brother and my father, so I want to stay in the Sydney area.'

'I think you need to rest and recover before you dream about doing anything my dear. Come along and I'll show you the spare room. I'll get pyjamas for you and make you a hot toddy.' Martha mixes a comforting hot cocktail with lemon, honey, whisky, and tea. She's used one herself when stressed and finds it can aid her sleep. She takes it to the spare room and places it on the bedside table.

The following morning, they share breakfast in the kitchen. After hearing more about the family problems facing Sarah, Martha understands her desire to stay undetected in Sydney. 'Why not call your father's nursing home.' She says. 'Surely the home gets lots of enquiries about patients.'

'I'm not game.' Sarah says. 'If the phone there's being bugged, they will recognise my voice.'

'Why not let me make a call saying I'm an old friend and I've just heard about his accident. That should give you a chance to learn his condition, and you can listen to his voice.'

'Would you do that for me Martha?'

'Of course. Do you know the number, or will I look it up?' Sarah gives her the number.

'Hello. Is that Nurse Geraldine? My name is Martha. I've only just heard about my friend George Fielding having an accident and that he's recuperating there. Can I talk to him please?'

'Martha, you say? You're not a family member by any chance?'

'No. Just a close friend. If he can't remember me, tell him I'm from Millmerran. That might stir his memory.'

'At this stage, I should only speak to family members, I'm afraid.'

'Is he that ill?

'I've been trying to contact his family. If you see any, could you let them know I would like them to call me straight away.'

'That sounds bad. I can call around and let Mrs Fielding know. I live very close.' She lies.

'It's good of you to offer. It's best for me to talk to her personally in the circumstances.'

'Oh God. What's happened?'

'He passed away in his sleep three days ago and I've been trying desperately to let the family know. If you could, would you please call around and ask Mrs Fielding to phone me urgently.'

Nurse Geraldine hears Sarah crying in the background. 'I know this is upsetting news, so please say nothing about his condition to Mrs Fielding. I'm sorry, but I have to be the carrier of this sad news.'

After a pause, Martha asks if the funeral arrangements have already been made because of the delay. Geraldine advises next Thursday at noon at the Sutherland Crematorium. Sarah hears all this and feels like something has punctured her lung. She collapses back into her chair, folds her arms across her chest, and sobs while ants run up her spine. Martha hangs up, pulls a chair close, hugs her with one arm, and pats her on the shoulder with the other. Sarah folds forward, hangs her head over her knees to avoid passing out, and weeps. It's some time before she feels well enough to sit up straight and face Martha. Her brain races with jumbled thoughts. *How can I talk to mum? Does she already know? Has someone already told her, and now she won't answer the phone? I hope she's not too sick to travel. She must attend the funeral. So should Clem and me. What can I do?*

'Martha, could you please try to call mum and ask her to ring Geraldine? I'm not game to speak, her phone's sure to be monitored and I don't want to give any reason for this call to be traced.'

Sarah listens to the call while holding a handkerchief to her face in the background. Martha does a good job, finding the carer at the mother's house, and passing on the request. The carer says Mrs Fielding is very unwell and hasn't been answering her phone. She apologises for not being able to spend the time she should to look after her and take calls for her. Sarah begins to shiver again, pimples creeping up her arms. She starts to rub them. Her world is collapsing.

'I don't feel well Martha, but I've got to find a way to go to Dad's funeral. Do you know anywhere I could stay safely till Thursday and then travel there in disguise? Or could you please let me stay here till then? At the funeral parlour, I could ask them to fetch the local police and get proper protection. If my friends are there, I know I'll be safe.'

'You've got to stay with me. You'll need more rest and good food after what you've been through. You're more than welcome and I'll drive you there myself.'

'You're so helpful, Martha. I really do appreciate your help.'

TWENTY-FIVE

Clem is still under police protection in hospital. Cheryl understands the problems associated with psychological trauma and she visits daily. Her duties at the Home have been helped by a part-time nurse who is attending an on-line tutoring course to advance her qualifications, and she is fully aware of the needs of Sarah's patients. She's arranged times with Cheryl to free her to visit Clem. Sarah has also requested the nursing association to try to organise a travelling nurse to replace her full-time at the nursing home for a few weeks to give her full time with Clem. She feels she is making good progress with his life traumas and also his recovery from drugs, and she wants this to continue.

She's become good friends with some of the nurses and the police on roster providing protection. Clem's main problem is a feeling of disempowerment. Cheryl knows the importance of restoring his relationships with others and has spent hours with him trying to establish his safety and reconnecting with herself. The hospital staff are providing strong professional support and are also pleased with his progress. She's been told it would help to have him recount his story of the traumatic events he's experienced.

The psychiatrist supervising his treatment has agreed that his drug treatment should continue.

He describes to Cheryl the stages of recovery to be expected and ways to build his autonomy. He has to develop coping strategies of patience and anticipation, and a little humour would help. Later stages will be identified by his willingness for greater intimacy, his desire to work with others, finally to establish a career, and perhaps build a family. While giving his advice to Cheryl she experienced a sudden rush of blood to her cheeks.

146

This caused him to ask how she's coping herself with the pressure, and he asks for more details about Clem's family. He says if any family members could visit Clem this would help recovery. Cheryl calls Engadine Nursing Home to report on Clem's attempted murder and the aftermath. She advises Geraldine of her time being spent with Clem, the arrangements she is making, and asks for a progress report on his dad which she can pass on to him. She explains her relationship with their family. Geraldine quickly assesses the situation and discloses the details for the funeral. After checking with the psychiatrist, Cheryl breaks the news of their father to Clem. He looks blankly at her. Cheryl asks if he would like to attend the funeral. He can't answer, splutters, covers his face, and wipes tears away. After he settles Cheryl arranges for police to accompany them to the funeral, and she advises Geraldine.

*　　*　　*

'It's Bill Pickings here from Pittsworth. Can Mr Goldman take my call please, I have some important information for him.'

'What's this news Bill, I'm very busy at the moment.'

'George Fielding died, and the funeral is at Sutherland next Thursday at noon. Mrs Fielding is asking around for someone to accompany her to it.'

'Christ Bill! That's sudden. Would you be able to do the trip?'

'You mean to drive her down?'

'Yeh, what else would I bloody mean? You're a mate of Clem, aren't you? She would know he delivered tobacco to you on a regular basis. You could say he was a good friend, and you want to go to his funeral yourself.'

'I suppose I could. Why would you want me to go anyway? And will you pay me to do it?"

'Of course. I might have some other favours to ask. I'll call you back tonight.'

'Before you go,' says Bill, 'I don't want to take any risks. I have my own family to look after. Can you tell me what these favours could be?'

'There's nothing for you to worry about Bill. I'm thinking that if his kids attend you could offer them a ride home. They know that football coach who has connections, and if he goes as well, they'll all believe this would be safe for 'em. Once they're home, we'll have a better chance to find what we're looking for.'

'Wouldn't they want police protection once they get home?'

'Probably would. It would still be easier for us up here.'

'I suppose I could then. Clem might think it's strange and ask me why I'm there though.'

'Use your brain. Make up some story if you have to!'

Bill is slow to answer. 'Okay, I'll talk to Mrs Fielding.'

Goldman hangs up, closes his eyes, and lays his head back pondering on his next move. The football coach could be a problem on the trip back if he travels with either of the two children. That coach must be dealt with. He decides he must phone Bill while he's at the funeral to learn the family arrangements and to give him orders for the route to use on the way back.

*   *   *

Cheryl calls Len and finds him sorting out his clothes after returning from Miami Beach. 'Len, I've just called George Fielding's nursing home from Boris's hospital. George Fielding has passed away. Did you know about this? And have you heard Sarah's gone missing again?'

Len sits on the bed, his brain spinning. *NO! Not more blows for them all!* 'Cheryl - - - it's all news to me. His kids are in enough strife already. I thought the police were about to pick Sarah up at Medlow Bath. That's why I came back here to work. This is just more bloody stress to the whole family.'

'Surely the police will track Sarah down.' Says Cheryl. 'They've got all the resources, Len, it's not up to you.'

'It's not that easy for me. I'm on a mission to get these bastards.'

'Well, the funeral's been set by the nursing home, it's to be noon next Thursday at the Sutherland Crematorium. I've arranged for police to accompany me and Clem. Clem's improving, but this hasn't helped.'

'I'd like to go. It would be good to see you and Clem again. I'll call the Home to see if there's anything I can do to help. Thanks for letting me know.'

They continue to talk about Clem's progress. Len then calls the Home. 'It's Len Gorski speaking. I've just heard about George Fielding's death, and I'd like to confirm the funeral details so I could drive down from Queensland to attend.'

'What is your interest Mr Gorski?' Asks Genevieve.

'I'm sorry, I should have explained. I'm a family friend and I'm in Queensland. I would like to drive down to join the family members.'

'I have already been advised that Mrs Fielding is being driven to the funeral by another family friend, a Mr Pickings. Perhaps you could accompany them?'

'Did Mr Pickings leave a phone number?'

'He did, he said it would be a one-day trip, down and back. He plans to leave early and return late. If that is convenient for you I'll text through his number.'

'I'll speak to him. Thank you for that and your assistance to care for George. This is a terrible shock for his family.'

'Is that Mr Pickings?' asks Len.

'Yeh. Who's that?'

'I'm Len Gorski, a close friend of the Fielding family. I contacted the Nursing Home where George was, and they said you've arranged to drive his wife to the funeral. Can I offer to take you both?'

'I've already arranged to make it a day trip and for someone to mind my shop for the day. He needs the money, so I still intend to drive down. I'll be setting off at the crack of dawn, I don't know who might want to come back with me, so it would be better for you to drive yourself down. Thanks for the offer, but I'd prefer we go separately.'

'I'm helping the family with problems Bill, and I would appreciate the time to talk with Mrs Fielding during the trip. I could bring anyone who wants a lift back to travel with me.'

'They'd surely want to travel back together if anyone else wants it. I've already fixed things with Mrs Fielding and I don't want to upset her. You make your own mind up. If you want to travel with me, be out front of the Millmerran pub at 6.15 AM.'

Bill contacts Goldman to tell him about his conversation. 'Look Bill', says Goldman, 'if that prick of a coach turns up, you take him. I'll want to know the arrangements for the return, got it? Call me from the funeral.'

Bill feels he's done his best to make his own job simple. Caleb's sure to have a plan and he's worried about being involved in it. Len, on the other hand, has become suspicious about Bill's reluctance to carry him. All the more reason for him to turn up.

TRENTY-SIX

Cheryl, Clem, and their police guard are first to arrive at the funeral parlour. Shortly afterwards Geraldine arrives accompanied by two people from the nursing home. Cheryl walks to meet them. 'Hi, you must be Geraldine. I'm with George's son. That's Clem, standing over there with the constable. Clem's not well and we've come from the hospital where he's recovering from injury. The constable is here for protection. Thank you for coming.'

'These are two of the patients of my nursing home who wanted to come. Did you say Clem has police protection?'

'It's a long story. Sarah would have told you some of the problems we've had. We can talk about it after the service. You said on the phone that refreshments would be available then.'

'There's a tea-room in that block over there.'

A small car enters the carpark, and two ladies leave it and begin to walk toward them. As they approach, Cheryl recognises Sarah and rushes to her. She leaves Clem. He's standing there resembling a witness waiting for his call, blank face, deep in thought. Sarah's heart vibrates her ribcage as the two women collide in mid step and dance around with each other. Then Sarah notices Clem and rushes to him. He's smiling now as it dawns on him who she is.

Her clothes are totally foreign to him and in a fashion unbecoming. They hug and Sarah can't swallow, unable to speak. Tears are flowing. Cheryl joins and all three hug, packed in like a scrum. Another car arrives and a man moves toward them. Cheryl turns to greet him. 'Are you a friend of George Fielding?'

'My name is Abel Turner. I'm the manager of the mine at Cobar where George has worked for years. We became good friends. I'll miss him. His accident happened at my mine, and I feel somehow responsible. He was troubled with memory loss, and I should have taken more care to watch his whereabouts.'

The group continues talking and they are approached by a minister. He introduces himself and asks if anyone would like to say something during the service. They look at each other with puzzled faces. Sarah volunteers, expressing her wish to say how much he was loved. They are all surprised when Abel also says he would like to say a few words about how valuable George's expertise was to the mine profits.

Geraldine joins the group and asks if they are aware that Mrs Fielding is on her way. She says she believes she was to be driven down with two close family friends, and asks if they know their expected arrival time, or have heard from them. During the discussion another car arrives. Len alights and is helping Mrs Fielding out. Another crying match begins in a rush to greet her. There's light in the sky for the family, the first time for weeks. It's a short service and they gather at the tea-room to describe their experiences.

After the family discussion has simmered, Sarah moves to Abel to learn more about her dad's work. For years when home from Cobar he would take time out to visit a local mine near Stanthorpe. She assumed it was to do with his hobby and was interested to learn more about his mine work.

'Your dad was clever.' Says Abel. 'From 2005 he provided consultancy to several mines, including my own. He consulted for my original complex, a couple of separate underground mines, copper being the chief mineral extracted. This complex feeds 1.8 million tons per annum through a conventional processing plant, and our copper concentrate is railed to Newcastle for export. Your dad improved the extraction of copper for us.'

'Your dad was involved in our exploration activities that included a wide-ranging geological survey that led to the discovery of major new ore sources. These were of particular interest to your dad because they were highly prospective for new base metal deposits.'

'I'd like to learn more about that. I only wish he'd spent more time with me in recent years.' Says Sarah. 'I idolised him. I could never understand why he was so interested in the mine at Stanthorpe instead of spending time at his home.'

'He was highly motivated, Sarah.' He says. 'That doesn't mean he didn't love you dearly. Many men have this same problem. He was a very sensitive person, perhaps a loner, but I know he loved all his family deeply. When he recognised his failing health, he told me he thought he should get treatment before he went back home. I think he wrote a letter to your mum as well. I told him about this Nursing home in Engadine. That's why I contacted Geraldine after his accident. I knew she would arrange whatever treatment he needed, and Sydney would have the best services available after his discharge from Liverpool Hospital.'

Sarah closes her eyes. She thinks back to her dad again, remembering him kneeling at her bedside telling stories. Her favourite memories.

Len phones Inspector Stone to say Sarah has turned up at the funeral and he describes the reunion. He hasn't heard her full story yet, but he wants to take her home with him. There's room in the car with her mother and they all need time to talk.

'Sarah needs full police protection now she's safe.' Says Beryl. 'I know you mean well, but it needs to be twenty-four seven. We talked about the resort as a good location. This is a quick decision, but it should be safe to take her back there with you if it's done quickly. I'll have police there by the time you arrive.'

The resort is designed to be secure. It was previously used by a mining magnate to illegally import young girls from destitute conditions in Uzbekistan and train them for prostitution. He used this as a diverse plan for when his coal mining enterprises declined over time to introduce renewable energy. Len and Boris played key roles in identifying the crime.

The resort is surrounded by security fences and was guarded by hired security personnel as cover for the operation. Inside the perimeter it is a high-class resort with five-star accommodation and an Olympic style swimming pool set in a palm tree garden.

'It's a good location.' Says Beryl. 'It's close to Millmerran and Toowoomba. I know the new management, and it will be very secure with police protection.'

*   *   *

Len talks to Bill to ask if Sarah could accompany them back to Queensland. Bill agrees, then moves away to phone Goldman.

'Could I speak with Mr Goldman please. It's Bill Pickings and the matter is urgent.'

'Bill. What have you got?'

'I'm calling like you said before I drive back. I'll be carrying Sarah, her mum, and that coach. Clem is still under police guard in the Liverpool hospital. I'll be leaving soon and with traffic, I expect to take about seven hours. It's been a long day and I'll get the coach to do some of the driving.'

'Well make sure you do the last leg. I want you to come via Texas and drive through Inglewood. Is that clear?'

'Yes sir. It's a long trip and I expect there'll need to be a pit stop or two. So, I can't give a reliable time of arrival for you.' They continue to discuss the trip with Goldman giving more instructions, one being to refuel at the corner service station as they pass through Texas at the Queensland border.

Cheryl tells the group she and Clem are leaving to return to the hospital and the group begins to break up. Geraldine leaves with the patients. Martha has a tearful short talk with Sarah before hugging her and leaving. The others walk to Bill's car. Sarah and Mum take the back seat of Bill's car. Len's asked to drive the first section until they stop for refreshments. Bill tells him to drive until they reach the Maccas outlet on the bypass through Tamworth. Then he will take over.

From Tamworth Bill drives the backway to Millmerran through the Inverell township and crosses the border at Texas. Bill tells his passengers he will refuel at Texas, where he knows the toilets at the service station are normally clean and tidy. Mrs Fielding expresses her thanks to Bill, she needs to use them. Len has an uneasy feeling because Bill's manner has just changed. He looks tense, which is unexpected, as they are now moving into territory closer to home. When they are back on the road Bill keeps taking quick glances at the roadside ahead.

After Texas the road is deserted except for the odd kangaroo feeding on the roadside grass and threatening to cross in front of an unexpected driver. This is a hazard at this time of dusk when knowledgeable drivers slow down. But Bill has slowed down already and has plenty of time to pass the kangaroos safely. Len's fine-tuned early warning signals bring the taste of cold metals that chill his lips. Without being noticed he slips his hand across the centre console and switches on the safety switch to disable the opening of all doors from the outside. He can't really understand his action, it's a reflex.

After passing a crest Bill sees a van parked on the roadside. A man moves to the road waving a torch and signalling for help. Bill stops behind the van, half on and half off the hardtop. The man approaches Len's window, now open.

'My front offside tyre's flat, but I'm not strong enough to undo the wheel nuts to fit the spare wheel. Would you be able to help?'

Bill looks across at Len. 'You look fit and strong. Would you be able to do the deed? My wheel spanner's on the floor in the boot. It's got a long shaft for leverage.'

TWENTY-SEVEN

Len nods, hops out, moves to the back, flips the boot, and reaches in for the spanner. His sensory alarm bells are ringing because of the way this was happening in such a remote location, with Bill's driving manner, with himself so readily available to do the deed, and the convenient access to a long-handle spanner. It's been all too easy. He senses the signals too late. He's struck a vicious blow to the back of his head. He passes out and falls to the hard-top with blood trickling from the earlier unhealed wound. Another man runs from the van to the car and grabs the door handle where Sarah sits. He can't open it and looks through at Bill.

Sarah turns squirms sideways and sees a third heavy-set man moving to Len. 'Where are we?' she screams. 'what's this place called? Quick!' She searches her bag for the phone, forgetting she has none.

She sees a flat-top utility emerge from the trees near the van and it backs up to the two men lifting Len. She recognises the ute as the type set-up for hunting kangaroos and wild pigs, with a spotlight mounted on a strong frame at the rear of the cabin. This frame is used by shooters standing on the flat-top. She remembers this from when Boris was driven to the Millmerran Hospital with his injured leg. She quickly takes the mobile phone from her mother's handbag.

Bill now realises Len has activated the door locks and he quickly restores them. His shout is garbled, and loud enough for those outside to hear. 'Sarah, tell the cops we're about five minutes from Inglewood and I'll go straight to the police station there.' He's trying to make it clear he wants no further involvement to those inside the car, but to signal that Sarah's now free to be taken by those outside.

'They'll kill him!' Sarah shouts to the emergency operator, and she begins describing the vehicle. 'The ute they've got is for bush shooters. You've got to trace it before they murder him. Call Detective Inspector Stone in Sydney too. She's chasing these animals!'

The man from the van drags Sarah's door open successfully this time, pulls her out, and struggles with her to the enclosed rear compartment of the van. He pushes her in and slams the door. His mates join him in the front, the van does a U-turn, and drives off Southward toward Texas.

Bill accelerates, spinning pebbles from the roadside, and hugs the steering wheel, heading North toward Inglewood. 'I'm getting out of here!' He shouts. In his rear-view mirror, he sees Mrs Fielding has turned ashen, she has one hand with frozen knuckles pressing on her heart, and the other hugging her mouth. She's about to be sick.

'Keep calm, Mrs Fielding,' He shouts. 'We'll get help quickly. I'll stop at Inglewood. The cops should be able to block roads in all directions.' Bill glares ahead with blood draining from his face. He holds the steering wheel tightly attempting to show Mrs Fielding he fears for his own safety and indicating he is not involved with what has just happened. He floors the accelerator burning rubber on the hard-top.

Bill drives to the Inglewood police station. It's unstaffed. He calls emergency again and is asked to stay there until help arrives. Mrs Fielding has passed out. The emergency operator tells him she will try to get a chopper involved in a search of the bushland and have roadblocks set up South. The chopper happens to be close by at Millmerran after chasing criminals escaping from a Pittsworth crime scene and leading a chase down the Gore Highway for the border at Goondiwindi.

Len stirs and finds himself stretched out and bouncing around on the rear seat of a double cabin vehicle. It must be off-road by the way it's being driven. It's dark. He can't see his bindings, but he can feel they are rope, but thinner than his little finger.

He's had bindings worse than this growing up in Termez. Soldiers would return from the war and were merciless. As children, he and his friend Andrei had been sexually abused, then abandoned. His attitude to sex was badly disturbed and is partly the reason for his failure to have lasting relationships until Jane changed him.

He and Andrei freed themselves when Len was able to wear through the rope by rubbing his cuffed hands against the back of a tree stump. The memories still distress him. That took him over an hour. Now, with patience, he's convinced he could chew through these bindings.

His head aches. His hands are tied in front, and he lifts them to feel his head. It's still weeping and there's some type of rug under his head to mop the blood. The bouncing around doesn't help and it's too rough to hold the rug tight to stem the flow. There's talking in the front seat.

'Now we've got him what are we supposed to do with him?'

'I was told to strap him down tight to a table in the old cowshed out on Thompson's property and leave him. They've got some guys they call the G-G's who are expert in disposing bodies and leaving no trace. Nothing that could look like murder.'

'I don't want anything to do with that. Let's just do what's asked and piss off. Murder is out for me!

'I told them that too. They said not to worry, the G-G's know their job.'

'I suppose they could take him up the Cape and feed him to the crocks. That would do it. But they said the G-G's have their own methods. They're on another job today. I was told to just make this guy secure and leave.' They hear a drone sound, getting louder. The passenger peers out, then up, and sees a chopper in the distance.

'Shit Dan,' he says, 'could that be after us?'

'No way. Cops couldn't get here that quick. They must be on their way to something else.'

Loss of blood weakens Len, and he loses consciousness. He dreams of Jane and her injury. He imagines himself lying next to her, sharing her pain, keeping her company into a new world. The chopper passes and the ute continues deep through the trees to emerge into a spindly grass meadow and drive to the cowshed on the far side. They struggle in with Len and use tension straps from the ute to fix him tightly to the table.

They leave him and the blood covered rug and drive away through the scrub intending to join Campbell's Lane to take them the back way into Inglewood. Just before they reach the Lane, they hear the chopper return and pass again. At the junction with the Cunningham Highway to Inglewood they're blocked by two police cars. The police inspection finds no trace of Len having been on board. Their licenses are checked and recorded, and they are allowed to proceed.

*   *   *

Hours later Len stirs. His head still aches. His body and legs are fastened tightly to a table by strong tie-down straps. He feels groggy. It's very quiet, so the two bushies must have left. His arms are free, but his hands are still bound. He reaches up and finds the bleeding has stopped. The rug has a wide spread of dried blood. He breathes slowly and deeply trying to get clear thoughts flowing. He thinks he remembers a chopper. Could that have scared his captors away? He begins to chew the rope binding his hands. It takes energy he's short on. He reasons that if he chews through one loop in the bindings, he will be able to unwrap his hands first, improve the position of the rug holding his head, then rewrap the ties loosely as camouflage. He plans to surprise anyone who returns. Once they're free he adjusts the rug clear of clots. He's beginning to feel better.

The chopper lands on a pad at the Inglewood police station and the navigator briefs the assembled policemen.

'We flew over a flat top utility heading through the mulga and went ahead to see if there was a meeting spot up front. But I saw none. We retraced and I'm sure I saw the same ute travelling through bush toward Campbells Lane. To me it just looked like shooters checking for animals on dusk when roos and pigs begin their foray. I radioed in and was told police had already been sent to search. That's all I can report.'

'We checked the ute and found nothing.' Says another of the police.

After discussion it was decided that the body could have been dropped. Alternatively, if the second sighting was of a different ute, the first may still have the captive and be covered somewhere under trees. A ground search will begin, but considering the magnitude of the area, this could take days.

Bill Pickings is directed to return to the Fielding home where they will be met by Millmerran police. Mrs Fielding will be offered safety to resume living there. She is considered to be not at risk. Bill is released to return home. Sarah's kidnap is reported to Inspector Stone.

TWENTY-EIGHT

Cheryl's managed to have a second bed moved into Clem's secure hospital ward. It is one of four separate wards within the hospital having ensuite facilities, this one guarded 24/7 by a policeman on roster. He sits at the entry to these units at the rear of the main hospital. These rooms are normally used by locum doctors. The security exists for any person wishing to gain access to these, which are all occupied at present, and to provide privacy for the patients and medical staff as required. The separate bed has been provided for Cheryl's full-time caring role.

Clem's traumas robbed him of a sense of power and control over his own life. Cheryl's challenge has been to develop coping strategies for things such as regulation of sleep, eating, and exercise. She is aware that his reconnection with ordinary life, and feeling safe, could take from days to weeks. Sarah has taught her well, and she is doing her best to follow her advice for drug rehabilitation. She is encouraged by his rate of recovery over the last week and the effect of the family reunion. She's had no trouble to fully regain his trust. She is pleased with his commitment to quit the drugs and how his confidence is increasing. She feels she is benefiting too from his recovery. It has given her a sense of success with the healing process and a boost to her own self-esteem.

Her feeling for Clem has blossomed. She thought he was hot way back in high school days. He wasn't like other boys interested in one thing only, to get into a girls' pants whether wanting to form a friendship or not. He was always polite and respectful when she visited their home to study for exams with Sarah. He was always helpful to Sarah and offered to transport her once he restored his car, whereas most other boys would have nothing to do with a sibling. Being so close now daily, she has seen more of his assets, including remarkable respect and tenderness.

I'm worried about the affect his dad's death will now have. I hope he doesn't regress after all the progress he's made from all his troubles. It's been a long road to get this far and I'm feeling proud of the role I've played. I hope he doesn't see this just as the role a nurse should play - I know now I've done this because of my growing affection, and in some way, I regret the blunt refusal I made to his advances soon after we met. I've never felt this way before about anyone.

Days later Clem wakes one morning feeling like a new man. He's lying in bed with a morning glory from dreaming about Cheryl and his attempt to woo her to bed back in their time at the Anna Nursing Home. It mystifies him now, because it is not his nature to try to take advantage with girls. It seems like months ago. She said she's had many propositions from patients. That makes him feel he acted just like one of them. He won't do that again. *I need to impress her by taking her out on a proper date like a gentleman. That would be a proper approach. I want to succeed. Cheryl is attractive in so many ways, she deserves the best I can offer.*

While he lays there stewing about their relationship, he hears Cheryl behind him rise to change. He rolls to see what she's doing. He's looking at her in her flimsy night attire, a lace crisscross sheer silk shorty nightdress. He immediately loses interest in why she's there. His morning glory begins to grow. His heart pumps faster and he swallows with difficulty. He swings out of bed and sits there admiring her backside and covering his erection. It's embarrassing him. She's startled and twists around. Something happens. The magnets have drawn their eyes, and neither can break the spell. He rises. But cannot move. Cheryl smiles. Clem moves slowly across the room holding his gaze. He takes her face in both hands and kisses her sweetly on the forehead.

'I don't deserve you, Cheryl. You're always there responding to my needs, reacting carefully to my moods. I've been such a burden for both you and Sarah. I feel calm in your presence, calmer and happier than I've ever felt before in my life. It's not fair that it's been so one-sided. You need to live your own life, enjoy yourself. It's not been fair on you to live like this. Find someone more responsible than I've been. I don't deserve your dedication.'

Cheryl can't speak. *Is he telling me I should leave? That I've now finished my role as his nurse? Why is he holding me like this and nothing more?*

'Cheryl. I've just dreamt about our relationship. My advances being rejected. I'm trying my best and I really do appreciate your special care. Cheryl, I love you. I love you for your care. I love you for knowing what to do and persisting with me. I wanted you from the time we met at the Nursing Home. I've never felt this way with any other person.'

She slowly lifts her face breaking the grip of his hands and looks to reconnect their eyes. He drops his arms and folds them around her waist, drawing her in. Their lips meet softly and their eyes close in harmony. He feels her muscles relax; she feels comfortable with his arms around her. Their lips lock, emotions flow, and their bodies meld together.

Clem then steps away; he will go no further this time. He feels he must first make up for his shortcomings and prove his worth. He feels his passion is unjustified.

'I have to prove myself Cheryl. I feel I'm a new person thanks to you. I don't believe I need hospital anymore and I'd like us to move to the resort if you will come too. I heard about security there at the funeral. Sarah should be settled in by now. I know I'm over it. I want to help catch these bastards for being so ruthless.

'I was only thinking about myself when I ran away, not thinking about my family and others. I feel responsible for Jane's death and the impact it has on Len. I want to help Len and give police everything I know about their operation. I've been too scared to give anyone else information thinking it might endanger them.'

'I don't know what to say.' Says Cheryl. 'you've surprised me.' On impulse she swings her arms over his shoulders, 'of course I'll come,' and she draws him into a deep kiss.

'Our relationship has not been a natural one Cheryl.' He says. 'I want you to see the real me.'

Clem phones the resort expecting Sarah to answer. The manager advises no one has arrived yet, police are already there waiting to hear from Inspector Stone. Clem phones Inspector Stone and waits to be connected.

'Inspector Stone, it's Clem Fielding here. The resort has just told me Sarah has not arrived. Is there a problem?'

'Yes, there is Clem. I've heard from Queensland police that their car was intercepted near the Texas township. Len was knocked out and taken into the forest in a shooters' utility. Sarah was kidnapped and taken away in a waiting van which has not yet been traced. It's a double tragedy and very worrying. This gang is well organised. I cannot understand for the life of me why they want Sarah too.'

'Oh God. This is terrible. I was going to ask Sarah if Cheryl and I could join her at the resort to save the cost of our protection here at the hospital. I feel well enough to leave hospital.'

'That was the plan, Clem. I can arrange police transport for you both. It could benefit your mum as well for you to be that close.'

'You hear that Cheryl? Sarah's missing again. Shit! I thought she was on her way back to the resort. And Len's been taken too. Poor bugger. They must have been good to get him, he's very well wired for emergencies. I'm told he has a sense for danger coming, and why in hells name do they want Sarah? I'm the one they want, not her or Len!'

'Keep calm Clem. Don't blame yourself. Drug trafficking has tentacle's everywhere, believe me. Beryl's onto it. She's in a position of power and will act quickly and I'm sure with success. It won't help you if this wrecks the good progress you're making.'

'I suppose you're right. But I want to help. I think I could do more if we were at the resort. Beryl said she'd provide transport. I want you to come too. Can you do that?'

'I think it's a good idea too.'

TWENTY-NINE

Beryl contacts Cheryl and says arrangements have been made for their accommodation at the Leyburn resort. The manager has a suitable suite for them and both security and staffing have been arranged and payments negotiated. It will cost them nothing for the time being. A police vehicle will take them there, its travel monitored, and immediate contact provided should any emergency arise. The driver will call her to provide the time for pick-up, but they should be prepared for short notice. Every precaution is being taken this time.

Cheryl advises Clem. 'Beryl's not going to let any slip-up. She's just told us to get ready straight away and be prepared for a quick trip to the resort. I'll start packing for us both. I'm sure our things'll fit into my travel bag. My stuff at the Anna Nursing Home can come up by normal transport. We really need to get you a new set of clothes as well. We can manage that later.'

'This is great news.' Says Clem. 'I haven't had a chance to give the cops all I know yet. I can help them better from the resort. Next time either of us speaks to Beryl I'd like to ask for a Queensland detective to pay me a visit to pick my brains.'

Later that day the call comes for the pick-up. The driver arrives in the latest addition to the NSW police highway patrol fleet, the type normally used for pursuit, a BMW X5 SUV (Sport Utility Vehicle), six cylinder all-wheel-drive petrol sedan. The officer introduces himself to the security constable and then to the couple. He's a bright young officer, polite and conversational, and makes an immediate impression. He helps with the travel bag and escorts them to the car. Clem walks around the car smiling and rubbing his hands.

'How lucky are you to have this masterpiece!' He says to the driver. 'You've got a racing machine here. Bugger anyone trying to lose you in a chase! I'd love to have a drive myself.'

'I've had special training to get this job. You're right about it too, it's a racehorse and lively. If you're serious about a drive, I'm sorry, but I can't let you. It would risk losing my job.'

'Understood,' says Clem, 'I've got an auto Engineers Certificate and work in a garage importing and selling luxury sedans and sports cars. That's why I'm interested. To tell the truth, one just saved my life because of its safety features. I'm going to enjoy this trip.'

'I'm going the back way.' Says the driver. You'll like it and it happens to be the shortest of several ways we could take. But it's still over eight hundred kilometres. We'll need a break, and I think Walcha would be the ideal place, a small town on the way.'

'I'm a Queenslander,' says Clem, 'What's this back route, not the New England Highway?'

'No. We do cross that highway. We'll be taking The Buckets' Way through Gloucester and then The Thunderbolts Way through Walcha to Inverell. From there through Texas to Leyburn along the Greenup Limevale Road. You'll see a lot of new scenic territory today so you both can sit back and enjoy the ride.

Clem's impressed with the car, more so with the silky ride provided by the driver. He shows patience on the highways, declining several opportunities to speed past slower drivers. Once on Thunderbolt's Way they encounter road works and a creek crossing before rising quickly up to the New England Plateau over very rough sections of unsealed roadway strewn with rocks. He picks the best speed for these sections confirming his skill.

Reaching Walcha he drives into the Service Station for fuel. He points to the restaurant saying he will join them there as soon as he refuels and parks. An attendant has come out to clean the windscreen and chat to the driver asking if he needs to check oils, water, and tires. The driver shakes his head. The attendant moves to the shopfront and takes out his mobile to phone the manager of the Southport Dealership.

'Duchy, I got news for you that you won't believe.' He says.

'Is that you Kenny?'

'That's me, boss. I thought you'd know my voice.

'You're on extended leave old boy. What do you want?'

'Of all the places I picked Walcha to be clear of those investigations about Clem till the dust settles. I'm staying with an old aunt. Well, Clem's just turned up here in a Highway Patrol car driven by a young constable.'

'I don't believe you. He was shot through the heart at point blank range.'

'It's him all right. He's travelling with a good looker, too. I went out to check the oil and water and clean the windscreen, and I asked the cop if there was anything he needed for the rest of his trip. I took a chance to chat, and he let slip they're going to Leyburn. What the fuck could be there?'

'All I know is there's a disused Yank airstrip there a mile long that was used by long-distance bombers in World War II. They might want to slip him out quietly somewhere for safety.'

'Nah. That can't be it. They could do that from Sydney somewhere. How does he look?

'He's fine. I'm sure he didn't notice me. He was too busy helping his floozie. I'll keep out of sight till they leave.'

'I'll tell the Boss straight away. Thanks for the info, Kenny. This could throw a spanner in the works.'

*   *   *

'Mr Goldman, it's Duchy. We've got a problem. Clem's still alive and right now is on the road travelling to Leyburn with some floozie in a NSW police highway patrol vehicle.'

'Impossible. He was shot dead. The shooter got him in the heart.'

'Boss, it's true. One of my mechanics saw him. It's legit. He used to work with him.'

'Shit! You say he's on the road to Leyburn. When will he get there? Do we have time to get a lookout there?'

'They're at Walcha having food. Could be four hours away. Bill Pickings could get there in twenty minutes. He might be able to find out what's going on.'

'This is serious. We need a plan B. Clem's gunna squeal like a stuck pig after two attempts to kill him! You need to make sure all your cars are clean. I'll make it urgent for all Clem's delivery points to clean their shops and stash their product somewhere safe. He doesn't know about our bulk storage, but I'll have a look at moving that too. I've got work to do. Will you get onto Bill Pickings for me and get him to sus Leyburn out straight away? Find out more about the town. Check for a strong lock-up Duchy. Get him to check the joint. And what about all those other cars you've had modified?'

'We don't need to worry about the private cars and their secret compartments. It's entirely up to the owners what they use 'em for. That's their problem. I'll call Bill straight away.

I'll call you later if I get anything.'

THIRTY

Len stirs. His head still aches, he's strapped tightly to a table by strong tie-down straps. He feels groggy. It's very quiet, so the two bushies must have left him. He reaches up and finds the bleeding has stopped. The rug has a wide spread of dried blood. He breathes slowly and deeply trying to get clear thoughts flowing. He remembers the chopper. They won't see him in this shed even if they do bring the chopper back. He starts chewing the rope binding his hands. It takes concentration he's short on. When his hands are free, he adjusts the rug for a comfortable position and clear of clots, and loosely rewraps the bindings. He's beginning to recover.

At last, he begins to take in his environment. It's a small, enclosed shelter with a large opening in one side. It smells of cow dung. The roof is corrugated iron with a small slope. The only other object he can see is an animal trough, but he can't see the water. He listens closely for animal sounds and hears none. It's very quiet, so the shed must be very remote. Every now and then he hears a bird or two fly past, but they make no calls. He knows roos and pigs exist in the bush near Millmerran, this area would be similar. The trough is too high for either of those animals to drink from, so the shed must be for either horses or cows. Most likely cows, they need little attention.

*   *   *

Grigor and Gustav are on their way along the Gore Highway toward Pittsworth. They've been told to call in to see Bill Pickings at his tobacco shop to learn the geography and how to find Len. Grigor's the spokesman for the duo, he's also the driver of their recently stolen Pajero wagon from Tura Beach in New South Wales. It has NSW number plates, and they've crossed the border at Goondiwindi and chatting part in their own language, and sometimes trying to use broken English..

'This bomb'll stick out like a hairy pussy in this country. We need new State plates.' Says Gustav, shuffling in his seat to relieve pressure on some of his hardened skin plates. 'Let's swap em over at the next place, Pittsworth.'

'No,' says Grigor, 'that'll risk more.'

Gustav's been squealing for this change ever since he learned their next job was in Queensland. Grigor tolerates him, knowing he's stubborn, but not all that smart with most things they do. He's trying to convince Gustav that they should just keep going. They've been on the road overnight.

'How long we got for this job?' Asks Gustav. 'We must not get stop by police; we have no papers.'

'Why I no speed. We have plan to hide on coast till flight out back home.'

When they arrive at Pittsworth, Bill gets his assistant to look after the shop and he takes the G-G's to the nearby café. Grigor is a heavy-weight and has a voracious appetite. When he's finished his fourth meat pie Bill spreads a map of the local terrain on the tabletop. By that time all Grigor has eaten is an apple, delivered by the young waitress who purchased it for him at the nearby fruit shop. He's not hungry. The human flesh he's eaten at Tura Beach hasn't properly digested. He can't take his eyes off this waitress. They follow her every move, especially when she bends to stack and remove used cutlery from other tables. 'More hairy pussy there,' he mumbles to himself.

Their first job since arriving was for the Mafia group controlling drugs in the NSW Irrigation area. The two are professional hitmen.

They had to escape from Columbia for a while following a hit they made on a man their Cartel believed was the major reason leading to the seizure of 450 tons of cocaine by international territories. This mission at Tura Beach was to dispose of the body of a man they kidnapped at Griffith, an inland regional town in the Murrumbidgee Area. The man was kept alive for the whole trip to the coast so Gustav could murder him and feed him to the sharks while still bleeding profusely. Gustav's gruesome addiction arose from mental torture due to his birth defect, but he is a significant part of the pair's modus operandi. To leave no trace of human cause of the death. Grigor's part is to knock them out, Gustav's part is to get rid of evidence.

They hired a half cabin launch at Merimbula, a town just South of Tura Beach. They loaded the body and cruised offshore while Gustav used his knuckleduster to tear off strips of flesh. The fresh blood was designed to quickly attract sharks. Failing that, should the body be fished out by any other craft or drift ashore, the injuries would look like shark bites.

It's late afternoon as Grigor drives the Pajero through sparse trees and mulga, chest high hardy wattle bush plants able to withstand long periods of drought. The vehicle frightens birds along the way. The G-G's have never seen some of these and are captivated by the pretty blue faced honeyeater variety. These contrast to the larger numbers of small black faced wood swallows. Human nature has endowed them with a strange combination of adoration and cruelty.

Grigor finds Thompson's cow shed. Len hears them coming and prepares. As they enter the shed chatting about this job, he feigns to be unconscious. They've been told where a wild pigs habitat exists by a small creek a short distance deeper into the scrub. Their role is to mutilate enough of Len's body to attract them, then abandon him. A familiar modus operandi. Bill Pickings gave them a backpack and hikers tent to leave with the body to camouflage the reason for him being there.

'We got a move in deeper.' Says Grigor, still trying to converse in broken English. 'Thick pigs there. Our job, leave him there tonight and head to coast.'

Len translates their broken English. He has no idea of his whereabouts but doesn't like their plan to go deeper into bushland. He decides it's time to act, even though his head is pounding. Grigor releases the tension straps, unties his legs, and grabs Len's feet to drag him along the table until his feet reach the ground.

He stoops to lift Len and shoulder him for the carry to the Pajero. He sees Len's loose bindings untangle and realises Len is now conscious and with free hands. But it's too late. Len rolls off the shoulder, grabs Grigor's arm, pivots to his left, dragging Grigor in close, and delivers a backhanded blow to his throat. Grigor sways away to the shock. Len follows through with a full-blooded punch below his ribs.

Grigor growls and retaliates. He seizes Len into a bear hug and squeezes hard to deflate Len's lungs and weaken him. Len stamps down on his foot, a gap appears between them, and Len delivers a knee to his groin. Len's arms come free, and he delivers a double fisted uppercut. Grigor steps back. Len launches himself airborne and executes his flying scissors kick striking Grigor in the ear with his right foot. A kick he specialised for striking lofted passes for shots on goal. Grigor's down and out. Len jumps back up to his feet from his follow through.

Gustav stands back and gazes open-mouthed at the action. He's never before seen his accomplice go down. He pulls out his razor-sharp knuckleduster. Len looks at this weed of a man wondering what role he plays. Len unwisely reaches out to grab his arm to tie him up with the twine. Gustav closes in wielding the knuckleduster and opens a strip of flesh from Len's outstretched arm.

Len jumps back with blood streaming into his hand. Gustav rushes forward aiming the knuckleduster at Len's face. Before the gap closes Len drives his boot savagely into his groin. Another strike, this one with the toe of his boot instead of his instep. Gustav heaves and vomits a foul-smelling concoction which happens to land all over Grigor's prone body. Len flattens Gustav with a Karate blow to his neck.

Len grits his teeth and rolls the layer of torn skin back over the wound to his arm and tries to wrap it with the twine. This stems the blood, but it still weeps. He rips a clean strip from the blood-soaked rug previously under his head, rewraps the wound, and binds it again. It's painful, but he's got work to do.

He seizes the knuckle-duster from Grigor's prone body and pockets it. He leaves them laying there and goes to the Pajero to look for a mobile phone. There's one in a dashboard clip and he calls emergency. There's already a wagon searching the mulga, and the mobile's GPS identity shows them immediately where to go. Before long Len sees them emerge into the clearing.

The police load the G-Gs into their wagon and head off for the Pittsworth police station. One of the constables drives Len to the Millmerran Hospital in the stolen Pajero and waits while he's treated.

THIRTY-ONE

The constable takes Len to where his car was parked for the journey to the funeral, and he drives himself to the resort. Len is met by the manager and the duty policeman and shown a room where Inspector Stone suggested he should stay. Len has a feeling Beryl would hope he stays there and keeps out of trouble. *She should know better.*

He showers and cleans up, but he has no change of clothes to wear and feels embarrassed when he leaves the room to join Cheryl and Clem for dinner. His arm is in a mess from his shower although he's rebound it with the wet bandage. It's the first thing Cheryl sees when she gives him a hug. Clem shakes his good hand, and they bump shoulders affectionately. Cheryl drags Len away immediately to redress the arm.

They chat throughout the meal, there's a lot to catch up on. Len is impressed with Clem's condition. He quickly becomes conscious of the new relationship between Clem and Cheryl. He thought Cheryl was very level-headed right from the first time he met her, and now he's beginning to rethink his first impression about Clem as a weak drug dealer. Clem describes the long conversation he had with Inspector Stone to provided details of the tobacco shops he made deliveries to, the high-class car distributor where secret compartments are installed for other deliveries and caches, and said he believes the syndicate is managed by a well healed Gold Coast leader who pulls all the strings. He suspects this because of conversations he overheard while working in the garage. He keeps remembering events over the past twelve months and believes there's much more he could recall if prompted by an inspector at an interview.

After the meal they move poolside to sit in deckchairs to enjoy the fresh cool air of the setting sun and to watch the stars emerge in the cloudless sky, conditions previously denied to the pair locked in the hospital. They've taken drinks with them, but it's an uneasy conversation because Sarah's still missing. Len describes the call to Boris to say she was safe from her earlier capture at Blackheath. Now she's missing again. There seems to be no end.

'That bloody gang wants Sarah badly.' He says. 'I can't understand it!'

He phones Beryl to see if the police have made any progress. 'Roadblocks were set up as quickly as possible to trap the van carrying Sarah.' She says. 'It wasn't seen though. Police know it headed South from the ambush point, the wagon you were in went straight off road, the car with Bill Pickings and Mrs Fielding stopped at Inglewood police station.'

'Where was the roadblock going South?' Asks Len.

'NSW police blocked the junction where that road joins the Bruxner Highway at the NSW border. There was no sighting of the van in the Texas township, and it was assumed it must have taken the Stanthorpe Texas Road. That road joins the New England Highway at Stanthorpe where we had set up another block, but no van passed through and there was no sign of Sarah. If they did get through, they could have gone either South toward Sydney, or North toward Brisbane and the Gold Coast. In other words, the police lost it.'

'God! Now we're back to square one! Why the hell would they want Sarah? They must know they've lost Clem by now. Surely, they don't expect trouble from her. Clem's the one who has all the information.'

'Could there be something else they want from her?' Says Beryl. 'The fact she can identify the people who abducted her puts them in jeopardy. They're ruthless, Len, I'm afraid her life's in danger. That end was meant for you too, remember. They want to eliminate all sources that may know their identity.'

'I can't just sit here doing nothing Beryl. I'm going after Sarah and the leaders. I know the Gold Coast looks like the focal point. That's where the goods are shipped to, the bent cops are Queenslanders, the garage and the tobacco shop are involved. I need to get the tracking device back and use it'.

'Be very careful Len. Your nature is to charge in like a bull in a China shop and as I told you so many times before, you could interfere with the work of the Federal Police. Police investigations are ongoing in the new search for Sarah, Len, there's little you can do.'

'Well, the police aren't making any headway and there's a life at stake Beryl. I'll do the best I can.'

Len hangs up and sits back in thought. *That prick Bill Pickings is tied up in this. He expected something the moment we crossed the border back into Queensland. He's the first to offer to drive Mrs Fielding to the funeral. I know she was surprised about that. Then he tried to talk me out of joining them – what did he know? That flag down after Texas had to be planned, the route known, as well as the timing. I'm going to pay him a visit. I wonder if the stop at the Texas service station was for someone to tell the ambush people we had arrived.*

Len has listened patiently to Cheryl's description of Clem's progress, and now he is fidgeting with his watch and steepling his fingers on it. He's enjoyed the reunion, not fully absorbing all the details, but pretending to be listening closely while his mind wanders. He can't get Sarah's safety off his mind, and he wants to do something. To get started again.

Len tells the others his plan now is to look for connections to the gang leaders. He decides to rise early in the morning, go to his unit in Toowoomba to get decent clothes, talk to the football manager, and then return to the Gold Coast. He's turning down the offer of police protection to stay with the others at the resort. Cheryl applies a new dressing to his arm and tells him to be careful with it.

In the morning his first stop on the drive back is at Bill Pickings tobacco shop in Pittsworth. He waits until all customers have left Bill on his own, he walks in, and turns the sign hanging on the door to say the shop will reopen in one hour. 'What the fuck are you doing?' Shouts Bill.

'It's time you owned up to your role in Sarah's kidnap and the plan to have me murdered. That's what I'm here for. I don't have much patience, Bill. I want a lot of information from you, and you'd better come clean with everything you know about this gang, or I'll show you just how serious I am.'

Blood drains from Bill's face and he sways to hold onto a chair for support. 'You've got no right to accuse me of anything.' He says. 'I was shit scared myself when it all happened.'

'Don't fuck around with me Bill.' Says Len as he grabs Bill by his shirt-front and drags him close. 'You've got contact with the suppliers of the drugs Clem was delivering. You picked the route for the ambush. I want the leaders. Who's giving the orders? That's who I want!'

Bill nods his head as much as to say he's prepared to talk. Len relaxes his grip, still glaring into his eyes. 'You'll be lucky to avoid a murder conviction from your part in all this if Sarah isn't saved soon.' He says. 'Think about that. Give me all the guts you know and help me find her.' He pushes him back onto the chair.

Bill squirms around, his eyes blinking rapidly. 'I'm just a bloody distributer, Len.' He says. 'I don't know who's calling the shots. The tobacco shop in Surfers' sends me tobacco with drugs to sell, and that's who I pay. I've got a feeling the car dealer's involved too. That's all I know, I swear. I drove back the way I did because that's the usual way. The gang leader must have a source of information in Sydney to know about our arrangements for the drive home.'

'How come you offered to drive Mrs Fielding to the funeral in the first place?'

'I knew Clem well. I knew she was unwell and being cared for. I felt sorry for her. That's why.'

'Bulshit!' Says Len. He knows Bill's life is at stake from the gang if he says more. Len can't take the risk of doing what he wants, to smash him senseless. He'll leave it to Beryl to interrogate him, an expertise she has is profiling, looking for facial and body clicks to know if lies are being told. *She'll trap him.* Len pokes Bill in the chest. 'I'll be back. Think about that.' He walks away and drives off.

He parks in front of the Gold Coast tobacco shop and walks over to read the sign on the door. "CLOSED FOR ONE WEEK." He returns to his wagon. *This bloke's panicked. I bet he's had a call from Pickings. I know where he lives, I'll drive past.* When Len drives slowly past there's no car and no sign of anyone home. *I'll risk another look at that warehouse. I hope they haven't shifted base.*

THIRTY-TWO

The back of the van Sarah's travelling in is fully enclosed, her only view of the world is through the rapidly disappearing landscape through the small rear window. She looks up in time to see Bill Picking's car spinning stones away. *At least Mum should be okay. The Inglewood police should see to that. I fear for Len and myself though. It's as if we know too much. I don't know what. Why do they keep asking for Dad's computer? These guys are crazy. The whole Queensland police force should be looking out for this van by now, and Inspector Stone will be urging them on. I've got to stay positive.*

Her arm is bruised and sore. Her head aches from how she was bundled into this van, striking her head in the process. She feels it with her hand. There's no blood, just a large lump that's sore to touch. There's no way to get comfortable. The tray is flat but there are no rugs or pillows, it wasn't meant for comfort. She contents herself to sit back against the partition to the front, face the back, and watch the road slide away.

She feels the van slow to enter the town of Texas, then she rolls to her left, reaching for support as the van turns abruptly. *We're heading East. It must be the main road to Stanthorpe. Surely the cops will block this road too!* Two kilometres on they pull to the side of the road. She hears men talking and loud voices. She feels a surge of adrenaline. *It must be the police!* The rear door swings open, her feet are grabbed, and she is hauled from this van and manhandled into the rear section of a large four-door wagon. During the transfer she sees a third vehicle, a car, and she realises the van is about to be either dumped or torched. Most likely the former because this will not attract immediate attention.

She is bound hand and foot, gagged, and dumped on the floor in front of the rear seats and covered with a heavy tarpaulin. It's very uncomfortable because of the drive-shaft hump.

The wagon drives off. She finds it hard to breathe covered by the tarpaulin. Her hands are cuffed at her front, and she tries to ease the weight near her face. Time passes and she wonders why the wagon hasn't been pulled up for a police check. She hears the muffled voices of the men in the front seat rise as they talk about a check point coming up.

There's voices from outside and she tries to scream through the gag, but that and the tarp are too much. She tries to wriggle her hands up through the heavy tarp to drag the gag down but can't make it. She's frustrated that the wagon isn't checked out. The front seat pair must have convinced the police they know nothing of the kidnaps and are genuine travellers. She feels the wagon move off, sensing it to turn into a new direction. They must have reached the New England Highway as the speed is now increased. She is unable to fathom whether they now head South or North.

Eventually the speed decreases and she feels more turns and curves and assumes the wagon has entered suburban streets. They stop and reverse, and she hears large doors being closed. There's more talking outside, the front seat passenger leaves the vehicle and slams the door. He removes the tarp, unties her feet from the bindings, and pulls her out to stand up. She struggles for balance; blood is pounding her ears. She stares at the captors. She will not forget these faces.

She is aware she is inside some kind of warehouse as she is led to an internal metal staircase. Held on both sides by the pair from the wagon she is led up to the landing above and through a door into a small staff room equipped with a small kitchen, two tables, a few chairs, a single bed against a side wall, and a lampstand alongside for reading in bed. There are two other doors, one in the rear wall of the building, the other an internal door which could lead to a washroom.

She's pushed into a chair and has her hands untied and the gag removed. 'We've been told to leave you here and go' Says one. 'I don't want to bind you to a chair like I was told, it's been hard enough for you already, and you should be free to use the facilities. I've got no idea how long you'll be here or who wants to meet with you. I'm sorry for how we've had to get you here. We're just following orders. Please don't try to leave or harm yourself.'

'You guys have already gone too far.' Says Sarah. 'You're being used. You're meant to be the fall guys as far as your gang is concerned. You should know a major police investigation is under way to get your leaders. It's all going to come tumbling down around your ears. No one will escape, believe me. Your best hope is to set me free or take me to a police station.'

'I've already been told police are tracking you down. We're being paid big money to do this, that's all I know.' They return to the door from the internal stairs and leave, locking it behind them. Walking down the stairs the leader says, 'mate, I'm sorry I took this job on now. She looks like a decent person. I was just told people wanted some information, then she would be joined by two wogs to be taken back to Columbia. I think I've fucked up with this one.'

Sarah is desperate to use a toilet and stumbles to the other internal door, and is lucky. She relieves the pressure and tries to tidy herself up, annoyed that a wavy plate of stainless-steel substitutes for a mirror. Then she begins to examine the rest of the main room. The external door is locked tight. All utensils are locked out of sight, most likely in the cupboard under the sink.

She runs the tap, washes her face, and gulps down mouthfuls of cool water. She takes a seat, runs her hands through her hair, then buries her face in her hands. She sits there mulling over her problems, wondering what time it is. The only window in the whole unit is the small one she saw in the washroom, and it's set high in the wall She returns, stands on the toilet seat to check the possibility of escaping through it, but it's too small and too high, and surely way above the ground.

She looks out at the scenery. Is there any way of attracting attention or signalling for help? She's viewing a desolate long concrete area to the rear of the warehouse, cluttered with rubbish bins, large storage bins full of industrial waste, and two piles of rectangular stepping-stones. Beyond that is a row of backyards to suburban houses of various vintages, mostly quite old and poorly maintained. No one is in sight. At one house a dog runs from a porch and chases away a bird sucking nectar from a red flowered bush. The bird lands on the back fence, patiently watches until the dog returns to the porch, then flies back for the nectar. *There must be residents at that place. Could I attract one with reflections from the sun with a mirror? Would they recognise an SOS?* She scans the sky for the sun and tries to work out the direction she is facing. She believes conditions could be right.

She decides to try to open the door to the cupboard and look for something she could use as a reflector. It has a hasp and staple lock. She lifts a chair and tries to smash the lock by hitting it with the seat of the chair. She tries repeated swings, but it doesn't work.

She sighs and sits back down, chews her lip, and strums her fingers on the tabletop. Daylight is beginning to dull, that opportunity is lost. She'll try again tomorrow if she has to. Time drags on. She hasn't eaten since the table food at the funeral, her spirit is flagging, and she's feeling tired. She tries the light switch and finds there is no power. *I'm not going to survive this. I don't have what they want, and they'll kill me trying to get it. I'm not going to give them any satisfaction no matter what they do to me. Clem and Mum should escape danger so long as police do their job.*

Len's really my only hope and God only knows how another life lost could affect him. He doesn't deserve any more suffering.

I've had a good life. I should be thankful. I've had doting parents, brotherly love, and I've made important friendships. I've enjoyed life at Millmerran, the community with the tidy-town culture, the rural community surrounding the town with it's hard-working and self-sufficiency. I've seen enough of city life to know I've had the best of it. My big disappointment is failing to keep closer contact with Dad and losing the opportunity to give him his dream.

She looks at the bed. The mattress is thin and covered with a heavy fabric which has not been washed for months, if ever. The pillow is the same. She lays down and soon dozes off.

*   *   *

After a restless night she's still in isolation. Mid-morning she hears footsteps on the stairs to the external door. The door is unlocked, and two men enter. Men she has not seen before. They look mean and are startled to find her untied. She tries to rush past them for the door but is grabbed by both arms. She twists and knees one in the groin. He doubles up and she knees him again. He staggers back. She uses her free arm to reach up quickly and claw the other man in the face, drawing blood. He howls and shouts telling her to calm down, then he punches her heavily in the stomach. With a righthand slap that snaps her head sideways, he sends her to the floor. The first man then shouts telling her to be sensible and tell them the truth. She passes out.

She regains consciousness to find they have seated her in a chair and bound her arms and feet to it. Handfuls of water have been thrown into her face and her blouse front is saturated.

'You're a nimble little chick, aren't you.' One scowls. 'We want to get this over as quick as we can, and you can go free.' Sarah knows he is lying. 'Others treated you too soft and you got away. I'll guarantee that won't happen this time and you'll tell us where your dad's computer is hidden.'

'I can't tell what I don't know. You're wasting your time.'

'Don't believe you, lovely. You've been caring for him, he trusts you. We know your brother or mother don't have it, so it has to be you. He wouldn't trust anyone else.'

'I promise you I don't know!'

The one who carried the haversack speaks. 'You think you can keep secrets, don't you. Well, we've got ways to change that. He takes two clamps from the haversack and connects them to each of Sarah's thumbs. He begins to screw them tighter bringing tears to Sarah's eyes. She refuses to scream; she won't give them the satisfaction. The tension is increased in increments, each time making her wince, but she remains silent.

'We can keep this up for as long as we like, you know. Soon you will have each finger so damaged amputation will be needed.'

'I've told you. I don't have it.'

Eventually shock sets in and Sarah passes out. 'We're getting nowhere with this Bro. Set up the drip and we'll come back tomorrow. Mental torture will get answers.' The table is cleared completely, the unconscious Sarah is lifted and laid prone, and her body strapped tightly with no chance of movement. Her head is placed in a foam mould and her face strapped tightly to the mould giving no room for the slightest head movement. The foam is also anchored. The light-stand is dragged to the table, a water bag is taken from the haversack, filled with tap water, and hung over Sarah with a slow leaking cap so that the drips fall directly onto her forehead.

The drips rouse her at first. 'You scum - - - wasting time - - - kill me now - - - leave my family alone.'

'Where's the laptop?'

'What --- laptop?'

'We'll leave you like this till tomorrow. You'll tell us then.'

Sarah tries hard to move her head so the drips don't flow into her mouth or nose. She's unable to do this fully, the water she consumes causes a gag reflex and creates a drowning sensation. She tries to remain calm, but her chest tightens, and her heart is racing. Before long she becomes confused and anxious. Her fuddled mind is trying to tell her to survive but her resolve is fading.

THIRTY-THREE

On his drive to the Gold Coast Len is agitated with thoughts of Sarah's safety and troubled by his arm, in fear of tearing the stitches. Cheryl treated the horrible gash and arranged a course of antibiotics because of the potential of the weapon being contaminated.

The police should have found Sarah. They didn't find the dumped van soon enough, and they should have been more thorough with interceptions. But that's history. I only know their orders come from here in the Gold Coast somewhere. They won't keep Sarah in something as obvious as a tobacco shop, and they don't know I followed the drug delivery to the warehouse. I'm going there to see what I can find.

Len reaches the warehouse mid-morning. He parks where he can maintain watch, and slumps down to reduce his exposure. Regular deliveries are made to and from the double-doors facing the street. A four-wheel drive wagon enters soon after he arrives and leaves shortly. A car stops at the curb near the warehouse and its two unruly occupants walk down the side of the warehouse. One is carrying a big haversack. This rouses Len. He is aware of the access to a staff room from the rear. He also believes there is access from inside the warehouse from the first time he cased the joint. He leaves his car and creeps down the side. He peers around the corner. No one in sight, they must have climbed the stairs and gone in. He knows work is still being done down below. *Who are these two and why go in this way? What's their business?*

He stands patiently at the corner wondering whether to investigate or back off, conscious of Beryl's wishes. But these two looked suspicious. Poorly dressed in worn street clothes and not built for heavy work. What were they carrying. *Should I go up and ask for advice? Could I ask if there's an office or another address where I can meet the owners? That I'm looking for storage space?* He hears raised male voices coming from above. It goes quiet. He waits, but then the external door opens, and the two men begin down the steps, not now carrying the haversack. He rushes back into his car. They go straight to their own car and drive away. *What was that all about? Why the raised voices? Perhaps there's more people up there. Was that a special delivery?*

He continues surveillance expecting to see others leave soon, the ones with the loud voices. He waits hours and there's no action. He feels he's waited long enough. It's time to do something. He walks to the back of the warehouse, climbs the stairs, and knocks. There's no response. He knocks harder, nothing. He senses sounds and he puts his ear to the door. A gurgling noise? He shouts, 'Is anyone there?'

Sarah recognises Len's voice. She tries to scream but achieves only a gentle monotone 'uh- -uh- - uh'. She tries again. Len's convinced someone inside is suffering. He tries to shoulder the door open but it's too solid. He can't run at it. There's no platform at the top of the stairs, so he can't put his boot to it with enough force. He puts his ear to the door again. The monotone noises continue, someone needs help. He'll try to get up from inside the warehouse. *Could it be Sarah?* He shouts and listens, 'is that you Sarah?' 'Uh—Uh—Uh', in quick succession.

He runs to the front, trying to remember if there's a tool in his car boot he could use to lever the door. He can't think of one. He turns to look at the warehouse. There's a single door beside the large double doors He opens the unlocked door and enters looking for the staircase.

'Hey! What are you up to mate?' A stern voice from behind a stack of crates. 'You can't come in here. We don't allow visitors.' The raised voice is coming from a tall man wearing orange coloured work clothes and a hard-hat. He walks toward Len.

'There's someone suffering badly in the upstairs room. I think a friend of mine could be up there. There's been an accident of some sort. All I want to do is check, then I'll go with no hassle. I saw two men leave the backway earlier, but somethings gone wrong up there. Come up with me to check.'

'The boss keeps that room for his own use, mate. We can't let you in. I'll look for the key to check for you, but you'd better wait outside.' Len makes a dash for the stairs. Another worker from behind the crates tries to stop him. Len shoulders him aside and runs up the steps two at a time. The two workers chase. At the landing Len runs at the door and using his momentum to strike the door with his right boot just beside the lock. There's a loud cracking noise, the door jamb splinters, and the door swings open. Len rushes to Sarah.

The tall worker is in next. He stops and gapes. 'Holy shit!' he says. 'What have we got here?'

Len kicks over the stand and water bag and begins untying Sarah. He disconnects the strap across her chin, there to keep her mouth open, sweeps away the plastic mould, and rolls Sarah onto her side. She spurts a spray of water out and starts coughing. Len pats her hard on the back. 'Get an ambulance quick he shouts.' The smaller of the two workers runs back to the door and down the steps for his phone. Sarah coughs up more water and lays there struggling to breathe properly. The tall worker moves to Len and gently takes his arm.

'I'm sorry mate. I had no idea what was going on up here. I hope she's alright.'

'We got here just in time. She could have drowned. Do you know the bastards responsible?'

'This is only our second day here. All the previous workers were laid off and we're here to move all those crates to a new lock-up. They want it done quickly for some reason.'

'Is this the first time you've done any work for this manager? Says Len.

'Yeh. It'll be the last, too, after this. Do you want me to get the cops?'

''No need.' Says Len. 'I'm working with them already. Just give me the address of this new lock-up and move the stuff. I'll handle it from here.'

The paramedics arrive and check Sarah's temperature, blood pressure and pulse rate. Len describes the action he took, and they seem satisfied with Sarah's condition. They ask if she vomited, and Len says only water was ejected. She's breathing freely. They sit her up and observe her condition and ability to speak now. They say they feel no further treatment is necessary, but her condition should be monitored for the next eight hours. Len says she's a nurse herself, and he'll take her to safety where there's another nurse. They're satisfied and leave.

*   *   *

There's jubilation when they arrive at the resort. Sarah phones her mother, and they have a cry together. After they hang up Sarah describes the raid on her mother to Len, with the gang looking there also for the notebook. Len offers to pick Mrs Fielding up to join the reunion and he decides he will also stay the night and join the merriment.

Sarah runs to the car to meet her mum as soon as Len drives into the resort. 'Oh Mum, it's so good to see you again. I'm sorry I couldn't talk to you for so long.'

'Give me a hug,' says Mrs Fielding, as she climbs out and is swept up by Sarah's rush. 'I've been so worried about you both. And then my house being raided. And then you were kidnapped again! It's been terrifying. Nightmares kept me awake. I've been so sick that a carer has been sent to look after me. I'm just so happy now you're both safe.'

Clem joins and hugs his mum. He apologises to her for being the cause of all this mess and not being able to contact her because of the bad cops monitoring calls. They go inside to tell their stories. They rest up and order dinner and drinks. Len comforts Sarah with talk about Boris's improvement and Beryl's agreement for them both to shelter here until the gang is destroyed. But he misses Jane and retires long before the others.

THIRTY-FOUR

The next morning, after others leave for the pool, Len and Sarah chat over breakfast. 'We need to find your dad's laptop.' He says. 'If he recorded something important, we need to know what it is.'

'I'll phone Abel Turner and find out more about Dad's work. I'm beginning to think it has nothing to do with the drug gang at all.'

'Now you and Clem are safe here, I'd better get back to my coaching job. Please call me if I can help in any way Sarah. I'm set on paying this mob back for Jane's sake, so please keep me posted with any news. Inspector Stone wants me to stay out of it but if I get a chance I'll do some snooping around.'

Sarah phones Able Turner seeking as much information as she can about her dad's work. He describes the role he had with the refining processes and says he spent hours in his own time experimenting. 'I assumed he was searching for new precious metals and ways to extract them. But he didn't talk much about his findings, except something he called Graphene. He described it as a material extracted from graphite and made of pure carbon. It consists of a single layer of atoms arranged in a hexagonal lattice nanostructure. The molecular forces holding graphite sheets are very strong.'

'A small metal plate deflected a bullet and saved Clem's life.'

'That could have been something your dad made.' Says Abel. 'I know he made a small quantity by pouring graphite powder into a blender, adding water and dish-washing liquid, and mixing at high speed.'

'Could this be something he was planning for his family to benefit.' Says Sarah. 'I know he had that ambition.'

'Not likely, I'm afraid. The way he said large scale production processes means changing all your machinery, retraining your people, and redesigning your products was enough to turn me off. Manufacturers won't do that unless there's a significant immediate financial benefit. He gave that thought away and went on with his other experimenting.'

'I've got to find out what's recorded in Dad's computer. Crooks are after it. It must be valuable.'

'After your dad died, I did receive a call from a businessman asking for the computer.' He says. 'I wouldn't have given it to anyone, but as a matter of interest I did have a good look and told him I couldn't find it anywhere. I said I knew nothing about the records he kept, and that he never talked about them.'

'Did he say why he wanted it?'

'He said he was a friend of George and that they had been discussing a business proposition he can help your father with.'

'Just as I thought. It's got nothing to do with drugs. Did he give a name?'

'He may have, I don't remember. I didn't like his attitude to tell the truth.'

'It looks like there's more to this. Thanks for your help, Abel, Dad must have been on to something big to attract the interest of a businessman. I'm trying to find out what's at the bottom of it all.'

Sarah wants to learn what her dad did when he was home and joins her mum. 'I think all my trouble has been about a search for Dad's computer, nothing to do with Clem and the gang. What did Dad do with his spare time when he was home?'

'He spent a lot of time visiting a friend at the State Heritage mine called Little Sundown Creek. It's not far from here. I think his friend's a geologist.'

'Did he ever say what they talked about?'

'Never.'

Sarah asks the manager if she could use a resort computer to do some research. He leads her to a special cubicle set up for this purpose. She searches for the Little Sundown Creek Mine and reads its history. Tin was discovered there in 1893. After a short period of stop-start mining in 1899, 470 tons of ore was smelted to extract tin and copper. It grew to become an important producer of tin, copper and arsenic, the primary product at any given time varying with the prevailing market condition. It was a small-scale version of forces that influenced the pattern of early mining in Australia.

The mine is listed as State Heritage and located in the Stanthorpe Local Government Area and registered under the Southern Downs Regional Council. Sarah studies the map and finds it close to Millmerran and easy to reach for Dad when at home. No phone number is listed, so Sarah calls those authorities. After two enquiries she learns the mine is no longer in operation, however, there is an old manager of the mine acting as caretaker for the site, and his mobile phone number is provided after she states her interest.

She phones Noel Collier, introduces herself, and asks him about her father. 'George Fielding?' He says. 'Of course I know him. It's a wonder he didn't tell you about me. We were great friends, and I was very interested in his work. You say he died - I'm sorry to hear this, Sarah. I would have come to his funeral if I'd known.'

'Mr Collier, Dad said so little about his work at home, and I'm trying to learn more about what he did.'

'That's disappointing. He was a very good chemist and very good at research to help the mining industry.'

'What was his interest in the Sundown mine? He spent a lot of his home time visiting there I believe.'

'He certainly did.' Says Noel. 'He asked me to help him set up a laboratory in an old disused building here so he could experiment with different ores. This area had several different sites operating over its active years and your dad would scavenge these for his experiments. He was interested in the range of slag, tailings, as well as the tailing sand above the dams in the creek. I warned him not to spend too long in those because of the strong sulphurous smell.'

'Mr Collier, would it be possible for me to visit the mine. I'm trying to come to grips with what he was working on. I know he had an ambition to invent something to benefit our family. It has to be something to do with mining. If I could see the mine, I might get a feel for what he had in mind. I know there are people wanting his findings, and they're desperate. It must be important.'

'I'd be only to pleased to meet you and show you over the old mine. It's not operating anymore and the site's a bit run down. I'm being paid a pittance just to keep check every now and then. Just say when and I could meet you there. I live in Stanthorpe now. Directions are not easy to find, I'll text you a sketch to show you the way in. Just make the turns shown on the sketch. Make sure the vehicle is okay for an unsealed road with many potholes. It doesn't have to be four-wheel-drive.'

'Are there more than one mine and will I need special clothing?'

'Wear good strong shoes Sarah. If you want to go into a couple of the workings, it would be a good idea to bring bonnet and wear clothes that are well worn and comfortable. You might have to rough it a bit.'

'I think I can borrow overalls; will that do?'

'That's fine. There are old hard hats and vests there, but I don't think you would like to wear them. We'll see when you get there.'

It's mid-morning as she waits for Noel's sketch. The moment it arrives she's tight-lipped and rubs her jaw as she studies it. The road winds around like a worm in motion. There's no indication of the terrain but it must be mountainous. She uses the resort computer to search for the site. She finds it in the heart of the Sundown National Park. The map shows a web of several walking tracks, but few designated as roads, and is dotted with a number of camp sites. The Severn River winds its way through the mountains with small creek tributaries, one close to the location for the mine. The closest campsite is the Resources Reserve. *This could be quite a hike.*

She pleads with the police minder to take her there straight away. He agrees, and she calls Noel back to see if this will suit him. They decide to meet at the mine in one hour. The police constable suggests Clem should travel with them rather than remain at the unguarded resort. They agree there's little risk because of the sudden decision, and he's keen to go. The national park is in a range of mountains heavily covered with dense growth. The road soon tapers to a rough dirt one-lane track that winds its way into a very rocky valley. Sarah finds it hard to imagine trucks using this route during the busy mining period. There must be other ways in.

Noel greets them and escorts them all to the first work site. They climb with him through boulders and smashed rocks to a rockface some ten meters higher. The face is rough and gnarled where pickaxes had smashed sections away. He points to a mottled blue section.

'That's called malachite. It's the ore prospectors have sought for their copper at various parts along this section of the valley. It's the most common type of ore and is copper oxide, found mostly near the surface. This is considered low grade and extracted in large quantities, crushed into large heaps, and leached by spraying a weak solution of sulfuric acid onto the heap to collect the solution containing copper sulphate.'

'Is there a higher-grade worth searching for?' Asks Sarah. 'Would this be what Dad was after?'

'Good question, Sarah. Copper sulphides are richer in copper and mostly found deeper. Tunnelling looks for this and follows the seam. Extraction is more complicated, using heat. The process steps include flotation, smelting and electrolysis. I can take you into a tunnel if you're willing.'

Clem and Sarah join Noel for a short walk to a convenient tunnel that opens straight into the rockface at ground level. Noel explains most mining begins as open pit, digging deeper using a series of step benches for extraction, then going deeper. A seam can then be followed for the sulphide ore. He shows where pickaxes have been used to dig out chunks of rock. Noel then takes his visitors back to the old office building to show them where George would spend most of his time. His room has benches, an array of dishes, beakers, containers, and a couple of Bunsen burners.

'I don't think Dad would be interested in the digging and crushing part.' Says Sarah, facing Noel. 'He would be more interested in the chemistry. Have you any idea what he was after?'

'We chatted a lot, but he always avoided talking about his experiments. He would say it's just a hobby. I'm pretty sure he was interested in the final part of the processing, looking for the most efficient way to get pure copper. He scavenged small particles everywhere, including the tailing sands at the weir. I think he was interested in collecting the last bit and wasting none.'

'What about his records,' she asks, 'that's what others are keen to get. They're looking to get his computer. Have you seen it Noel?'

'I've got it. He was very worried about his failing memory the last time he visited. He said to me his work was finished, he'd gone as far as he could. He had a very satisfied look about him, said he'd finished his life's work. He gave me the notebook PC and thanked me for my friendship and support.'

'Oh my God,' says Sarah, 'Is there any sign of his work!'

'I've had a good look, Sarah. There's nothing in the PC. He said there was every chance his findings could be valuable for large mining corporations, and he wanted any profits from his findings to go to his own family. I believe I was one of his very few close friends. He would sometimes bring a sample from the mine he worked for in Cobar. I know he used a gas burner in the lab here. He used it to boil the billy for our tea when we chatted. He was always interested in the various metals, and we would talk about what they were used for and their market value.'

'I'm sorry Mr Collier. I'm at a loss to know what he's done. Maybe he already had some corporation interested. I believe there was a businessman asking questions. I appreciate your help. Thank you so much for what you've told me, and I appreciate the friendship you had with Dad. I know he had an ambition of some kind, I'm sure he was not just playing with things as a hobby. If anything turns up, would you please contact me? You've got my contact number. It's been really nice meeting with you.'

On the drive back to the resort Sarah's fidgeting and twirling a strand of her hair. *Noel Collier has no idea where records are or what they contain. All the likely places have been searched by the gang, and none of us has a clue. Would Dad have copied or printed records and stored them in a fixed*

deposit box? If so, where? Post office? Banks? I'll talk to mum again about this,
she might think of something.

Back at the resort Sarah looks for her mum and they discuss likely
places. Mrs Fielding says the only box she is aware of is the one at
the post-office, but Dad also had two bank accounts.

THIRTY-FIVE

During that night Sarah remembers Abel Turner saying her Dad sent Mum a letter when he recognised his memory was failing. *Could it be possible Dad's letter was to tell Mum the whereabouts of his records?*

During breakfast Sarah asks her mother what was in the letter Dad sent. Her mother has no recollection of the letter, she's been too sick to visit the post office. Sarah tells her about her visit to the mine and asks if she will accompany her to check the post-office box on the way to take her home. Sarah stares at her mum feeling goosebumps rise on her exposed arms. She rubs them. *Surely Dad would leave a clue as to where the records are and what to do with them. Abel Turner said Dad wanted the family to benefit from his years of work. It must be the letter. It gels with Noel Collier's remarks.*

Sarah arranges for the constable to accompany them to Millmerran. If records are there, she'll take them back to the resort for safety. Sarah's heart is racing as they enter the post-office and move to the suite of boxes. But she's disappointed. There's only a plain sealed envelope addressed to Mrs Fielding containing one single page. Sarah's hands are trembling as she hands it to her mum, who recognises that it's written in Dad's handwriting.

Dear Mavis

I haven't come home for some time because I've been sick and did not want to trouble you. My memory loss is a problem too. Some days I can't remember what I did the day before. I find myself stumbling into things. I can't find where I've left things, it's a worry.

My long-term memory is a bit better, especially my memory of the feeling I had around my heart the first time we hugged. It warmed me and sent nice ripples through me. I still dream about it. My love for you will never fade and I realise I should have spent more of my time with you and the children.

I know I've been selfish with my own work. I've kept it private even from my friends for fear of its value being stolen. I know I'm on to something. Somehow word has got out about the potential my work would have on mining and I've had enquiries from a businessman wanting to help. But I've been too sick to follow this up. He was very anxious about it.

I don't feel up to continuing further with my work and would like our children to use the value of what I've discovered for their own futures. I've done my dash and enjoyed life. I want the same for you and them.

You'll find the history of my work where I would tell bedtime stories to Sarah. She and Clem should take over, I know they can. Please be careful, I feel there are predators.

Love,
George.

'You read this Sarah.' A tearful mum passes the letter into the quivering hands of her daughter. 'I think Dad meant this for you and Clem as much as me.' Sarah studies it.

'I don't know what Dad means, Mum. What's my bedroom got to do with it.'

It suddenly springs to memory of her father mumbling about a bed when she visited him at the nursing home. 'He tried to tell me something the last time I saw him. Can you think of what this letter means Mum. Can you think of anything to do with a bed?'

Mavis clasps her hands after wiping tears away, slowly shaking her head. 'The gang searched both bedrooms and found nothing. They pulled out all the drawers and tossed everything onto the floor, bedclothes, and mattress as well.'

'But they were looking for a computer. Something bulky. Could they have missed something smaller, like a small diary, or a reference?'

'Dad built that bed for you, Sarah.' She says, standing still, staring steadily at Sarah. Then her eyes light up. 'You watched him build it. If you take out the back drawer completely and feel in on the right side with your left hand, there's a secret compartment. That's where I kept my jewellery many years ago.'

'Oh my God,' says Sarah, 'that's it. Let's look now while we have security with us.'

They drive to the family home. It's a fifteen-minute drive and Sarah talks non-stop all the way. She remembers the secret hide from childhood now and being told never to take anything out before asking her mum.

'If there's more secret directions there, I'll take them back to the resort for safety. I'll be able work out what to do next. Perhaps Dad's records could be sold for a tidy sum.'

'Didn't the letter say a businessman was talking to your dad about wanting to help?' Says the security man.

'Maybe he was looking for a joint venture.' Says Sarah. 'Most of these businessmen are only interested in their own personal gain. If that's the case, I need an independent assessment first. It's out of my league.'

Sarah kneels at the bed, slides out the back drawer to remove it, and reaches in to recover a small, sealed, plastic envelope holding three small USB plug-ins. These she knows are flash drives holding millions of digital data. She jumps to her feet and dances around holding them high. Mum decides it's time to celebrate with fresh coffee and biscuits and leads them to the kitchen to sit down and discuss what to do next.

When the discussion ebbs, their driver goes outside to clean the car. Her mum leaves for her bedroom to change into casual clothes, and Sarah sits back and runs her fingers through her hair, her thoughts reviewing all her terror and confusion. *What a treasure Len's been for us. Even after the personal loss of Jane devastated him. It could change his life. Could we be like a new family for him? He's never married, he has no children of his own, and he's lived the life of a nomad seeking to fulfil his football ambition. Jane told me his background. He doesn't remember his dad who died when Len was a baby in an accident in the Soviet Military camp near where they lived. His mother remarried and seven years later died in childbirth when his sister Samira was born. He's never been lucky to appreciate childhood stories like those I enjoyed with my dad.*

She snaps out of it. Now she knows why it's been her they wanted as well as Clem. It's the reason for brutality and crimes and attempted murder and putting so many people in danger. Her mother returns from the bedroom. 'Mum, did Dad have any friends who could give me guidance about what's recorded in these chips?'

Mum screws her face and sucks her lip. 'Nothing comes to mind.' She says. 'I think he was well respected and had no enemies, but he was a private man. His only close friends and ones he could trust were Noel Collier and Abel Turner. I do remember way back when I first met your dad, he had a friend at uni doing a geology degree course with him. They would visit each other often to talk about their studies. I think their friendship continued but just faded over the years. I later heard he was a Professor at the Toowoomba University. His name is Fred Finder.

Sarah rings the University straight away. A friend Geologist is just what she needs. Her heart rate quickens while the receptionist tries to locate the Professor. She's told he's been contacted, he's busy, but said he would be available later in the afternoon. Sarah asks the constable if he would accompany her to the university. He nods agreement, he's become interested himself now. Sarah arranges a time to meet Professor Finder.

When they reach the entrance, they see the notice board with the list of Administration Officials and Professors. One is listed as Professor F Finder PhD and the faculties in which he works. She knows her meeting is to be with a Fred Finder, can this be him? She goes to the reception desk. 'You did say on the phone I was to meet Mr Finder, is that the Professor with PhD after his name?'

'Yes. The Professor has a bachelor's degree in science, majoring in geology, and he went on with post graduate study to qualify for his Doctorate Degree in Geoscience.'

'Oh gee. I hope I'm meeting the right person.'

'I'm sure you are. When I mentioned you were George Fielding's daughter, he sounded anxious to meet you.'

Sarah is warmly greeted by the Professor. He's sorry to learn about the death of her father. He would certainly have attended the funeral had he known. Yes, they spent many hours together years ago, he and George were friendly competitors for first place at graduation. He's shown the packet of drives.

'These are 128 GB Flash Drives. That's a lot of data to study, Sarah. I'd like you to leave them with me overnight to have time to study the gist of your father's research. I know George well enough to know how brilliant he was.'

'I'm reluctant to part with them Professor. You've no idea how much trouble other people have caused to get their hands on them.'

'Have no fear. I'll study them here. This place is locked up like a battleship at night.'

Sarah is convinced of the Professor's sincerity and agrees to return in the morning.

*   *   *

While eating breakfast the following morning Sarah receives a phone call. It's the professor, he's excited. 'Your dad's a genius!' He says. 'I've spent all night going through the files. If his test results are correct, and I believe they would be, he's made some extraordinary advances in the technology for extracting precious metals.'

'I know nothing about his work. Can you describe the basics for me please professor?'

'For most people, a pile of mine tailings is simply waste.' He says. 'For those that extract the mineral copper, the heap leach process is common. They sprinkle reagent on a heap and wait up to ten months to get all of the deposit. What your dad has done, using his chemical experience, is to experiment with ion-exchange resins and finds it can be extracted in a day!'

'Sounds good,' she says, 'so this would make the process much more profitable?'

'Yes,' says the professor, 'but that's only the beginning. He's developed different resins for different metals, such as battery metals nickel and cobalt, as well as for rare earth elements needed for green energy transition and hi-tech equipment.'

'What does this mean I should do. Should I try to sell the information?'

'Certainly not, in my opinion.' He says. 'These processes reduce the times greatly to produce the metals, but also to extract them from much larger particle sizes. Both these will increase the payload enormously. My advice would be to arrange one company only to use these discoveries and patent the processes. It could be undertaken as a joint venture with yourself, or a family trust. That would produce an ongoing income for you and your whole family.'

'I can't believe this.' Says Sarah.

'I also found work your dad did with a product called Graphene.' Says the Professor. 'It's a material extracted from graphite and made up of pure carbon. It's tough, flexible, light, and with a high resistance. It's beginning to be used instead of Kevlar for body armor by the army.'

'The manager at Cobar Mine told me about this Graphene and said it could stop a bullet. It saved Clem's life.'

'It can. While other types of armor can do the same, they weigh more, and often cannot take multiple impacts.'

'Clem was saved by an engraved metal plate Dad gave him. The Cobar manager said Dad gave Graphene away because of large-scale production costs and marketing, and that Dad was more interested in his other experiments. If I decided to follow your advice, would you be willing to be the advisor?'

'I would. And I agree there's much better prospects with your dad's experiments with other metals. I suggest you first see what prospects you have to borrow money for investment purposes.'

'I can't thank you enough for this help professor.'

'It's my pleasure. I've been thrilled to go through the files. It would have been great for your dad to be well enough to set it up for you. He was a good friend, and I will do all I can to help. If you run into trouble convincing a bank or a mining company about the value of these findings, please let me know.'

Sarah's hand is shaking. *Abel Turner's operation at Cobar might be interested. I should talk to a large mining company first to get an idea of the potential and learn what capital I would have to borrow to form some sort of partnership or joint venture. I'll use the resort computer and look up large Australian mining companies.* Sarah has never been conscious of her own intellect or motivated to use it. Growing up she was content to become a nurse, even though at high school the career advisor told her that her test results showed she would be a walk-in to do a degree course in medicine or finance. Now she sees an avenue that could lead her into business that could benefit the whole family for many years to come. The thought has energised her.

THIRTY-SIX

Sarah's research has found Cancer Copper Mining Corporation based in Brisbane. It has extensive estimated ore reserves and mineral resources, supporting a mine life in excess of 12 years at each of the operating assets. The mining leases cover 2,800 square Kilometres, indicating the scope of their operations, and the production mining rate averages 1.9 million tonnes per annum. Most of the sites are in Queensland, but they also have a strategic tenement in Chile, the world's largest copper producing country.

What interests Sarah is the range of metals extracted at some sites. The Security officer agrees to take Sarah for a dash visit to the company headquarters provided they return the same day.

'I don't want to make any commitments today,' she says on the way, 'just get enough knowledge about the company and if they would consider some form of financial agreement for what I say I have. I want to talk with Professor Finder then to see what he thinks. I know for sure he'll want me to get the best deal possible.'

'I can see how excited you are about this.' Says Security. 'From what I've seen you've got what it takes to manage this through to something.'

'The main problem I see is how long is it going to take others to copy. I wonder if I can protect the use of these unique ion-exchange resins. Patent them if that's possible. The Professor should be able to advise on this. I don't think I should mention the use of ion-exchange resins today, just test the water with what the new processes could achieve. Let's go see what they think.'

They are expected at reception and are taken to talk to a strategic manager. He politely listens to Sarah's description of what her father has done and what can be achieved, and what she is prepared to negotiate with the Professor's advice. He sits back slowly, his bottom lip squeezes over his top lip and he tilts his head back.

'Ms Fielding. I know many people worldwide are searching for new ideas. We too have teams of experts to guide us on extraction methods, it's a very competitive industry. Cancer is a multi-million-dollar company. We would see little value in making any form of partnership or joint venture based on what you have described, as it would require large scale development at a number of sites on our part. I have every respect for your father and his work, however, I'm sorry to disappoint you. It may have been his lifelong hobby, but the practicality of him earning lots of money from it probably means he did not understand the business prospects.' He says.

'The experiments he carried out and his records are very convincing.' Says Sarah. 'Professor Finder was excited about them. I could give you the Professor's number if you wanted his personal opinion.'

'I don't think this would help, Ms Fielding. I've found academics are seldom practical. It would be a waste of my time to take this further, I'm afraid.'

She thanks him for his patience to hear her out, and leaves. 'What an officious prick he was.' She says as they leave the building. 'I should go back to the Professor and tell him about his refusal to even see the test results. I don't think he really understood a word I said.'

She wastes no time to arrange another meeting at the university that afternoon. The university is on their way back to the resort. The Professor greets her and is disappointed with what she tells him.

'I think it's right that you should seek patents. You may have a better chance to do this with a particular company. You'll need to try to get some protection for his work. I agree with a comment your dad wrote, that when mining corporations learn about it, it will lead to a 'race to riches.' The sooner you can act the better. All these mining wastes could be a valuable source of metals and there's a lack of a productive and economical method to extract them.'

'Your Dad's new technology may require large scale processing modules.' He says. 'Yes, the Cancer Strategy Manager may have a point. If so, perhaps a smaller company with decades of waste tailings from an array of close by sites could see profit in extracting several different metals with just the one module using your dad's methods.

'Thanks for your support, Professor,' says Sarah, 'I'm encouraged by your interest. I'll have to give it more thought before I talk to you again.'

I wonder if Able Turner would be interested? He would trust Dad's findings, I'm sure.

He has many small mine sites closely located which would have millions of tonnes of waste. And he's producing more all the time. If he took the lead with just one plant, maybe he could keep ahead of the pack. And could there be secrets in the tailing sands? They would be easy to get.

*   *   *

There's a phone call when Sarah returns to the resort. 'Sarah, I've got good news. I'm about to be discharged from hospital. I want to join you. Please tell me how.' Boris says.

'Oh Boris, I've been waiting so much for this news. Clem and Cheryl are here at the resort too and we have police protection. Len's gone back to coaching. So much has happened, and I've got heaps to tell you. I can get you picked up at the Toowoomba Airport. Come as soon as you can and give me the flight details.'

'I will. Prepare yourself for a big reunion!'

On his arrival at the resort Sarah runs to the car to greet him, almost knocking him off his feet. She takes his face in both hands and plasters it with kisses. He has no walking stick. He wraps both arms around her and pulls her close. A little unsteady, he holds her close and prepares to meet Clem and Cheryl, now standing by with huge grins. They move to the restaurant to tell their stories.

An additional policeman has been added to guard the gate into the resort which is surrounded by high Colourbond fencing and an array of security camaras. These were part of its former role. Boris remembers the luxury well. Few rooms, small lounge and dining area, and the courtyard well-manicured with an inground pool and sunbathing lounges. This was heaven for the migrant girls from Uzbekistan. He was part of the attack he and Len made to capture the mastermind here. Sarah had been aware of the future plans for these migrant girls and was instrumental with its downfall.

Clem and Cheryl join them to celebrate his arrival and wine is provided by the resort manager during dinner. They chat for a while and soon retire to their room for the night. Boris will move into Sarah's unit. Both have suffered badly and faced death, crimes that interrupted their plans for their coming wedding. They enter their room and embrace again, hugging each other tightly for minutes while both try to eliminate bad memories of terror and pain. Neither wants to talk about them, just to absorb the love and comfort of the other.

They relax and sit at the foot of the bed holding hands and gazing into each other's eyes struggling to find words. Sarah speaks first. 'I thought of you all the time Boris. At times I feared for my life, but my greatest fear was losing you and our future together. I treasure the way you met my wishes when you took me to Toowoomba that night. Our work and family problems have kept us apart too long.

'Believe me, I remember the next morning well.' Says Boris. 'I craved you so much. This separation has been agony for me. My body's the problem now. My ribs still hurt from the fractures and my broken leg won't take my weight if I try to kneel. I'm sorry, but I'm still very fragile.'

Sarah's not prepared to have him suffer more pain. He's had enough of that. She has a plan of her own. She pulls him to his feet and begins to strip off his clothes, making him naked. She helps him to lay flat on his back on the bed. She strips off herself and crawls alongside, then gently rolls on top.

Boris holds her warm body fondly with his arms wrapped around her. Having been separated in the past due to their respective work locations, then the traumas that followed, this is the first time since that morning in the hotel room they've shared a bed. At first, they're both a little tense, and Boris moves his hands to cup her face and draws her into a soft kiss. Sarah's body softens and melts into Boris. The effect on Boris is immediate and he moves one hand to gently massage her back. Sarah kisses him more firmly then moves on to nibble an ear and to kiss his neck. The effect on Boris is blissful and unbearable at the same time, which Sarah realises, and she slides her body to reach down and direct his erection. She lays soaking in the ecstasy of the connection. Boris is struggling to contain himself.

Sarah begins to squeeze. It's too much for Boris. He comes and Sarah rides him. Boris experiences euphoria as their bodies synchronise. His head and shoulders stretch back hard onto the pillows. When their energy subsides, Sarah rolls to lay alongside, both wallowing in the bliss of the union.

THIRTY-SEVEN

Len's finished his morning break after coaching attack with emphasis on the front third of the field and particularly as the game gets close to the attack penalty area. Here the priority is to get a shot on goal, for an attacker with possession to accept responsibility and take on defenders using clever footwork, screening with the body, and bursts of speed. Creative passing between attackers is the order of the day. He asks Mark Ranger, the physio to take over with the players and organise a friendly small-sided game in one half of the field. He will carry out a functional coaching session for the two main strikers at the edge of the other penalty area.

He chooses the goalkeeper, 'Soapy' Cellarman, two defenders, one a normal midfielder, the other a solid centre-back defender, and he takes them to the other goalmouth. He asks his centre-back to stand aside for the beginning session. He places one attacker, with back to goal just inside the penalty area, close marked by the midfield defender. The challenge he sets is for the second attacker to serve a pass the centre-attacker from ten meters back, the first attacker then has to take-on his defender one-on-one to get a shot on goal. The server cannot assist the first attacker.

At first, he allows free play, each attempt to score started with the ten-meter pass, and repeated after a goal is scored past Soapy, or an attempt fails. At the beginning the defender prevents a shot on most attempts. Len takes over the position of the attacker and demonstrates new techniques. The first is to replicate the method the centre-forward was taking, trying to screen the ball while turning to create enough space to take a shot. But Len demonstrates heavier back pressure on the defender together with tricky changes of direction and back-heels to unbalance the defender.

Len then demonstrates another method. This time, the instant the pass is served, he pushes back into the defender to unbalance him, sprints toward the pass, spins with the ball at his feet to face the defender, and prepares to take him on and sashay past him for the shot. Using clever footwork and feints he is able to succeed about half the time.

The session continues along these lines. The attackers change roles and the centre-back replaces the midfield player to offer stronger defence as the skills improve. The session ends when Len's satisfied with the progress. The players gather around him discussing the session and praising what Len has just delivered. Len calls a halt to the free game at the other end, assembles the whole team, and comments on his satisfaction with the team's progress. He thanks them for their passion for learning and forecasts a successful performance in the coming competition if they can continue on this track. They've worked hard at it for five days in a row, and Len decides on a two-day break.

Len's anxious to spend time describing the team's progress with Boris and he phone's the resort. He returns to his hotel to shower and pack a change of clothes to take with him and is about to leave when his phone rings. It's Beryl Stone.

'How are you coping Len, and how is your arm?'

'I'm getting there. The arm's fine thanks. Life'll never be the same without Jane though. How's the investigation going. Have you scraped anything yet from those captives?'

'That's the purpose of my call. Thanks to you we *have* made some progress. The driver's licence you took from your Sydney attacker shows he lives on the Gold Coast, and he travelled to Sydney to make a delivery to a Sydney Brothel. Most likely drugs. His mate probably travelled with him. More drugs were found in their wagon. Most likely they were for delivery to other sellers like the Nazi types from Blackheath. We don't believe they were in any way crucial to the gang, just users for hire. Nevertheless, they are sure to be convicted for their crimes.'

'The Gold Coast again,' says Len, 'just as we thought.'

'I've more,' says Beryl, 'My investigation has found those two policemen dressed in Queensland uniform were most likely two who had taken two days off from the Ipswich Police Station to visit Sydney.'

'Queensland again eh. Not so close to the Gold Coast though. I wonder what that could mean.'

'They might just be users too.' Says Beryl. 'But they could be somehow involved in all the call tracing. We've got to get to the bottom of that yet. But here's something that got you a few brownie points with my federal counterparts. The freighter off the coast at the time those drugs were dropped has been traced with the help of marine shipping records. Its name is not for release, but they're using this knowledge with overseas authorities in the search for the source.'

'That's great news Beryl. I've been busy with my coaching commitment, but I still would like to look into matters at the Gold Coast. I've got good leads there to follow up.'

'You know my wishes there Len. The feds were so pleased with the info about the ship they asked me if you would be interested in part-time work as an undercover agent from time to time. I've been reluctant to tell you, but you should know about the offer.'

'That's not part of my life ambition as you know. I take it as a compliment, but my life is fully committed to my coaching role. All these other things have just been unnecessary diversions, I'm afraid.'

'I'm pleased to hear that. You deserve to work without all the disruptions to your friends. I appreciate your help. Leave the rest of this to the feds now. You know, our friendship has shown me we both need to concentrate more on our own lives. You will remember I have a young boy of my own. Well, he has just turned five. You must meet him some time. He knows all about you and keeps asking. It wouldn't hurt for you to have more friends after your tragic loss. Please keep me posted. 'Bye till next time.'

Len reaches the resort in time to sit for dinner with the whole group and to listen to their stories and plans for the future. He's interested to hear of Sarah's mine visit, the value of the records George kept, and the prospect of benefit for the family. What suffering Sarah has had might finally be worth it. After dinner, drinks follow, and Len and Boris talk about the football team until they decide it's time to retire for the night.

THIRTY-EIGHT

'**M**r Goldman's office, can I help you?'

'I'd like to speak to Mr Goldman please.'

Mr Goldman's very busy, can I tell him the reason you're calling?'

'Just tell him it's Kieran. He'll speak to me.'

'Yes Kieran. This is a surprise, you calling me here at work.'

'What the fuck's going on Caleb. You're way behind with your work and it's stuffing the business up.'

'My work for you's getting harder all the time Kieran. I've got a problem with the Perth Mint being put under scrutiny. Politicians are squabbling over what form investigations should take. There are two independent investigations already underway. The first worries me. Australia's financial authority, AUSTRAC, will assess the mint's level of compliance with anti-money laundering and counter-terrorism financing laws. The investigation could look back as far as 2006.'

'The mint's also under scrutiny from overseas,' he continues, 'the London Bullion Market Association being one.' He draws breath. 'They're not my only problem, either. The Government's imposing stricter rules for banks for overseas money transfers. And the Casinos are being investigated for money-laundering. Already heads have rolled. I don't want my head in that category.'

'You're pissing me off. You haven't told me yet why you wanted that nurse kidnapped, especially after we knew Clem was in safe police hands. She knows fuck all. What's going on? You've cost me men and they're hard to get. You're creating risks I don't need.'

'I'm sorry Kieran. I'm not aware of how you operate.' Says Caleb.

'That fucking coach guy barged in to rescue her again and now the cops have got two more of our lackies. If any blab, you'll be in real trouble. Forget that shit about money laundering. You're the one who gave them the job to interrogate her. I'm sure that bastard's got the ear of that detective inspector Sheila. I bet he's humping her.'

'In case you don't know,' he continues, 'call monitoring needs Attorney General authorisation. I've been able to get around that with people I know. They don't know it isn't authorised and the telco boss will drop to this if we continue. So, I'm closing it down. You don't realise the risks I'm taking with all this call tracing and monitoring bullshit.'

'I'm grateful for your help Kieran. We've lost her to the police now, so I'll have to use a different approach. I won't need tracking anymore.'

'That fucking football coach has cleaned up the G-G's as well.' Says Kieran. 'They know shit about us, so they're no risk, but we don't know where he'll turn-up next. I don't like the way things are going, they're not in our favour. To cut it short Caleb, you've been a pain in the ass. Why's this bird so important for you?'

'I've got a family problem Kieran. I haven't told you about it, but it means I need to rebuild my retirement nest-egg. When you first asked me to help with your finances I agreed for old times' sake. I'm not in favour of the source of the money but I needed your commissions because of this family problem. Now money laundering's getting too dangerous for me. I've got to get out of it and find another source to refinance my retirement. That's where this nurse comes in.'

'What the fuck is this family problem?'

'My nephew, the only son of my only brother, has been diagnosed with Rasmussen's encephalitis. It's a very rare condition that involves long-term worsening inflammation of one side of the brain. It causes frequent seizures, mental decline, and weakness or paralysis on one side of the body. There isn't a cure, but certain treatments can help manage seizures. He contacted Covid which aggravated the condition with complications that can lead to severe disability and death.'

'An American surgeon claims some success with a brain operation,' he continues, 'he looks for some specific antigens and employs stem cell infusion. But it costs a fortune. I had no option, Kieran, I had to use my retirement savings for this treatment. You would have done the same.'

'I'm not too sure about that. You're a softie, Caleb.'

'Your offer of commissions was just too good for me to knock back.' Says Caleb. 'I had money laundering knowledge and could also take messages for you, and I tried to help, even though it mostly went against my grain. I'm sorry, but with the current investigations into laundering I've got to give your work away.'

'How's this nurse sheila gunna help?'

'I want the research data from her father's records. He's just died after losing his memory. I know he was on a winner in the mining industry. If I could have found those records myself, I was sitting on a fortune. But she's smart, and now my only chance is to get her to form a business partnership with me.'

'I don't understand your generosity for your brother, but I see your problem. I knew something was up, so I've started expanding my distribution. I want more users to become distributers for a commission, and to deposit profits into selected bank business accounts as payment for mythical consultancies. It's giving me better access to tough field groups I can use like the ones I've let you use. It's slow work, and I'll miss you. We've been friends a long time. I'll do my best to protect you from the cartel. You should be safe because you're in deep shit yourself if they get onto us. I suppose you'll continue with your day job for a living, and I might get your advice from time to time. And I hope that other plan works out.' Kieran hangs up.

*   *   *

In the morning the resort receives a phone call. 'Is that the Holiday Resort at Leyburn? There's no advertised phone listing, but I would like to speak with a Ms Sarah Fielding, and the Millmerran post-office gave me this number.'

'Who shall I say is calling, and what is the purpose?'

'I'm a good friend of her late father.'

'Please wait.' The resort manager speaks to Sarah who's resting in the lounge trying to read about the history of copper mining in Australia.

'Hello, this is Sarah Fielding.'

'Ms Fielding. I'm Caleb Goldman, Manager of the Southport City Bank, and a close friend of your late father. I'm very sorry to hear of his passing. He was secretly confiding with me about plans he had to establish a new processing method for mining. He asked me if I would take on a joint venture, as I have the business experience needed. I liked George very much, and I would like to consider making an offer to continue down this track with the family.'

'It's good of you to call me, Mr Goldman. I don't know exactly what my dad had in mind.'

'Do you have any record of his work?'

'I do now, and I think it must be valuable because a gang has been after it.'

'That's terrible. However, it's a sign that it's worth commercialising. Would you be interested in meeting up with me here at the bank to discuss possibilities?'

'I suppose so. I'll talk to my friends and call you back. The Southport Bank, you say?'

'That's correct. I look forward to meeting you.'

THIRTY-NINE

Len overhears Sarah's call from Goldman. He rises and walks over as Sara's discussion with the bank manager is about to end. 'I couldn't help but hear that guy wanting to talk to you about your dad's work.'

'It came out of the blue.' Says Sarah. 'I wonder if he's the one I've already heard about. I wonder if he knows about my talk with Cancer Mining. These businessmen can be very crafty. I was worried why Cancer showed no interest. I wonder if there's a connection.'

'Do you feel well enough to visit this bank manager today? I could take you down and back on a quick trip that should be safe enough. I won't let you out of my sight this time! I'd like to help if I can.'

'I feel okay. What about yourself. You've been battered too?'

"My head's good to go. I'd like to shower first then have you dress my arm. I'll be fine to drive."

Sarah later takes dressings for Len's arm and sits on the bed to wait. When he leaves the shower with a towel wrapped around his waist she is suddenly impressed by his natural charm. *His emerald eyes are like magnets to mine, and I want to hug him. I've got to turn away. Poor Len. Poor Jane.*

Len and Sarah are invited into the Manager's office and offered seats facing him across his desk. The room is well furnished and is located on an elevated floor of a large shopping complex. From his high-back leather chair facing a large window there's a panoramic view across the Gold Coast Highway to the shoreline of the Broadwater. There's no clutter on his desk, and the side table holds his desktop computer such that he can conveniently pivot his chair to use it. He invites them to sit opposite, across his desk, in two plush visiting chairs.

'Thank you for coming Ms Fielding. I'm very sorry to hear about your dad's death. He was very excited about his discoveries, and he described them to me as best he could over the phone. He wanted my advice on the best way to commercialise his findings for the benefit of yourself and family. I believe it was his life-long ambition, and I'd like to help achieve his dream.'

'Your call came as a surprise to me Mr Goldman. Dad never talked about his work at home. But I've had advice from a professor friend he had years ago to go ahead because he valued Dad's expertise, and he liked what he's seen.'

'I have contacts in the mining industry,' says Caleb, 'I will certainly be able to have them value the worth of his findings. Do you wish to sell them?'

'Well no. My advice has been to try to earn a portion of the profits from implementing the new methods Dad devised.'

'Well, what can I do to help?' Says Caleb, looking and smiling at Sarah. 'I would be prepared to use my contacts to advise the best way to sell, to invest, or to form a business partnership. But first, if you propose to partner a development, you may need a loan to contribute to the costs for the plant design and the equipment to use.' He looks at Sarah who is struggling to respond, and he decides to proceed.

'If you are asking for a loan from this bank, I will need to know more about your assets, employment, and earning capacity to make repayments. Do you bank here?' He asks.

'No. I live in Millmerran, but I'm getting married soon and will live in Toowoomba. Later I may move to Sydney depending upon the career of my husband.'

He looks to Len. 'What plans do you have?'

Len is rigid. He's wearing a long sleeve shirt which covers his damaged arm and it's clear that Caleb does not recognise him as the problem coach. He takes a time to respond. 'I'm just a friend of her future husband. I don't know his plans.'

Len rises and turns to Sarah. 'I don't think we know enough yet to make any commitments till you talk with Boris.'

Sarah senses a tremor in Len's hand as he takes her arm to lift her prematurely. She looks into his face and sees his eyes are narrowed and his face hardened. She rises slowly, apologises to the manager for taking his time, saying she will return as soon as her future husband can be involved. She leans forward to shake his hand. Len hurries her out through the door.

They leave the bank and Sarah stops Len and stares into his face. 'What the hell was that all about. You know Boris's plans better than anyone?'

'I'm positive that man accompanied the shop manager on the drugs pick-up night. I've got to talk to Inspector Stone about this.'

'Beryl. I'm sure I'm onto something. I'm positive that the manager of the Southport bank was at the drug shipment pick-up that night. I had a good look as the car drove past me. He was reading something with the interior light on. His name is Goldman.'

'You're sure?

'Positive.'

'He must be laundering money for the cartel.' Says Beryl. 'I'll check his internet and phone calls. This could be the break we need. I'll get back to you.' She hangs up.

This inaction doesn't sit easy with Len. He wants to get on with it. He decides to visit Southport. He wants to learn more about Goldman and his associates. The manager of the garage where Clem worked must be involved too.

*   *   *

For Sarah's trip back to the resort her head is in a cloud. The roadside scenery blurs past and she's unaware of talking between Clem and the driver while Len's on the phone. *Surely not! A reputable bank manager working with the cartel! A witness to the drop of a drug shipment! Someone in financial control and crimes of kidnap, attempted murder, and torture. How many powerful allies has he got? Inroads to cops and phone control. How do you smash crime so meshed as this? I can't deal with something this big, but I'm not going to let them stop me fulfilling Dad's dream for his family.*

From the resort she phones Abel at Cobar. 'Mr Turner? It's Sarah here. We've just discovered the businessman who called you that time about Dad's records. He's the manager of a bank. He's a crook in control of the crimes we've experienced.' There's a lengthy pause.

'Sorry Sarah. I had to sit down. That's hard to fathom. He'd be well off, have large assets, why would he need to get involved with drugs and crime? And Sarah, forget the mister bit, just call me Abel next time.'

'Thanks Abel. But I'm still determined to fulfil Dad's dream, his life work. We have all his records now, they're in the custody of a professor at Toowoomba University, another old friend of Dad's. He's convinced they could revolutionise mining. I've discussed the findings with him, and with his guidance, I believe substantial profit increases are possible. I would like your Cobar mine to be the pilot and share the rewards.'

'That's generous of you Sarah. I trust your dad's brilliance and if that professor is excited about them, of course I'd like to do whatever I can. I would need to discuss all this with the professor.'

'The professor wants to patent the process, and he's offered do that and provide guidance. He's a geologist, he says a new type of processing plant will be needed and that an engineer would be needed to set it up.'

'I have an excellent civil engineer employed here at Cobar, and I'm sure he could handle it. He manages everything for us, the equipment maintenance and repair for the mining, the crushing, and structural work for expansion.'

'Would it be possible for you both to come to Toowoomba for a meeting with the professor?'

'I'm sure I could arrange that.'

'We would need to first of all estimate the cost to build the prototype. I will have to borrow finance, that was our intention when Len and I discovered the crook bank manager. I guess the cost for plant would be a job for the engineer. But we all need to sit down with the professor and work our way through it, the new process, and the design of the plant. I'm very excited, Abel, you can probably sense that.'

'Loud and clear Sarah. I'm keen to find out what your dad's come up with myself now. The professor's excitement must be contagious. I'll talk to my engineer and if you give me the professor's contact details, I'll talk with him to see if we need to do some spade work before we meet.'

FORTY

Len goes to Clem to chat about the Southport set-up. 'That Goldman guy has no idea who I was. That means the two guys that attacked me in Sydney haven't given them a good description, and neither has any of the hoods at the Inglewood hijack. Bill Pickings knows me well, but maybe he's been too frightened to provide a description. You can forget the G-Gs. So, I should be able to travel incognito to look at the Southport set-up. What do you think?'

'They mightn't know about your arm either.' Says Clem. 'All I can say I know the manager of my garage must be in the know. He provides the drivers for deliveries, and he modifies imports to conceal drugs. That's where I think you could start.'

'I'd like to get my tracking device back off the MG sports car first. Last time I looked the shop notice said he was on vacation for a few weeks. He must be shit-scared now he knows you're alive and well after two attempts to be killed.'

'He could have left it parked at the garage and shot through. He knows you're onto him. He could have skipped the country for all I know. He's not got much confidence with his role, I know that.'

'If he's still around I'll find him. I know where he lives. If I get the tracker, I'll follow Goldman around for a while. He's in it up to his eyeballs. What did you do with your own car before you were pushed off that cliff?'

'I left it parked in the back of the garage workshop where I always left it on workdays.'

'Do you think I could pick it up for you? Would you need to ring to say you were sending a friend for it?'

'That would get you in. But the manager would be suspicious. You should pick a time when he has his day off. Problem is, he picks days at random. If I ring him about the car, he'll make sure he's in – best if I don't.'

'What about your mate. The one that got you that job. Would he shop you if you called him?'

'They'd all know I'm in protection now. I suppose it would be natural for me to want my own car back. I could call him. He's got nothing to worry about really, he just does what he's told. I'll see if I can casually find out the manager's next day off. What would you do if you did get in Len?'

'I'm not sure. I just want to do some snooping to start with.'

Len drives back to Southport and parks at the tobacco shop. The sign on the door is the same, the shopkeeper is on holidays. He drives to his home address. The house looks deserted. Garbage cans have not been put out, the lawn is overgrown, and weeds are peeping up. Len casually walks up to ring the doorbell and wait. No response. He walks to the rear and there's still no sign of life. Len goes to a next-door neighbour to enquire. The lady that answers the door says she's been worried about him. All she knows is that he's gone on an unplanned holiday without asking anyone to look after the place, and she's frightened about attracting vandals.

Len phones Clem. He's already phoned his mate, and the manager is not in, he's taken today off. Len drives to the garage and parks out front alongside other cars in for repairs. He enters the workshop area and looks around, searching for someone to speak to. No one can be seen. He sees Clem's car parked at the rear of the workshop, and walking toward it he is surprised to see the MG driven by the manager of the tobacco shop. It's not back with Clem's car, probably indicating it must be there to be worked on.

It should have the tracker still attached. He's anxious to recover that before a mechanic sees it and he kneels at the rear to unclip it and slip it into his pocket. A mechanic returns from the restroom. He sees Len rising from the back of the car and signals him to come down to the vehicle where he's working. Len smiles broadly at the mechanic, reaches out to shake his hand, and nods toward Clem's car.

'I'm a friend of Clem Fielding,' he says, 'I've come to pick up his car to take back to him.'

'Yeh. That's Clem's car. He had an accident, and we haven't heard anything about him. I rang his home some time ago and his mum said she was waiting to hear from him as well.'

'He's convalescing from injuries at present and asked me to do this as a favour. Ring Mrs Fielding again if you need to.' He holds out a photo to show him standing with her preparing for the drive home after the funeral.

'What were you doing at the rear of that other car?' Asks the mechanic.

'I'm after a better car for myself but I'm not keen on second-hand dealerships. I much prefer to deal privately. That's why I was looking. I saw that one regularly in front of the tobacco shop, and I think he wants to upgrade, so when I saw it, I decided to have a look. I wouldn't mind seeing the service records if that would be possible?' He says, raising his eyebrows. 'Is it for sale or for hire, do you know?'

'You'd have to ask the owner about that.' He says, 'As for the service records I can't see that would be a problem. The manager's not in. I know the vehicle, come on, I'll show you.'

This is better than Len had hoped for. He remembers the registration and quotes it to the mechanic. His attitude influences the mechanic to show him the service manual that contains mileage records, servicing, and repairs. Len glances at ownership details and is surprised. The car owner is a Mr K Casters, someone in Brisbane. He memorises the details. *Why would a drug distributor be given this fancy car to drive by another person.* He looks at the owner's address thinking it may be a company. He decides to drive there to take a look.

FORTY-ONE

He arrives at Fortescue Street Spring Hill, finding it quite close to the Central Business District of Brisbane. Len drives slowly past the car owner's address. It's a home, not the business building he expected. It's well-appointed and modern compared to others he passed. It has a two-car garage facing the street.

Len does a U-turn well past and parks several houses away with a good view of the house. *Well, that's it. Nothing special, but the land value would be high due to its location. Expensive, like his car. I wonder what he does for a crust and if he has a family. He'd need some sort of camouflage to hide his income from drug distribution. It's not the sort of place I'd like to raise my family. No yard to play in for kids and no close parks.*

Thirty minutes later the front door opens, and a middle-aged man skips jauntily down the front steps and sets off leisurely in the direction of the business centre. He's dressed in pricy casual wear. No tie, but a cobalt blue linen cotton stylish jacket and wearing classy black leather upper walking shoes. Len follows well back on the opposite side of the street. Before long he turns into another street, more congested with pedestrians. Len maintains contact at a safe distance. They're soon in the heart of business, and the man enters the head office building of the major telco. Len follows him into the lobby and sees him catch a high-level lift on his own. A guard approaches Len as he stands casually watching the level at which the lift stops.

'Can I help you sir?' Says the guard. 'A pass is needed to go further, where is it you wish to go?'

'I'm from Toowoomba looking for a friend of mine who said he worked on the twelfth floor here.'

'You will have to return to the reception desk around the corner and ask her to contact him. He will need to come down and sign you in for a visitor pass.'

Len walks back to the receptionist. 'I'm a friend of Bill Pickings and he asked me to visit him here. He said he worked on the twelfth floor.'

She looks at Len and arches an eyebrow. 'Sir, you must be mistaken with what he told you. That floor is for our chief executive and his staff. There's no one there by that name.'

'Could you tell me if a Mr Casters works for your company?' Asks Len.

'Sure. He's our CEO. Is that who you wish to see?'

'No thanks. It's just that my friend happened to mention the name when I was talking to him about visiting Brisbane. Thanks for your help, I'll have to talk to my mate again and get things straight.' A glance at the telco's notice board behind her confirms the CEO is Mr K Casters.

'Our computer records here show your friend does not work here, I'm afraid,' says the receptionist, raising her eyes to face him. 'he must have given you the wrong address.

'I'm sorry. Thanks anyway for your help. I'll try a couple of the other high-rise buildings.'

Len walks casually back to his car and phones Beryl. 'I've got some interesting news for you.' He says. 'The owner of the tobacco manager's car at Southport is the CEO of the country's major telco and he lives in Brisbane. His name is Casters, Mr K Casters. I got the lead when I called in to check out the elite car dealer. What do you think? I'm sitting in front of his home in Fortescue Street right now.'

'Oh my God.' She says. 'Whatever you do, go no further with this Len. This is unbelievable. But it may well explain how all this call tracing and monitoring has been done. I can check this out from here Len. I'll check his own calls as well, but I'll have to be very careful about that. I should have no difficulty getting his call records, but little chance of what the conversations have been about without him finding out. Please don't do anything further Len, you've been a good help with this. Don't spoil it now.'

Len acknowledges her advice, but he's in Brisbane and in a position to be able to do some surveillance on this CEO. He has the tracker in his pocket. If a chance presents itself, he could use it on whatever the CEO drives for himself. He's likely to have his own company chauffer, but surely any covert activities would be done in private. He leaves his car and looks for a café where he can have a meal and think about what he should do next.

While eating, his phone rings. It's Beryl. 'I've had some secret work done about these two new suspects. Goldman has a reputation for being a bit of a philanthropist in the past, giving to charities. And he's committed a huge sum of money for surgery in the U.S. for work on his nephew. These are not consistent with criminal activity. I can't obtain any info on monitoring calls, but his call record does show contact to some strange people, including that Pittsworth tobacco shop manager, Bill Pickings.'

'I'm positive he was there for the drug drop. He has to be involved somehow.' Says Len.

'I'm having his bank's records examined in a search for money laundering. This could be his downfall. I'm checking for calls to police establishments, Ipswich in particular, but nothing has shown up as yet.'

'Thanks for letting me know.' Says Len. 'I suppose it's a bit harder to trap our CEO suspect. But I've still got that tracer and I'm sure I could sneak it onto his own private car when I get a chance.'

'Be very careful about that. It's possible he would have some security features installed.'

'My car is still parked a few doors away from his home. I'm sure I could do some covert surveillance without attracting any attention.'

'Don't take any chances to upset the progress we are already making, Len. I know you're good at this, so please be extra careful.'

Len returns to his car. He slumps in the driver's seat and pretends to be napping. After his full lunch he nods off a couple of times, expecting that he would be roused by any activity. Hours later he sees a police car pull up in front of the house. Two constables knock on the front door and are admitted. *I must have missed the CEO walking home.* Soon they exit carrying a large parcel each. The parcels look the same as ones carried from the Southport tobacco shop. *Are these the bastards responsible for Jane's death? There must be more drugs stashed here and that would be damming evidence. I'll have to call Beryl, but I've got to make sure the evidence stays put.*

With his head down trying to contact Beryl again the two constables surprise him at his car door. The one at Len's window indicates for him to wind the window down. 'Step out. You've been spying on a resident across the street. We're taking you in for questioning.'

He opens the door, pulls Len out, and is about to cuff him. Len swings around and pushes him back. The cop pulls a gun. Len knocks the gun arm away, but he's taken in a headlock from behind. He lurches forward headbutting the gun holder and lifting the one behind off his feet, loosening his grip. Len back-heels him in the knee, spins and strikes him with a savage right cross sending him to the ground. The first gunman's quickly back on his feet and he pokes his gun hard into the back of Len's neck.

'Stop or your dead.' He shouts.

Len recognises the feel of a gun. He ducks to his right to get out of the firing line, swings around lifting and forcing his left arm over the gun arm. He straightens up and strikes the attacker in the face with his elbow. Len locks the gunman's arm under his own and knees him in the groin. He doubles over. Len snatches the gun and strikes him under the chin with it sending him down. After fully overpowering them both, Len returns these two toward the garage at gunpoint. The one hit with the uppercut is still staggering and has to be assisted by his mate. On the way Len asks to look into the boot of their car, then for one to open one of the double doors to the garage. He sees ten more boxes against the far wall.

Both men are resigned to their fate and follow Len's orders to sit against a side wall.

The man who Len followed suddenly pushes open the inner door and fires a handgun at Len, winging him. Len ducks behind a car. The homeowner calls to his men to bring Len out into the clear, holding his gun out pointing to Len's location. Len has crouched, but as soon as the only one able gets within range, Len takes him into a bear hug as cover and rushes at the gunman. One shot is fired which flies over their shoulders, then another that wings his own man. Len pushes him into the gunman and karate chops him in the neck, a debilitating blow, serious enough to give injury lasting for weeks.

Len has all three down now and is in full control. He takes cable ties from the garage bench, laces them all hand and foot, and sits them against the wall. He takes the owner's wallet and checks the licence. Mr Kieran Casters. The telco boss. This will interest the inspector.

'Inspector Stone, is that you Len?'

'It is, and I have some more information that will surprise you.'

She can hear him breathing heavily. 'Tell me what's up Len?'

'Good news this time. I've found a drug stash in the CEO's home. He's also the owner of the car the drug distributor in Southport's been driving. We've got the Mr Big.'

'What's his name.'

'Mr Kieran Casters.'

'Stay put.' Says Beryl. 'I'll arrange immediate help. Then I'll check out the history of this Casters guy. I'll check his police records and his profile. This is the break we needed Len. Sit tight till help arrives.'

'Don't forget I've got two policemen cuffed up here. Make sure my backup is safe and aware of the situation.'

Len checks the credentials of the two cops sitting on the floor and records the details. In quick time two police vehicles arrive. The three captives are bundled into the van and driven off. Two detectives stay with Len to wait for a forensic team to arrive to case the joint.

Beryl calls Len back. 'Len, the CEO's name is Keith Casters. He's well known and has a clean record with no charges or convictions. It's not likely he's involved, but the mystery is about the illegal phone work.'

'This guy's licence says Mr Kieran Casters, and he's just come from the office of the CEO.'

'If one has been visiting the other, they're got to be related, most likely father and son. There could be another family member connected, but not as likely. I'll check the records for this Kieran.' Says Beryl.

'I've got the licenses of these two cops as well.' Says Len. 'I'll read them to you. You said you planned to look up police records to see what Queensland Cops could have been in Sydney when Jane and Boris were attacked. It would be interesting to know if these were the two from Ipswich.'

'I can do that.' Says Beryl. 'I've already told you federal police are checking with authorities in other countries to trace the source of the drugs. We're on a winning run here Len. Once more I have to thank you for your contribution and the risks you've taken.'

'I just hope you properly punish the gang members and those responsible for Jane's death. The drug gang's important, but it's Jane who changed my life. I'll be forever grateful if they are properly locked up long-term.'

FORTY-TWO

After weeks of investigation, it is deemed safe to discontinue police protection for those at the resort. The government will no longer cover the cost of staff and accommodation, leaving the boarders to do their own thing. These past weeks have been enjoyed and celebrated by all four lovers and with sharing visits from Len, Mrs Fielding, Able Turner, and Professor Finder. The management here will now be free to reopen and satisfy the requirements of other clients and tourists seeking to enjoy the peace and relaxation afforded by the luxury.

After months of investigation and court cases, the telco CEO is cleared of any involvement in the crimes. He is criticised for not being aware of the illegal use of his staff and equipment, especially due to the extended time period. His son is found guilty of the control and distribution of the illegal drug shipments, and for orchestrating the associated crimes. He is given a thirty-year sentence. Federal police are still cooperating with foreign countries regarding the source of the drugs.

The shipping company has been heavily fined for the use of their freighter.

The two policemen caught by Len are convicted of the crimes that caused the injuries to Boris and the death of Jane. Both are given twenty-year sentences. Len accepts this, but at first regrets that he did not know when he had the chance to take his own retribution in the garage. Now he accepts that would have been a mistake.

Three Investigation Branch members involved in the call tracing and monitoring are identified and fired by the telco CEO. They receive no court conviction. The court accepted their claim that the son usurped the authority of his father when they believed attorney

General authority had been given. The son's frequent visits to the Telco boss bore credence.

Most captured members of the gang and their distributors, including Bill Pickings, are given jail sentences for crimes that include the cause of grievous bodily harm and drug offences. Ill-gotten possessions are recovered, and fines imposed. Goldman is sentenced for thirty years for his money laundering and criminal acts.

Negotiations with Able Turner have reached a decision for his company to finance the cost of building the plant needed to implement George Fielding's extraction methods, and to share the increased profits equitably between the company and the Fielding family. It was agreed that Sarah should play a major role to manage the finances, the trading, and chair a bi-monthly meeting for that role. Professor Finder has convinced Sarah to take a business management course in Toowoomba.

Professor Finder has agreed to become company advisor, for a small consultancy fee, as required for the design and use of the resins, and for patent applications.

Boris and Sarah are now keen to move back to Boris's former hotel accommodation in Toowoomba where Sarah can obtain part-time employment at the regional hospital in addition to attending the business course. They will search for a rental property as soon as able, but wedding plans now take first priority. Both have suffered major setbacks for weeks, both now bathing in the glory of their romance and the prospects for their future together.

Clem and Cheryl decide to live with Mrs Fielding. Clem will return to work at the Pittsworth garage where he did his apprenticeship. Cheryl has been invited to join the staff at the Millmerran hospital where they have been struggling to recruit nurses. They've started their own wedding plans.

Len returns to his coaching ambition. First priority is to prepare his Darling Downs team for A-league entry. Commitment to this team will now consume his time and energy. He hopes concentration on this will provide some escape from the grief he is suffering. Jane's memory will stay with him for ever. Football has been his life since he was a teenager, his nature has always been to improve his ability and to continue his climb to the top.

He's learnt that coaching players to learn new skills and achieve recognition enhances their self-esteem and their enjoyment of life. His own self-esteem gets a kick as well.

Len recalls the conversation he had with Beryl when she rang to thank him for the work he did to identify the freighter, to provide identities for his Sydney attackers, and to tell him of the offer to do undercover work, which he rejected. That pleased her, and that's when she reminded him of her own five-year-old son and her realisation that they both needed to concentrate more on their own private lives.

Was Beryl making any hidden suggestions with this? I've learnt women can be very devious, using ways I don't understand. In some ways Beryl and I come from similar moulds. We hate crime. We strive to protect people we've never met before, to lead and inspire others. Is she saying we should think more about ourselves in future or does she want me to stop interfering with police work. Both our lifestyles are fast-moving, neither consistent nor stable for different reasons. Or is she suggesting we should spend more private time together?

THE AUTHOR

Ron McCarthy was State Manager for Telstra Australia. He played State grade football with an Australian legend, and golf against Sitiveni Rabuka just weeks after his Fijian coup.

He's thankful for his achievements in sport and business and the rewards of pleasure and excitement. But it's the advice learnt along the way he's been able to give to others that he's most grateful for. To accept change, learn new skills, be creative, achieve more goals, and enhance self-esteem.

He's proud of the lifelong love and support of his wife Jann, the architect of a healthy, supportive, and successful extended family.

Milton Keynes UK
Ingram Content Group UK Ltd.
UKHW030909271124
451618UK00013B/353/J

9 798369 497777